PUT IT
— to —
REST

To Janet
Thank you for
your Support!
Erin Mullahy

ERIN MULLAHY

Fulton Books, Inc.
Meadville, PA

Published by Fulton Books 2021

ISBN 978-1-64952-659-5 (paperback)
ISBN 978-1-63710-010-3 (hardcover)
ISBN 978-1-64952-660-1 (digital)

Printed in the United States of America

To my family,
Darran, Jack, and Frank.

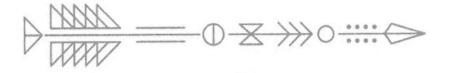

CHAPTER 1

Helen approached her front door with suspicion, as always, and knocked. She had been a slave to this mind-numbingly tedious ritual for so long now that it had become her norm. Living alone, isolated and without a soul to confide in, she had been left to her own devices, creating a home reentry ritual to cope with the overwhelming anxiety she felt every time she returned home.

No matter how short her absence, Helen couldn't shake the uneasy feeling that welled up in her gut upon each return. It was the haunting feeling that something awaited her inside. It drove her to knock repeatedly on her own front door, wait, then walk across the street to watch her house for a while before going back to repeat the whole cycle over and over again until it felt right. It was an exhausting habit, but Helen couldn't fight the compulsion. Her ritual had never failed her. It had rewarded her every time by getting her back inside safely, quelling her anxiety. Knock, wait, repeat, observe from across the street, knock, wait, repeat.

Of course, neighbors couldn't help but notice Helen's odd behavior. She'd been shamelessly spied on over the years. The small-town gossip surrounding her was like another living being in itself. People talked about how many times they had seen her knocking on her own door, how long she would take to go back in. They wondered if they would ever see the day when she would just go in on her first approach. It didn't seem likely.

Helen was well aware that her neighbors watched her. It annoyed her, but she had to admit that she understood the draw of her eccentric ways, especially in such a small town. There was really no way for her to blend in with such provinciality. A reputation had been built for her, at least that was how Helen saw it. It felt ever-present, like it would always precede her. It made her feel powerless, but it took a back seat to fear. This fear was something that resided in her so persistently that it had become her life's sad priority. She lived in fear that something awaited her inside her home, that whatever it was, it was ever-present, and that it waited for her to leave home only to psychologically torment her when she returned. It felt so real. She couldn't remember if it had begun from something real that had happened or if it was a runaway worry she had indulged to the point of believing it.

Over the years, Helen had heard the rumors. People thought she was paranoid, mentally ill, a complete psychopath. Few had any true concern for her. Once while in a hardware store, she overheard a man say that he wondered if there was some real danger Helen was in. Other than that, no one had bothered to actually try to help or to even try and talk to her about why she did what she did. She understood it was an uncomfortable subject to broach, strange as it was, and she also knew she carried herself in a way that conveyed a no-vacancies kind of air, making her rather unapproachable.

An uglier realization occurred to Helen: that neighbors had developed their own rituals of watching hers. As she would knock, wait, observe, then repeat, she would catch curtains fluttering and heads bobbing in retreat as neighbors spied on her from their windows. She had become a guilty pleasure for them, one they looked forward to witnessing and didn't want to disrupt for fear it would go away. It provided too much mystery and entertainment to their small-town lives.

Helen did her best to ignore it all, trying to force herself to believe that their opinions were none of her business. But it was a tough pill to swallow, to know that people considered her home reentry ceremony a pointless, indulgent compulsion, an urge she couldn't help but repeat. To her, it wasn't. She didn't want to be doing it either, but she was stuck in a loop. In the end, it always made her feel safe; but lately, it had been wearing on her. The anxiety was taking a toll on her nerves. She could feel something changing in her or that a change was coming, but she couldn't tell if it was coming from her or from something else.

Today, on this bright, sunny late Saturday afternoon, Helen deviated from her pattern, something that happened ever so rarely. After she knocked on her door, she leaned over the rusty metal railing at the top of her crumbling concrete steps and peered into her living room window. It didn't feel like enough, so she walked the perimeter of her house. Her anxiety was exceptionally high today, and this added measure seemed necessary.

Deep down, Helen knew it was only a false sense of control she gained from these repetitive tasks, but she couldn't admit it to herself. She was a slave to it and to that familiar ominous gut feeling that kept her going. Whatever it was, it drove her emphatically today.

"What's this? She's walking around her whole damn house today," Bruce Feller reported to his family, gazing out of the kitchen window. The Fellers lived three houses down from Helen. They had been watching her eccentricities for years. Her oddball behavior was a familiar amusement, nothing more.

"Really? Now she'll take forever. How long for her to go back in you think? What's your bet?" Bernice asked her father as she watched Helen from an adjacent window to where her father watched.

"I'd say forty-five minutes," Bruce wagered.

"Okay. I say a half hour. What are we playing for?" Bernice asked.

"One hour hard labor whenever I ask. No complaints," Bruce proposed, setting the timer on his silver wristwatch.

"Fine. And I'll take fifty bucks when I win."

"*When* you win? Presumptuous little twerp. And fifty dollars? What are you, nuts?" Bruce joked.

"Yeah, that's right. Fifty dollars *when* I win," Bernice fired back, rife with a ten-year-old's cheekiness.

"Bullshit! *If* you win, it'll be five dollars. Fifty my ass! Who the hell do you think I am, Rockefeller?" Bruce retorted, donning phony anger and exasperation. Bernice enjoyed these exchanges with her father. The playful banter came so naturally to them.

"Who's Rockefeller?" Bernice asked, smart aleck-like but with an honest ignorance of the name.

With exaggerated disgust in his voice, Bruce said, "Get a life, would you? Read a book or something. Do I have to teach you everything?"

Bernice giggled and digressed. "Fine, five bucks. But I think I am worth more than five dollars an hour for hard labor."

"God, you're clueless," Bruce said, chuckling.

"Duck!" shouted Bernice, dropping down to her haunches so her head was below the windowsill. "I think she saw me!"

Bruce didn't duck. He had played this game too many times before. He stood his ground and remained looking out his window, occasionally switching his gaze to the sky, giving the impression that he was merely contemplating the weather or was deep in thought. There was no way Helen would even think that he would have the nerve to spy on her, he surmised.

As Bruce stood by the window, he could see Helen standing across the street from her house. She was looking in his direction. He wondered if she could feel eyes upon her, so he gave her a casual wave, as he sometimes did, and then returned to his bogus attention to the clouds, missing Helen's wave in return.

Feeling he had held his position in the window long enough to satisfy any suspicions Helen may have had, Bruce turned away from the window and announced, "She's too busy looking for ghosts to have noticed us."

Bernice sat at the kitchen table and kept Helen in her periphery. She had to keep watch. She was confident she would win the bet today. To a ten-years-old, this hobby of spying on Helen was a harmless game. It was a diversion from monotony and a game she shared with her dad. She was too young to understand that their game came at the expense of Helen's neurosis.

Bernice's mother, Irene, grasped the underlying apathy in their game. It seemed Helen was a mere oddity to them, void of a personality that could be hurt. Irene couldn't deny that she was just as intrigued by Helen as everyone else, but she wouldn't make a game of it. It was cruel. She had rebuked her husband and daughter for spying on Helen but was met with eye rolls. "You two are awful, getting your kicks off poor Helen's suffering. Bernice, go find something else to do."

"Mom, she doesn't even know. How is it mean to her?" Bernice asked, defending this game her dad had started. She couldn't imagine her father starting a game that intentionally hurt someone. It wasn't something she had considered until her mom mentioned it. Now she was torn between watching Helen and getting her mother's approval.

"Oh, come on. You think she doesn't know she's being watched? That woman is so paranoid. There's no way she wouldn't pick up on that," Irene said.

"Hey, don't act so innocent. You're as guilty as we are. Sure, you don't play along with us, but you get a kick out of her. I've seen you," Bruce countered.

"Well, it's hard not to notice. I don't get a kick out of it, and I certainly wouldn't make a game out of her paranoia like two other people I know," Irene rebutted.

"What exactly is paranoia?" Bernice asked her mom, inadvertently changing the subject.

"You know when you ducked below the window when you thought Helen saw you, but you weren't sure, so you stayed down, then you thought twice about coming back up because you weren't sure whether she would be looking this way or not? That's paranoia. Like constantly second-guessing yourself, I guess. I wonder if that's how Helen feels all the time. Imagine living like that," Irene said, shaking her head as she bit her bottom lip, hoping her daughter would understand and put herself in Helen's shoes.

Bruce crushed any chance for empathy, spewing a patronizing retort. "Yeah, yeah, bleeding heart. You don't fool me. You're feeling guilty because you know you can't resist watching her either. Besides, she's a grown woman. If she doesn't expect to get a few looks, then she's got a few screws loose. For Christ's sake, you have to admit it's funny. We ain't hurting her. It's not like we are enjoying her problems. We're just having a little fun amongst ourselves. Besides, it's my house, and I can look out my goddamn windows anytime I damn well please, so there!"

Bruce had a way of putting Irene back in her place under the guise of humor. Most of the time, she let it roll off her back. But when he did it in front of Bernice, she felt belittled and embarrassed. She didn't want to start a fight in front of Bernice, so rather than stand up for herself, she would either change the subject or just laugh like it didn't bother her. She was afraid to push back and show anger. She didn't like feeling so defeated by Bruce, but keeping the peace was more important to her than being right. Like Helen, she was stuck in her own loop of just smiling and rolling her eyes to diffuse Bruce's anger and avoid a fight. Bruce took it as a playful reaction, but it was really contempt disguised as a harmless gesture.

"It smells like poop downstairs," the Fellers' five-year-old son, Will, announced, bounding upstairs from the basement.

"Why? Did you shit your pants?" Bruce teased.

"Really, Bruce?" Irene said, annoyed by Bruce's crass choice of words. "Come here. Let's make sure it isn't you, although you're far too big to be having accidents like that anymore."

"It's not me, Mom. There's dirty water down there again," Will explained.

Irene and Bruce exchanged a knowing look. Bruce trudged down the steps, turned the corner, and was hit by the unmistakable stench of sewage. He peered into the basement bathroom and saw sludgy brown water all over the floor, seeping over into the other rooms.

"Aw, Christ!" Bruce grunted, grimacing as he used his T-shirt collar to shield his nose from the putrid stench. He shouted upstairs to Irene, "Damn it. He's right! It backed up again."

Irene pressed her fingertips into her temples. This was the fourth time their sewer had backed up in four months. She called down the stairs, "Can we just call a professional this time? It's obvious we can't fix it."

"Get the buckets and old towels from the garage and bring them down. Don't forget the bleach," came Bruce's dreaded answer to Irene's plea.

Irene slammed the garage door behind her as she went to retrieve the cleanup supplies. She was beyond annoyed. She already had a full

Saturday of house cleaning after a full week of work. She had made a huge breakfast for her family, something she did every weekend to make up for the guilt she felt for being absent during the week while she worked. The last thing she wanted to do now was clean up after yet another sewer backup.

Foreseeing this problem happening again and knowing Bruce would never call a professional, Irene had bought face masks. She removed one and stretched the elastic band around the back of her head and covered her nose and mouth with the flimsy felt cup. She lugged the buckets and cleaning materials downstairs to Bruce, who stood over the drain in the floor. He removed the grate covering the large opening and peered down into it, a look of confusion mixed with irritation on his face as he stood nearly ankle-deep in sewage.

He thought back to when he and Irene had first looked at this house before they had bought it and remembered the red flag that had gone up in his mind when he saw the foot-wide drain in the basement. He had asked the real estate agent why a drain that large would be inside a house but never received an answer. His wife's excitement over the new house had made them both overlook the drain problem, regrettably.

Bruce looked up at Irene dangling a face mask up to him by her index finger. Bruce recognized the vexed look in her eyes. "I don't want to be doing this any more than you do," Bruce said, snatching away the mask.

Bruce's remark disarmed Irene a little. "Is it really worth our time and energy to do this ourselves again? We're supposed to go out later. I'm not even going to have the energy to get ready after another one of these cleanup sessions. Please, can't we just call someone this time?" Irene begged.

"You know what the issue is. First of all, no one's gonna come look at this until Monday. And trust me, I'd love to pay someone to do this for us just as much as you, but where do we come up with the money for that? You know the kind of money they'd charge for this."

If you cut back on booze and cigarettes, we could afford a lot of things, Irene wanted to say but bit her tongue. An insinuating comment like that right now would send Bruce through the roof. "You're right," Irene forced herself to say just to keep the situation from getting any worse.

As she mopped, Irene considered how often she had had to bite her tongue over the years and was surprised she had any tongue left. She bit back hard on her anger to avoid clashing with Bruce. Most times, Bruce was good as gold, Irene rationalized. But he was either clueless or didn't care about the hoops Irene jumped through to keep him happy. Whether it was keeping her opinions to herself or whether it was covering for Bruce's drinking, Irene was unaware that she had lost herself in the act of enabling her husband. She thought she was keeping the peace, believing she was doing her best.

She defended Bruce against all odds. They lived in a very small town, and Bruce's fondness for drink was no secret. Bruce didn't care one way or another what people thought of him. Irene, on the other hand, cared quite a lot. Lost in her denial, she thought she was succeeding in keeping her husband's drinking problem under wraps.

Bernice knew there was a problem. She lived with it, and people talked—family, her friends, and her friends' parents. She was tired of the questions from her friends, wondering how much her dad drank every night. She just wanted them to mind their own business.

She tried to ask Irene about some of the things she had heard, but instead of talking to Bernice about it, she became angry and had shut down, telling Bernice not to talk about such ridiculous things. Since it wasn't safe to talk about, Bernice quit asking—not just about that subject but also any subject with some emotional weight attached to it. So she kept quiet and played along in silent uncertainty, hoping everything would be all right.

Bernice didn't quite understand that Irene was playing along as well, acting like she shared Bruce's opinions most of the time. Even in this moment, as Irene forced herself through the motions of mopping up the disaster in the basement, feeling like she couldn't take another second of it, she just kept going. It was easier than fighting for what she really wanted, namely a professional to rectify this ongoing problem once and for all. But it just wasn't worth it, and Irene didn't have the energy to speak up. Not today.

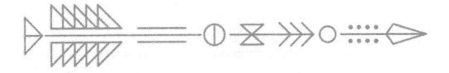

CHAPTER 2

With the perimeter check complete, Helen returned to the sidewalk across the street from her house to have yet another look. A quick movement from the Fellers' window distracted her. She glanced over to find Bruce staring back at her from his window. He waved, so she waved back. *Now go ahead and pretend to watch the clouds*, Helen thought.

Of all the people in Helen's neighborhood, the Fellers took the most interest in her business. It annoyed her, but for the most part, she knew the Fellers were good people. The reason she knew this was because she had decided to take an interest in their business just as they did hers. In fact, she took it a step further by documenting the everyday occurrences of the Fellers, devoting entire notebooks to them. Do unto others as they do unto you, she reasoned.

Years of observation had given Helen quite an insight into the Fellers' lives. They had their problems as families do, but the good seemed to outweigh the bad. The Fellers would be surprised and likely creeped out at what Helen had figured out. Patterns had developed. Helen knew when Irene and Bruce came and went to work. She knew Irene got groceries on Saturday mornings. She knew Bruce and Irene met friends at the local bars every Saturday night. She had even forced herself awake some of these Saturdays to see what time they would return, unintentionally bearing witness to the couple quarreling on quite a few occasions.

Two small houses stood between Helen and the Fellers' house, making it easy for her to hear Bruce and Irene's raised voices from her open window. The couple argued outside in their driveway or in their truck. Most arguments were about Bruce's drinking.

Helen felt guilty for having discovered such personal things. She gleaned no joy from such knowledge but kept making records out of concern. Helen didn't have friends, but even if she had, she would never divulge the sensitive information she had on the Fellers.

Helen also recorded how long Bruce and Bernice watched her and from where. Usually, it was from their dining room windows; but sometimes, it was while they pretended to be working in their garden or fiddling with something in their garage.

The rare times Helen ventured out of her home and into public places, she would make mental note of anything she might overhear pertaining the Fellers. Upon returning home, she would record the information in a notebook. The small-town gossip helped fill in the gaps and added tasty tidbits of information she wouldn't find out otherwise.

Since Helen kept her findings a secret, she deemed her journals harmless. Doing it gave her a sense of satisfaction and fairness knowing she had significantly more information about the Fellers than they had on her. It also gave her a sense of power and control that she so rarely felt in every other aspect of her solitary life. She was an isolated, lonely forty-something who was nearly crippled by the mere thought of social interaction. She was quite content with the quiet life she led at home, at least that was what she told herself.

Helen figured the Fellers saw her as a reclusive, crazy spinster. They never saw a visitor go to her house, and she rarely ventured into public. The Fellers didn't understand how excruciating it was for Helen to psych herself up just to leave the house for anything at all, especially on days she needed to go to a store for necessities. She dreaded those days and planned them well in advance, making sure she had a list of things she needed so she wouldn't have to make any return trips if she forgot something.

Helen knew she had earned the stares from the townspeople. She had heard their snide remarks about her strangeness and heard the heartless cackles of the younger kids as they watched and mocked her. She tried her best to ignore it all, but some of it always found its way in, and she took it to heart. She coped with the hurt by keeping a keen ear out for any town gossip she overheard about anyone and documented it in one of her many notebooks. Helen had overheard her share of "Poor Irene" stories. Helen wondered if Irene had any idea how many people pitied her because of all she put up with in her marriage.

In a small Midwestern town of less than three thousand residents, everyone either knew one another or knew of one another. It was difficult to have any sort of privacy, but Helen had somehow managed to isolate herself but at a cost to her reputation. She didn't envy the position the Fellers were in, unaware that everyone knew their secret.

Helen naturally went against the grain of what was socially expected. She didn't mix with others or go out of her way to say hello. She wasn't a churchgoer. She wasn't married and had no children. She didn't work, not anymore. She didn't join town committees or participate in community service activities. She had lived in Ramsey her entire life as had her parents, yet she chose to live like a hermit. It was nearly impossible for the townspeople to let someone so unconventional just be.

Helen chalked up the townspeople's insatiable appetite for gossip to boredom. Their unbearably dull lives caused them to salivate over Helen's eccentric behavior. They spun vicious stories about her. Some were hurtful, some were amusing, and some were so wildly untrue it made her head spin. Maybe she played herself into the rumors, she thought, by remaining reclusive, wearing black, having no religion, having no friends, not dating, and knocking on her own door. But one rumor was so cruel that it made her sick each time she heard or thought of it. The townspeople actually accused Helen of somehow having a hand in her own father's death a couple of years ago.

Helen had lived alone with her father for the past thirty years, ever since her mother disappeared without a trace in 1956. On the day of his death, Helen had come home to find her father dead on the bathroom floor. She assumed that he had a heart attack or had fainted and hit his head on the tiled floor. There was a strange scratch that ran up the inside of his left forearm in a zigzag pattern. The cops investigated for foul play but came up inconclusive. But in that small town, word got around, and Helen was as good as guilty for her father's death. Even if it wasn't true, it was entertaining to wonder about.

Helen's eccentric and reclusive behaviors arose after her mother's disappearance, becoming more pronounced as time went on. After her father's shocking death, her compulsions took over her world. When her mom first disappeared, the townspeople were ruthless in the stories they spun about how and why she disappeared. They said she had run off to be with another man. They said she had to escape from home because of how strange her husband and daughter were. They said she was crazy, which would explain Helen's behavior. It must have been inherited.

The disappearance of Helen's mother was still a mystery to everyone, especially to her husband and daughter. They had been a happy, content family. When Helen and her father went fishing on that fateful Saturday back in 1956, they couldn't have imagined that when they returned home by dinnertime, she would be gone forever.

Normally, after one of Helen and her father's fishing trips, Helen's mom would have dinner ready for all of them to enjoy together, but not that night. As that particular night wore on, Helen had helped her father clean and gut the fish. They worked in silence, trying to ignore the worry that was setting in as the hours ticked by and as the sky went from light periwinkle to deep cobalt. It was not like Helen's mother to leave without a note saying where she had gone and when she would be back.

They had searched the house and found that only her shoes and purse were gone, nothing else. They had driven around town in search of her before calling the police, who told them they had to wait twenty-four hours before they could consider it a missing person's case.

After a sleepless night of pushing their worst fears out of their minds, Helen and her father started the next day with as much worry and confusion as they had the night before. They could no longer deny that something was horribly wrong when the cops finally did investigate after the twenty-four-hour mark.

The urgency of the investigation turned into a weak, passive search as the weeks turned into months and months grew into years without a trace of Helen's mother. No one claimed to have seen her that day. A body had never been recovered. No sightings of her had ever been reported since. It was like she had vanished into thin air.

Helen and her father lived an isolated, purgatorial existence after the disappearance. Early on, they looked for signs around the house, reasons why she may have left. They scoured her drawers, finding nothing but her neatly folded clothes. Their suitcases were still in storage. Her toiletries all sat in the medicine cabinet as though they anticipated her return as much as Helen and her father did.

As the years wore on, Helen and her dad lived on the edge of fully accepting that her mother, his wife, was gone and that they would never see her again or would never know what had happened to her. But without proof of anything, hope held them hostage.

Helen's father had been destroyed by his wife's disappearance. The only time Helen left her father's side after that was to attend high school. Her father was her priority. She even decided to forgo college to stay with him, a decision that both disappointed yet made her father proud. He knew that Helen possessed an extraordinary intelligence, that she was capable of so much more. Selfishly, he also needed her. She was all he had after his wife disappeared. With Helen's intelligence, her father reasoned, she would be able to find a job in town with no problem, college degree or not. He just worried about how people would treat her.

The sad truth was that Helen was even more destroyed over her mother's disappearance than her father was, but she wouldn't show it for the sake of her dad. Helen's loyalty toward her dad became the crutch that stopped her from pursuing any kind of independent life for herself. She was crippled with anxiety. She was so traumatized by it that she couldn't have pursued her scholarly pursuits even if she had wanted to. The best she could do was to work inconspicuously at the quiet local library, reading voraciously on her own and making enough money to supplement her father's income as a carpenter and general handyman.

They had gone on like that for nearly three decades. They had been able to save an impressive amount of money since they only bought the bare essentials and never vacationed. It came in handy when Helen's father was diagnosed with Alzheimer's about two years before his death. He was unable to work any longer, and Helen had to quit her job at the library to care for him full-time.

It was a soul-crushing time for Helen that she endured alone, but that was the only way she knew how to cope. As her father hurled deeper into the unrelenting downward spiral of Alzheimer's, Helen contended with her caretaker's guilt. She hoped he would just die in his sleep so he wouldn't have to keep suffering and so that she wouldn't have to witness the agonizing destruction of her once-capable father. But she also didn't want to be alone.

The caretaker's guilt transformed into survivor's guilt when Helen's father finally expired. Though the circumstances of his death were still a mystery to Helen, she had to admit that she felt relief that he was finally gone. He was free from his pain and suffering. Helen no longer had to care for her father, but she felt anything but free.

Left with no one and no distractions, Helen felt the rawness of her isolation. The years of stigma she had endured after her mother's disappearance coupled with the mystery surrounding her father's death drove her even further into her anxiety-ridden seclusion. At only forty-two years of age, Helen was resigned to the belief that she would spend the rest of her days alone, imprisoning herself inside her own home like a dried-up old maid. She had been reduced to a life of overplanning necessary outings—like the grocery or drugstore visits and the agonizing return-to-home ritual she had developed to quell her anxieties about what may await her inside—and the recording of her neighbors' social lives in her journals.

Helen didn't like living this way, but she had grown accustomed to the discomfort. She was doing the best she could and couldn't handle anything more. The thought of change of any kind was exhausting. She didn't enjoy being spied on by her neighbors, having to act like she wasn't aware of it. Recording their information in journals wasn't really a way of evening the score, Helen knew, but it was something to pass time.

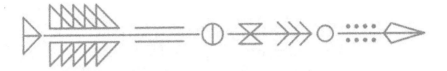

CHAPTER 3

"Thirty-five minutes gone, and she's still going! She's knocking again," Bernice yelled downstairs to her parents, who were busy with other things more pressing than Helen's ritual.

Bruce shouted back, "That means you lose. Now get down here, and I'll take that hour of hard labor you owe me."

Bernice knew this was coming but was hoping that maybe she wouldn't have to help clean up this time around. "Coming," Bernice yelled back before shooting a look of resentment toward Will, who sat at the kitchen table, snacking on his grapes, all too self-satisfied and content. He was only five, Bernice reasoned, but it still felt unfair that he got to sit and eat snacks while she had to help her parents sop up raw sewage in the basement yet again.

She bounded down the stairs as quickly as possible, grabbed some towels without being told, and began mopping the murky water. Normally, Bernice would argue that her father had not yet won the most recent Helen challenge, that the forty-five minutes weren't up. She would love to point out how unfair it was that she had to clean up disgusting shit water while her little brother got to watch cartoons and stuff his face. But she knew better than to argue with Bruce when he was in bad form. Bruce was a moody guy. Bernice learned early on how to read his fluctuating moods.

The second time their sewer had backed up, Bernice's response to her father's request to help with the cleanup was, "I'm not cleaning up that shit while Will sits upstairs and scratches his ass!" Big mistake. Bruce approached Bernice swiftly, slapped her cheek with a force that felt as though her skin had split, then grabbed her upper arm so tightly that it felt as though his fingertips would poke right through to the bone. He spun Bernice around and gave her a hearty swat on the ass. He released her arm, grabbed some dry towels, and shoved them into Bernice's trembling arms. His face was beet red as he spoke. "I'm not asking you. I'm telling you. Now clean!"

It left Bernice with a ball of fear festering in her stomach. It wasn't the first time she felt it and, likely, wasn't the last. This type of outburst had happened before and was happening more frequently. The bite of each incident scared Bernice enough to know that when her dad was serious, she had to act accordingly. She had grown acutely self-aware of how she interacted with him based on his moods. When Bruce was in a jovial mood, like he had been earlier that day, he lavished Bernice with playful banter and had an anything-goes sense of humor. But when Bruce was sour and down, "anything goes" transformed into "his way or the highway." Bernice learned to keep her head down and her mouth shut, just like she planned to do during this cleanup.

As Bernice worked, she could feel her father's irritation in every move he made as he threw the wet towels in the corner of the room with force, kicked tools out of his way, and occasionally punched a wall to get some aggression out of his system. She didn't understand why she felt she was to blame for his bad moods. Anytime he was angry, that sick, nagging feeling welled up in her, that feeling that she should know how to make things better for him. She felt like she was the cause of her parents' problems. She constantly second-guessed her instincts and wondered why her own feelings could be so wrong. The heavy burden of it made her a perfectionistic in everything she did. Even in their basement that Saturday, she cleaned with a speed and efficiency that was a little too intense for someone her age.

Bruce won the challenge that day. It took Helen just over forty-five minutes to finish her house reentry routine. After her usual jostle of the keys in the lock, she opened her front door and walked into her house, exhausted and relieved. She had just returned from her monthly trip to the pharmacy to pick up her prescriptions: one for depression, one for anxiety, and beta-blockers to lower her blood pressure. Helen chose Saturdays to retrieve her medications because those were the days Irene Feller was off at the pharmacy. It gnawed at Helen knowing that Irene likely knew of the medications she took. It was hard enough to have to take them in the first place. Helen didn't need Irene's judging eyes on her. Having to speak to her at the pharmacy would be torture. She imagined forced conversation and niceties mixed with piteous looks from Irene. She avoided it at all costs.

Helen dropped her canvas bag to the floor and removed the white paper bag from the pharmacy and brought it to the bathroom. She ripped it open and removed the three new bottles of meds and stored them in her medicine cabinet above the sink. Before closing the cabinet, she withdrew a tablet from each bottle and drew herself a glass of water.

It was 1986, and the sentiments around mental illness, especially in such a small town, were archaic and harsh. Helen wondered how many people knew she took medication to treat it. If they did, it was another strike against her that she didn't need. A tinge of guilt always slid down her throat along with the pills, thinking of the things the self-righteous bitches in town thought of her: "Maybe if she went to church and found God, she wouldn't need to rely on medication to make her happy"; "She's certainly attractive enough to find a husband, but maybe she doesn't like men. A husband and some kids would do her good"; "If she would just wear something colorful and stop acting so strange, then maybe she'd have some friends."

Helen knew she shouldn't give it so much thought, but her mind always set to defending itself. A part of Helen wished people knew that she didn't want to have to take the meds, that it had been a last resort. But when it had become impossible for her to function and she couldn't bear to white-knuckle it through another day, she finally accepted her doctor's suggestion to take the mood stabilizers.

Helen's isolation fed her depression and anxiety, she knew, but it also insulated her from the people's harsh judgments of her. She told herself that she was handling her mental issues responsibly with medication. She knew she wasn't the only person in town with mental issues, and she thought of the irresponsible ways in which they chose to cope in order to avoid the stigma of being labelled mentally ill.

Her thoughts turned to Bruce Feller. She had witnessed his mood swings many a times. She wondered if his drinking was the cause of them or if the drinking exacerbated them or if drinking was his quick fix for whatever else was causing his temperamental state of mind. Whatever the reason, Helen didn't judge him. She sympathized. She had educated herself about her own struggles, so she felt like she understood him.

Even though Bruce and his daughter watched her like hawks, she didn't dislike him. In fact, he was quite friendly to Helen. He waved anytime he drove by in his beat-up pickup truck. He would yell a "Hello" to her if they happened to be outside at the same time. There were times she had caught Bruce gazing out of his dining room window, deep in thought. He would sometimes stare at her house, a look of concern and sympathy on his face. Helen wondered if he saw something of himself in her and if it scared him. Or maybe he was just feeling guilty for spying on her and for bringing his daughter in on it. Maybe Helen just hoped he felt guilt.

Helen's thoughts were interrupted by the familiar gurgling sound coming from the open drain on her bathroom floor. The usual banging and screeching noises followed. Helen looked knowingly into her open-lid toilet and waited for the giant bubbles of air to arise and for the changing of the water level from low to high and back again. This was yet another habit she had developed in response to something else that had occurred in her home during the time her father died.

Helen opened the medicine cabinet and removed a long, narrow cardboard box, lifted its lid, and rummaged through the trinkets inside. She chose a few thimbles and nails from the box. She chucked them into the toilet and flushed. She closed the toilet lid, replaced the cardboard box in the medicine cabinet, and retired to the comfort of her living room sofa.

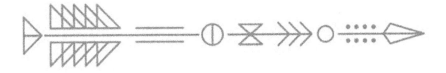

CHAPTER 4

Bernice watched Bruce feed the metal snake through the open drain. Irene had been relieved of the sewage cleanup duties about an hour ago so she could take care of Will, make dinner, then shower and get ready to go out with Bruce.

Alone with her dad and feeling confident she had satisfied her hour of hard labor plus an additional two more hours, Bernice said, "I hope you find what's clogging this thing." She knew her dad was tired and irritated and hoped that her wish would let him know that she didn't want him to have to do this again. Obviously, she didn't want to have to help again either. Mostly, though, she was afraid of Bruce's dark mood, and cleaning up another basement flood brought that side of him out.

Bruce didn't answer. He didn't even acknowledge that Bernice had spoken even though he had most definitely heard her. She was too afraid to repeat herself. The sound of metal on metal and a grinding noise broke Bernice's train of thought. The snake had hit something. Bruce quickly flipped off the switch, and a look of concern crossed his face.

"What the hell was that?" he said, stepping back. He waited a few seconds before switching the snake into reverse. Bruce looked at Bernice, who shrugged her shoulders in response to his question. He was hit with guilt, remembering how harsh he had been on her. Her eyes told him that she was afraid of him and that she just wanted to please him and not make him angry. She wanted her happy dad back, and he knew it. He was sorry for making her feel that way but couldn't make himself apologize for it. Bernice had just spent over three hours of her Saturday afternoon wiping up raw sewage and did it without stopping and without a complaint. Bruce was proud of her for it. "You were a big help today."

Bernice was flooded with relief hearing that short and sweet praise from her dad. She needed it from him more than Bruce knew. Bernice understood that his compliment signaled a good shift in Bruce's mood. She was so satisfied by Bruce's praise that when Bruce suggested she go on upstairs and get cleaned up, she happily declined. "I'll wait to see if you pull anything out if that's okay with you."

"Suit yourself, but head up anytime you want now," Bruce said as he looked at her with a hint of a smile.

With the snake in reverse mode, Bruce flipped the on switch. The snake began to recoil as usual, but then it screeched to a halt. The motor fought furiously to keep pulling the metal coil out of the drain, growing louder, emitting smoke. The smell of burning oil against hot metal began to fill the air. Before Bruce could reach the off switch, an earsplitting snap came from below. The motor revved, and the metal coil whipped wildly out of the drain. Bruce hit the off switch as the coil finished wrapping itself back around the loom. As the motor slowed, Bruce was baffled by what he saw. The end of the metal coil was frayed like a flimsy piece of yarn. *What could have done that kind of damage and how?* he thought. Bruce's thoughts were replaced by the gurgle of the drain and a forceful suction noise coming from it. It seemed to be coming from deep within the ground.

"Does that mean it's cleared?" Bernice asked, hoping her father could quell her fears about what was going on.

"I really don't know" was all Bruce could offer. He was exhausted after hours of nonstop cleanup and worry over how and when this sewer problem would be solved. As dumbfounded as he was about the state of the mangled snake coil, he didn't have the energy to give it more thought right now.

"Does that happen very often how the coil broke like that?" Bernice asked.

No, it never happens like that, Bruce thought, shaking his head no to answer Bernice's question. Bruce looked worried, so Bernice worried. Bruce noticed the look on her face and tried to subside her fear. "I think that suctioning sound was the drain unclogging. There's no water coming back up. Why don't you go upstairs and shower now before Marie gets here. I'm going to keep an eye on it while you shower to make sure it doesn't flood. Tell your mom to stand by in case I yell to turn off the water."

It took Bernice no time to switch gears from thinking about the hellish work she had done in the basement to anticipating the arrival of her favorite babysitter, Marie. She would be there at 7:00 p.m. to watch her and Will while Bruce and Irene escaped for their regular Saturday night out with friends.

Bernice thought of Marie as more of a friend than a babysitter. She was five years older than Bernice, but she treated Bernice as an equal. Bernice loved her style and her taste in music. She wore charm bracelets that Bernice desperately coveted. She loved Duran Duran and Tears for Fears, so Bernice liked them too. The nights Marie babysat, they stayed up late to watch music videos after Will fell asleep. Most of all, Bernice loved that Marie gave her so much attention. Bernice wasn't even jealous when Marie gave Will attention, who loved her just as much as Bernice did.

As excited as Bernice and Will were to have Marie babysit, Bruce and Irene were just as excited, if not more, to finally have some time out for themselves. Even though they were both exhausted from the work week and from the basement cleanup, there really was nothing that could stop them from going out for a few drinks with their friends.

Irene had showered and was busy doing her hair and makeup when Bruce announced he was going to pick up Marie. As usual, Bernice was ready to go with him for the short five-minute drive to Marie's house, her anticipation not permitting her to wait at home.

With Bruce and Bernice gone and Will playing quietly in another room, Irene was able to finish getting ready quickly without interruption. Her energy level was almost magically transformed. She had been exhausted stepping into the shower. But as she got dressed, applied makeup, and primped her hair, she magically revitalized. She was always amazed at the transformation, especially after a day like today. She was thankful for it because she felt that her Saturday nights out with Bruce were crucial in keeping harmony within their marriage even though she loathed the fact that alcohol had to be involved.

The front door burst open to the sound of Bernice and Marie laughing followed by Bruce yelling, "Irene, you ready?"

"Five minutes!"

"The car is running. Hurry it up," Bruce urged.

Irene hated being rushed, especially when she was just as eager to get out the door as Bruce was, and he knew it. She emerged from the bedroom dressed and ready to go, looking pretty but receiving no compliments.

"Where's Will?" asked Bruce.

"Playing in his room," Irene said.

Bruce checked Will's room. "Not there."

After shouting his name a couple of times, Will responded to his father's calls. He had been downstairs. He marched back up with his case of stuffed animals in tow.

Irene asked Will, "When did you go downstairs? Didn't I tell you not to go down there?"

Will shrugged in response. He couldn't resist checking things out after whatever excitement happened there all day. He wondered why he was the only one who didn't get to help. The smell of shit had kept him out of the basement earlier, but the odor had waned, and he couldn't resist but investigate for himself.

Bruce ordered Will firmly, "You are not to go down there until I tell you it's okay to go back downstairs. Got it?"

Will nodded. Bruce held out his hand in a high five to seal the deal, and Will accepted with a slap, throwing all his five-year-old might into it. Bruce reacted like the bones of his hand had been shattered by the force. He dangled his hand limply and groaned as though Will had caused him immense pain. Will loved when his dad acted like this and laughed until tears ran down his little cheeks.

Irene told Marie, "Our sewer backed up downstairs today. It's okay for now, but please don't go downstairs at all tonight. You know how big that drain is, and the cover isn't on it right now. It wouldn't take much for one of the kids to slip and get a leg stuck in there. So just stay upstairs please. Of course, if it starts to smell like poo, give us a call at the bar."

"Poo, Mom? Really? You think Marie hasn't heard *shit* before?" Bernice assured her mom.

Irene, too tired to argue and too eager to get out of the house, just smiled at Marie and said, "See what I get for trying to be appropriate?"

"I'll keep them upstairs. Don't worry. We'll be fine," Marie assured Irene.

"She's got it under control. Let's go," Bruce said, coaxing Irene out the door.

Bernice was as excited for them to leave as they were to go. The door had barely closed behind her parents when she asked Marie if she had brought her cassette tapes. "No, but I found something for you. Close your eyes," Marie said.

Bernice squeezed her eyes shut and smiled, giddy with excitement. "What is it?"

"Hold your horses," Marie said, pulling a small piece of white paper from her bag. "Okay. Arms out, palms up."

Bernice opened her eyes when the paper touched her hand. She brought it closer to her face to examine it. "Oh my God! The Michael Jackson glove sticker! Where did you find it?" This sticker was *the* sticker to have right now. It was white, fuzzy, and adorned with fake rhinestones, and now it was Bernice's.

"I found it at Spencer's. I remember you said your mom won't let you go in there, so when I saw it there last week, I had to get it."

"I love it! You're the best!" Bernice said, then scrambled to her room to add the sticker to her collection as soon as she possibly could, securing it there forever. Marie followed her and was pleased to see how happy her small gift had made her.

"I smell shit," Will's little voice arose from behind Marie. Marie and Bernice laughed at his choice of word. He was a little annoyed at being laughed at but smiled as he said, "What? I do."

Bernice said, "The stink from downstairs is probably still in the air. That's probably what you smell, Will. I was downstairs helping clean up while Will got to stay upstairs, so I got used to the smell."

20

"You got used to the smell of shit?" Marie asked.

"Not a hundred percent," Bernice said.

"I helped too," said Will. Bernice looked at Marie and shook her head in opposition to Will. Will saw Bernice's look of denial and explained, "I didn't clean up the shit, but I stopped it from coming back."

"You were nowhere to be seen downstairs the entire day! You're full of it!" Bernice countered.

"Oh yeah? Go look!" Will said.

Marie intervened. "All right, guys, enough. Actually, I smell it too, Will."

"Yeah, me too," Bernice had to confess. "It's definitely getting stronger. I wonder if it's overflowing again. Maybe we should take a look."

Marie shot Bernice a look. "You know what your parents said about going downstairs."

"Yeah, but it's only a quick peek. Besides, if we see that it's over-flowing again, my parents said to call them right away. Trust me. They'll be glad if we did," Bernice said.

"I suppose. But just a quick look, then we're right back upstairs. Got it?" Marie said.

They nodded in agreement and descended the steps, the stench of feces growing ever stronger. All three of them instinctively covered their noses by pulling up the necks of their shirts. Marie dry-heaved, and the kids couldn't help but laugh at her while fighting off their own urge to do the same. Bernice led them into the room with the drain. They were surprised to see steam billowing up from its edges. It looked like something was clogging its center. Whatever the block-age was, it heaved up and down, almost like it was alive and needed to belch. Bernice boldly edged closer to get a better look.

"Not so close!" Marie warned, but she couldn't stop Bernice from getting closer. "How can you stand the smell? And why didn't your parents put the cover back on?" Marie asked Bernice through back-to-back gags. Bernice didn't answer. She had spotted a rubber glove she had used for cleanup earlier that day and snapped it onto her right hand. Using her index finger and thumb like tweezers, she grasped something hairy at the very top of the drain and pulled. It came loose, and she flung it in the air, sending it splatting against the wall. She screamed, causing Marie and Will to follow suit. "It's a rat!" shouted Marie.

"It's Rocky," Will corrected.

"Rocky?" asked Marie.

"It's my dog. He helped me fix the drain," Will explained.

Bernice went back over to the drain that was still heaving up and down and spewing more steam. She stuck her hand down the drain a little farther and pulled out yet another sodden, furry wad. This time, it was a stuffed parrot. She held it up in her pincher-like grasp and examined it. "And here's Paco," she said, dropping it to the floor and plucking another furry friend from the drain. "Oh, and Francis," Bernice said, holding a soggy stuffed frog.

"They all helped me. Tuck and Brewster are still in there, but they're still working. See? You're ruining it! The steam's getting bigger!" Will complained. The steam was intensifying, heaving furiously now.

Bernice asked Will, "Did you stuff these down here when Mom was getting ready?" Will nodded. Bernice explained to Marie that Will must have shoved his toys down the drain while she and her dad had gone to pick her up. "I should probably get the last two," Bernice said, bending down.

"No, Bernice. We aren't even supposed to be down here. What are your parents going to say when they find out we came down here in the first place? And what if you pull out the other toys and the steam burns you or it explodes in your face? Please, just get away from there," Marie ordered Bernice.

"The steam isn't even hot. It just stinks. It'll be quick. They have to come out eventually," Bernice said, completely dismissing Marie's wishes. Holding her breath and squinting, Bernice leaned her body away from the drain and stretched her arm farther down and pulled up a filthy, soggy turtle. "Tucker," she said and dropped it on the floor. She reached back in one last time, expecting her fingers to meet with another saturated stuffed animal, but she was surprised to feel something smooth. At first, she thought it was some sort of pipe, but whatever it was moved. It felt like a large snake, muscular and undulating. Bernice's hand quickly recoiled. Steam was no longer billowing out of the drain. It seemed that whatever was down there had blocked it.

"What's wrong, Bernice? What is it? Get away from it, okay?" Before Bernice could answer Marie, Brewster, Will's stuffed toy horse, slowly rose to the top of the drain. It was resting on top of something.

"Grab it!" Will commanded Bernice.

"I'm not touching anything else. It's yours. If you want it so bad, get it yourself."

Before Marie could tell Will not to touch the sewage-soaked toy, he was already next to the drain, reaching down to retrieve his last toy helper. When he lifted it up, a hand was exposed. The palm was up, and the fingers were held together so that it made a kind of platform for the toy. The hand shot up out of the drain, exposing a long, almost graceful arm had it not been covered in a glistening tar-like sludge. Before any of the three could react, the hand grabbed Will's left hand and violently pulled him to the drain, taking his arm down with it, pinning Will to the floor.

He let out a bloodcurdling scream as he lay helpless, pinned to the ground. Marie feverishly tried pulling Will away, grabbing at his flailing legs. Bernice moved up to Will's shoulder, grasped it with both hands, and pulled with all her might, but he wouldn't budge. Whatever had him was too strong.

Over Will's screams, they could hear the clinking of metal coming from below, and then the hand simply released him. Will pulled his arm out quickly, and the three of them moved to the far corner of the room, away from the drain. Will's hand and arm were covered in the thick, greasy sludge. As Marie and Bernice were about to take a closer look at Will to make sure he and his arm were all right, a piercing screech sounded from underground. Then a stream of sewage mixed with the greasy sludge shot straight into the air like the force of a fire hydrant just opened. They all screamed and scrambled back upstairs, covering their ears from the shrieking noise. And then it stopped as suddenly as it had begun. No more noise. No more spewing water. Just an eerie silence remained.

The three kids stood breathless and terrified. Will sobbed with fright. Marie held him tightly and tried to assuage him the best she could even though she knew he could feel her trembling uncontrollably. Flooded with adrenaline, Bernice grabbed the phone and thrust it at Marie.

"Call my parents!"

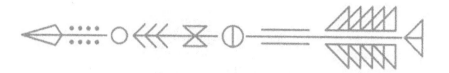

CHAPTER 5

Bruce ordered a whiskey sour and slid a few bills across the bar. Patsy, the longtime barmaid and friend to most everyone who frequented Nelly's Bar, reached for the money and teased Bruce. "You think I don't know what you want after all this time?"

Patsy looked forward to Saturday nights when she would get to see the regular crowd, the fun crew Bruce and Irene ran with. They were a welcome change to the sad small-town regulars she tended to on weeknights, those downtrodden, defeated, pitiful souls she feared becoming one day. She wondered how it happened for the weeknight regulars. When did their enjoyment of a drink turn into an enslaving daily necessity?

When the Fellers would come into the bar with their usual crowd, Patsy would spring back to life. Seeing Bruce gave her a rush she felt horribly guilty about. He was the ringleader of the rowdy bunch, and Patsy was drawn like a moth to a flame by his charisma.

"If I don't ask, you might just give me the whole damn bottle," Bruce fired back.

"For your own sake, that's never going to happen," Patsy said as she poured an extra shot of whiskey into Bruce's sour mix, sliding the concoction over to him with a wink.

How could you not like this woman? Bruce thought. Any woman who began his night with an extra shot was pedestal worthy.

"Now what can I get you tonight?" Patsy asked Irene, who sat perched upon a well-worn red leather barstool next to Bruce. She had been watching the playful exchange between her husband and Patsy, and that same old feeling of amusement mixed with unease crept up on her.

Bruce is a shameless yet harmless flirt, Irene thought. Or, rather, she hoped. Still, she couldn't shake the feeling she had about her suspicions where Patsy was concerned. She and Bruce got along a little too well, joked a little too freely, and looked at each other a little too long at times. Irene told herself she was reading too much into things. After all, Patsy's looks had faded rapidly over the years. The deep wrinkles and crepe-like skin from years of smoking and heavy drinking had left their marks on her once-beautiful face. It gave Irene a strange sense of satisfaction knowing she, at least, had her beat as far as looks were concerned. She couldn't compete with Patsy's wit, but she had her well-whipped in the looks and brains department—at least that was what she told herself. She considered her vanity and snarky judgments and ignored how superficial it made her feel because they served to quiet her suspicions.

A few years back, Irene and Bruce had helped Patsy out of a particularly rough patch in her life. They had become constant companions in her life since they had helped her get away from her abusive husband. When Patsy's son, who had learned his father's traits quite well and took it out on his mother, finally moved out of her home, the Fellers made sure she never felt alone. A strong yet regretful friendship had come of it. She felt guilty for even thinking that Bruce and Patsy had developed something even deeper, but she sensed it.

It all began one Saturday night at that same bar when things were particularly horrible for Patsy at home. That night, Patsy decided to confide in Bruce and Irene. She didn't know where else to turn and felt in her gut that she could talk to them. She had been bartending for well over a decade in that same small-town bar, every night listening to the alcohol-induced confessions of her patrons. That night, she decided she needed to confess her own demons to someone she could trust. Patsy was desperate, and the Fellers were in the bar that night, and since they were the most genuine people Patsy knew, she took a chance on them. She never could have predicted developing the feelings she had for Bruce. The guilt of it sat heavy with her. Falling for a married man was never her intention.

"What the hell. Whisky sour for me too. It's been a hell of a day," Irene said.

"Whoa, that's a change!" Patsy exclaimed, surprised not to receive Irene's normal order for a light beer, any brand. Patsy set the cocktail in front of Irene and said, "Who couldn't use a good stiff one once in a while?"

"What kind of ideas are you trying to put into my wife's head?" Bruce faked disgust at Patsy's comment. The alcohol had loosened his lips, the suggestive comment dropping from his mouth with ease.

Patsy deflected the comment, saying, "Ease up on the whiskey, Feller, and get your head out of the gutter." Had Patsy thought about how she had just responded to Bruce, she never would have let the words escape her lips. She knew Bruce's sense of humor and should have seen the naughty comment coming, as they usually did, much more frequently the more the alcohol flowed. Patsy enjoyed his playful comments, even the tawdry ones. Usually, Irene was out of earshot for the exchanges. Having Irene there for this one was awkward, and they all felt it. Irene forced an artificial laugh and rolled her eyes.

The phone rang from behind the bar, interrupting the threesome's banter. Patsy answered and used her index finger to plug her other ear so she could hear over the music and bar chatter. "Who? What happened? Sorry. I can barely hear you. Who you looking for?" After a few seconds of strained listening, Patsy passed the receiver to Irene. "What do you know? It's for you."

Irene already knew that it was either one of the kids or the babysitter. Usually, they would call once or twice with some random bullshit question or wondering when they would be home. But they usually didn't call this early on in the evening.

"Seven twenty-five, really? We're barely out the door, and already we're needed," Irene said to Bruce and Patsy, annoyed, before she spoke into the phone. "Hello, Bernice. What do you want?" Irene answered.

"Mrs. Feller, it's Marie. I'm really sorry, but you need to come home right away," Marie stammered, failing to cover the hysterical trembling in her voice.

Irene was taken aback by Marie's tone. She could hear Will crying in the background and Bernice's voice trying to soothe him. "Marie, what's going on? Is everyone okay?"

"Um, yeah, we're fine, but you really need to come home. The kids are really upset, and I want to go home," Marie said with increasing urgency.

"My God, Marie, what happened?" Irene urged Marie for an answer as her own panic arose.

"Just please come home right away, and I'll explain. I'm sorry. I really want to go home."

"We're coming," Irene said and left the receiver on the bar. She grabbed her purse and yelled to Bruce, who was looking all too comfortable as he sat in Patsy's company. "We gotta go. Something's wrong at home."

Annoyed at the interruption, Bruce retorted, "Aw, Christ! What sort of shit did they come up with this time?" He didn't get an answer. Irene was already making her way to the door. Bruce looked longingly at Patsy and asked her to hold his spot, that they would be right back. He got up in a huff and went after Irene. "Are you kidding me? You're just going to cut and run after their first call twenty minutes into the night? You don't really want to be here anyway, do you?" Bruce said to Irene, practically begging for an argument.

When he saw the seriousness and worry in Irene's face as she heaved herself into the driver's seat of their truck, Bruce shut up and got in the passenger's side. "What the hell happened, Irene? Are the kids okay?"

"I don't know. It was Marie who called. She was so upset. Will was crying in the background. She wouldn't tell me what happened, damn it! She kept saying she wanted to go home."

The short drive home felt like an eternity as Bruce and Irene were left with the uncertainty of what they would find when they got home. The truck was barely in park as they flew out the doors and into their home. They found the three kids sitting at the dining room table. Bernice held Will, rocking him to soothe him. Her face was filled with terror. Will's tearstained cheeks were smeared in what looked to be mud. He was trying to breathe normally, but involuntary sobs wouldn't allow it.

As soon as Marie saw Bruce and Irene, she bolted up from the table, saying, "Good. You're here. Please, take me home now!"

"Whoa, whoa, slow down! I'll take you home. Don't worry. But we gotta know what happened around here. Look at the state of you guys! Is everyone all right?" Bruce said as he scanned the kids' faces, locking into a stare with Bernice. Bruce stared at Bernice accusingly. True, she may have been the one to convince everyone to go downstairs, but she couldn't have foreseen what happened. He couldn't possibly blame her for that, she reasoned. Will lunged for Irene's arms and clung desperately to her now sludge-smeared clothes. Bernice sprang into a chaotic, manic explanation.

"Will said he smelled shit, so I thought the sewer was overflowing again, and I told Marie we should check it in case it was and that if it was, we should call you right away. I was just trying to save you another day of cleaning up! When we got down there, the drain was letting out steam, and there was something clogging it. Will said that he helped stop the flooding by sticking his stuffed toys down the drain, so I thought pulling them out would help! Then Will..." A lump in Bernice's throat choked her. She swallowed hard and tried to continue in vain as she started to sob.

"Then Will what, Bernice? What?" Bruce demanded.

Marie spoke up for Bernice. "Then Will ran to the drain before I could stop him, and he...he...slipped, and his arm just, like, went into the drain. We...had to pull him out."

Bernice caught the omission. "What about the hand that grabbed Will? You saw it too. Admit it!" Overcome with nerves, Bernice covered her face with her hands. Will was crying again as he remembered being pulled down to the drain and held there. He put his hands up to his ears as though covering them would make him forget what had happened. Marie shrugged. She didn't want to talk about it anymore. She just wanted to get home and away from the Fellers.

The blood drained from Irene's face, leaving her white as a sheet, terrified. Bruce, on the other hand, was boiling with anger on the inside, his default whenever emotions ran high. "What the hell did you just say? Did you say a hand came out of the drain and grabbed Will? Are we supposed to believe that? Or did you just make this up to save your asses from being down in the basement in the first place?

Didn't we tell you not to go down there, damn it?" He slammed his fist down hard onto the counter, shaking everything on top of it.

Irene didn't know what to believe, so she sided with Bruce. That was always easier when he was angry anyway even if it meant going against her children. Marie hadn't seen this angry side of Bruce before, and it scared her. She tried defending Bernice.

"Mr. Feller, Bernice didn't do anything wrong. I agreed to check the drain with her. She was right that if it was overflowing, we should call you right away. We didn't know what was going to happen." She stopped, and tears formed in her eyes as she trembled in fear. "Just please take me home. It wasn't Bernice's fault. I shouldn't have agreed to go downstairs in the first place. I don't want to talk about it anymore. I just want to go home!" she screamed.

"All right. Just calm down. Get your shoes, and we'll go right now," Bruce said. Bernice went to get her shoes on as well, thinking she would ride along since it was still early. Bruce was quick to stop her. "Uh-uh, you're staying here with your mom and Will. You best get your story straight by the time I get back."

Bernice's heart sank. Besides being terrified by what had happened, she was now forced to think about how she was going to squelch her father's wrath. She had no idea what to do. All she had was the truth, and she couldn't lie about what she had seen. Will was backing her up, but it didn't seem to matter. *Maybe if her father hadn't reacted in such anger, Marie would have felt safe enough to tell the truth as well,* Bernice thought. She had had full faith in Marie, and it stung to know that she hadn't defended her, but she couldn't blame her.

Bernice was used to the fact that Irene always took Bruce's side when he was angry, but she was desperate to tell her mom what had really happened. She had to try. "Mom, I swear I'm telling the truth. I know what I saw, and Marie and Will saw it too. It's the truth. Please believe me! I'm afraid for Dad to come back," Bernice tapered off and began to cry.

Irene wouldn't look at her daughter as she spoke. She didn't offer any comfort or solace but treated her as though she was a lying, conniving brat who was always causing problems between her and Bruce. She had enough to worry about and didn't need Bernice adding to it. She stared blankly at the wall as she half listened to Bernice. She continued to cradle Will and console him like she was throwing it in Bernice's face that she wouldn't offer the same comfort to her. It cut Bernice like a knife.

"Just stop, Bernice. You heard your dad. Get your story straight. You already ruined our night out because of your lie, and you've managed to terrify your brother and Marie because of it. She'll probably never come babysit again."

Bernice stepped in front of Irene and begged, "Mom, look at me." But Irene coldly and cruelly looked past her. "Okay, if you won't look at me, then look at Will. Just look at his face! Look at his arm! Listen to what he's telling you!"

Will spoke up. "The hand pulled me down, Mommy. It did!" He began wailing again.

Bernice asked Will, "You saw it with your own eyes, right, Will? See, Mom? I didn't make this up!"

"She's telling the truth, Mom! She saved me from the monster!"

Irene had been examining Will's arm as her children pleaded with her. She was looking closely at Will's wrist. "What the hell is this? Just what the hell are these marks?" Irene said accusingly to Bernice, thrusting Will's wrist in front of Bernice's face to see. She hadn't noticed before because of the sludge covering Will's arm, but now Bernice could see scratches and some deep gouges taken out of his wrist. The cut had a zigzag pattern.

"Oh my God. I don't know. Oh my God, Will, does it hurt?" Bernice was truly concerned.

Irene erupted, "Save it, Bernice! Is this what you're really trying to cover up? What the hell happened to his wrist? What the hell did you do?"

Bernice was speechless and completely defeated. She tried desperately to explain that she would never hurt Will, especially like that. She questioned why her mom would even think that of her and why she wouldn't listen to them.

"You know what? Just go to your room, Bernice. I can't listen to you anymore, and I don't want to look at you. Go wash yourself up, and get to bed. Maybe you need the night to think about things. Go on," she said with an iciness that gutted Bernice.

Bernice did as she was told. She had no fight left in her. She knew she hadn't done anything wrong, but she felt ashamed and guilty. The fact that both her parents were so quick to discount her and make her the problem was too much for her to bear. She felt ganged up on by the people who were supposed to make her feel safe.

Bernice went to her bedroom and closed the door behind her. She pulled her light summer pajamas from her top dresser drawer, changed into them, then crawled into bed. She clutched her stuffed elephant, Hazel, which she had had since she was three years old. She took solace where she could get it right now, and the only places she could find it were in the inanimate form of Hazel, the softness of her pajamas, and the familiarity of her cozy bed. She took deep breaths and tried to calm herself down. She heard Bruce's truck pulling into the driveway and waited in dreaded uncertainty.

CHAPTER 6

Helen sat in the dark, enveloped in the sanctuary of her living room. Nestled into the bright-orange and yellow flowers of her well-worn sofa, she opened the notebook on her lap and uncapped her pen. While other forty-somethings were out in town with their husbands or maybe looking for one on Saturday nights, Helen chose to devote her Saturdays to keeping watch on her neighbors. *The Lawrence Welk Show* played on the public access station. The kitschy tunes and schmaltzy waltzes reminded her of her parents, who never missed the show.

Helen tried not to admit to herself that her Saturday nights were sad and lonely, but the truth was that they were blatantly pathetic. But it had become her norm. She couldn't force herself to socialize like other people seemed to do so easily, yet she had an urge to know what made people tick. Spying on her neighbors helped her glean information about them without the chore of really having to participate. Helen skimmed through some earlier journal entries.

April 9—Flat tire on Jim V.'s car; threw wrench at the garage door

April 23—Berg family searching for their dog again; yelling "Dodger!" for hours; dog is never leashed!

June 11—Fellers leaving for the bar later than normal; both look angry; Bernice looking out window, sad

June 12—Patsy drove past the Fellers' five times
today, slowed down each time

Helen didn't consider herself nosy. She thought of herself as
more of an armchair anthropologist. She was just observing what
people did and wondered why they were doing it. After all, it was
only fair, really, since she was so overtly watched by them. It gave her
a sense of retaliation. It also gave her a sense of peace to know of her
neighbor's regular habits, providing some constancy and familiarity.

Helen saw the Fellers' pickup truck pass by her house the
usual three times between 6:00 p.m. and 7:00 p.m. She knew their
Saturday nights like clockwork by now. The first truck passing was
to pick up their babysitter. The second was to return to the house
with said babysitter. Finally, Bruce and Irene drove to the bar. Helen
usually missed their return home as it was usually well into the wee
hours of the morning. She was surprised to see the Feller truck speeding past her home only about a half hour after it had left home. She
took note of it.

> August 11—Fellers speeding home from bar
> early; Bruce brought babysitter home; angry
> when he returns and slams truck and house
> doors; arguing with Irene in kitchen; 11:10 p.m.
> Bruce looking out kitchen window, looks con-
> cerned. What's going on?

Helen watched the Fellers for another half hour or so. Their
lights had gone out, so she closed her notebook for the night but
left it on her coffee table, figuring the Fellers' saga may continue in
the morning. Helen had sensed tension growing with the Fellers in
the last few months. Something was eating at Bruce and Irene. Even
Bernice seemed to notice. Whatever was going on, Helen hoped it
would pass.

Bruce was fuming as he burst through the front door. Out of pure habit, Irene focused on diffusing his temper. She brought her index finger to her lips and motioned toward Will, who was nearly asleep on her lap. It calmed Bruce for the moment, and he lowered his voice. "Where's Bernice?"

"I sent her to bed. I couldn't listen to her lies anymore. Just leave her alone for the night," Irene said. She didn't want Bruce going after Bernice in the mood he was in. She had lashed out on Bernice to stay on Bruce's good side. She was afraid of going against him. In fact, she couldn't imagine anything worse than that. Bruce stood in silence in front of Irene, head bowed, hands on his hips. Irene listened to his breathing, praying it would slow and that he would relax.

"I suppose I better check things out downstairs. Fuckin' drain!" Bruce cursed.

"I'll get Will cleaned up and lie down with him until he falls asleep. Then I'll be down."

Bruce smoothed Will's hair gently, which finally seemed to disarm the worst of his anger, and said, "Get some rest, Willie boy."

Tucked in her bed, Bernice strained to hear her parents' conversation. Adrenaline flooded her veins when she had heard Bruce come back, hearing the door slam violently behind him. She trembled as she listened for Bruce's heavy footsteps, dreading he would make his way down the hall to her room. She feared what punishment could be coming her way.

She heard talking instead of yelling. *Good sign,* she thought. She still didn't hear footsteps. Tears of relief escaped the corners of her eyes and rolled down to her ears, making little pools in their crevices. Maybe she would be spared tonight, she thought. She prayed to God. "Please, please, please let this be over for the night. Please, please, please."

But the footsteps came down the hallway, getting closer and closer to her bedroom door. She was relieved to hear Will's voice and knew it was just her mom. She listened as Irene washed Will, her voice soft and soothing as Will did his best not to start crying again. But he whimpered when Irene cleaned his cuts.

Will's cries died down again, and Bernice listened as Irene took him to her and Bruce's bedroom. Bernice felt a deep longing and loneliness as she lay alone in her room, desperately needing some reassurance or comfort at that moment but only hearing her mother in the next room enthusiastically giving that warmth and love to Will. Maybe that stopped the older you got, Bernice reasoned. She couldn't remember the last time she had hugged her mother and felt it reciprocated. It always felt like Irene stiffened when Bernice tried hugging her, like she just tolerated it until it was over. Either that or she would end the desperate embrace of her daughter so she could get on to more important things, like cooking or cleaning or some other work.

After about fifteen minutes of stories, songs, and cuddles, Will was finally asleep. Irene quietly crept to the door and made her way downstairs. Halfway down, that familiar putrid smell engulfed her. She found Bruce squatting next to the snake, examining the coil and the motor. A pile of dirty, wet towels had already accumulated in the corner, and more clean ones awaited her to continue yet another cleanup. She grabbed a towel, sighed, and began the tedious task of soaking up the sewage. She looked over at Bruce and noticed how mangled the end of the coil was. The drain was eerily quiet, like it was listening to Bruce and Irene.

"What the hell happened to that?"

"That's what I'm trying to figure out. It happened earlier when Bernice was down here helping me. It sounded like it got snagged on something, so I reversed the motor, and when it finally budged, it whipped out like a shot and ended up like this," Bruce explained.

"What could do that kind of damage?" She studied the shredded pieces of metal splayed out and noticed that the edges were cut in the same pattern as the cuts on Will's arm. She pursed her eyes together tightly and looked closer. "My mind must be playing tricks on me," she said.

"What are you talking about?"

"Well, I noticed some cuts on Will's arm and—"

Bruce cut her off. "What do you mean you saw some cuts?"

"When you left to bring Marie home, I noticed some cuts on his arm. Bernice was chattering away in front of me, trying to explain what had happened, and I held his arm up to show her, and she looked shocked, like it was the first time she had seen it. I think it was, but I snapped at her, and I guess I half blamed her for it. I mean, I know she would never do something like that to Will, but I guess I thought maybe she knew something about it. Oh hell, I was just so mad I yelled at her and sent her to bed."

Irene tilted her head to the side and rubbed her forehead. "I know she didn't do it, Bruce. She has never hurt Will, and she was so scared when she stood there and tried to explain what happened tonight. So scared. That's not her, Bruce, and you know it. She's never scared easily. You know what she's like."

"Yeah, I know what she's like," Bruce said, smiling with pride over how tough he considered his daughter to be, but adding, "Sly as a fox."

Irene confessed. "I feel awful how I left things with her tonight."

"She's not made of glass. She'll get over it. It's not like I did any better with her. I'll go talk to her," Bruce said. Before he went upstairs, he asked, "What was it you were saying about the cuts?"

"Well, I know it sounds strange, but if you look at the frayed ends of the coil, you can see tiny zigzags. The cuts on Will's arm have the same pattern. Weird, right?" she asked Bruce, a look on her face that seemed to be questioning if Bernice's story was true.

"Come on now. You don't actually buy into her bullshit story, do you? I mean, I'm sure she didn't do anything to hurt anyone, but a goddamn hand coming out of the drain and pulling Will down? It's nuts," Bruce pushed back. "I'm going up to talk to her."

"Please go easy on her, Bruce."

After Bruce left, Irene noticed something dripping on her. She looked up to find the ceiling dripping with sludge, concentrated in the area directly above the drain.

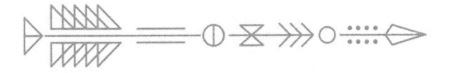

CHAPTER 7

From upstairs, all Bernice could hear were her parents' muffled voices. Images of the hand as it grabbed Will kept flashing through her mind, replaying incessantly. She worried about her parents in the basement, wondering if they would see it or if they were in danger.

Bernice was startled to hear the sound of her father's unmistakable heavy footsteps coming up the stairs. Her mind raced with anxiety, and her heart pumped furiously. She feared being slapped or scolded or maybe worse. She saw the shadow of Bruce's feet from under her door. She closed her eyes and pretended to sleep.

Bruce gently turned the knob and opened the door. He walked over to Bernice and sat at the edge of her bed, smack in the middle, making the bed sag so that Bernice rolled into him.

Bernice's red, swollen eyes popped open. She looked at her father, scared to death. Bruce reached his hand up to Bernice's forehead and slicked her hair back. Her fear was replaced with a relief she felt in every cell of her body. Bruce's comfort didn't come easily, and those times it actually happened were few and far between. But when he offered it, he meant it, and Bernice soaked it up. She tried desperately not to cry but couldn't stop the river of tears that kept flowing from her tired eyes. She hated to cry in front of him.

Bruce was filled with regret at the way he had spoken to Bernice. It was one of many times that he had let his anger get away with him, and she had been on the receiving end of it. The effects of his anger haunted him, especially where his family was concerned. "I bet you haven't slept a wink, huh? I'm sorry I came at you like I did. I know it's scary when I get like that."

Bernice knew her father meant his apology and that he really did feel bad about his behavior, but it was getting harder and harder for her to accept it. The angry outbursts kept happening and were getting worse. Bernice wasn't as forgiving as she used to be when it came to Bruce's apologies. She pretended to accept them just to quell his anger, but internally, she was defending herself against more hurt and anger.

Bruce tried to explain his behavior to Bernice, saying he was tired from working on that damned drain all day and was pissed off he had to come home early. Bernice was nodding her head, but Bruce wasn't sure if she bought it. "Bernice, I don't know what the hell happened down there, and I don't want to think or talk about it anymore tonight. We all need to get some sleep."

Bernice lay silent, waiting for Bruce to speak. She was surprised when he placed his hands on either side of her head and leaned in to kiss her on the forehead. She couldn't remember him ever doing that.

"Now get some sleep," Bruce said, leaving abruptly.

Once outside Bernice's bedroom door, Bruce fought back tears of his own, frustrated at his inability to control his anger. *If they would all just get off my back,* he thought. *I work hard to provide for my family. I don't beat them or abuse them, so why the hell are they so sensitive about a couple of drinks?* It wasn't something Bruce could admit, but he resented the hell out of his family for seeing a problem. He also couldn't admit that a life without alcohol terrified him.

Bruce's twisted rationale prevented him from seeing the cost of his problem. His family was paying for it more than he could ever imagine. It never crossed Bruce's mind that his family may be entitled to something better than being held hostage by the uncertainty of his ever-changing moods. He was oblivious to the anxiety they felt over having to cover for him, making sure the family secret of his drinking was hidden, when they really weren't fooling anyone but themselves. They couldn't acknowledge it to others, which meant they couldn't acknowledge it among themselves. It had to remain unspoken, creating a deafening silence of denial. Bruce forced these unpleasant thoughts from his mind and went back downstairs to Irene, who was busy piling towels into the laundry room.

Irene hadn't heard any yelling, so the talk must have gone well. She was relieved because when it came to taking care of any messy emotional aspect of parenting, especially as Bernice was getting older, she always deferred to Bruce. Irene went along with Bruce's decisions on parenting and punishment, whether she agreed or not, so that she wouldn't have to challenge him. She couldn't oppose him.

"It's as dry as it'll get. The drain's quiet, and I left the fans running. Let's call it a night. I'm beat," Irene said. Bruce nodded and leaned over to take one last look into the drain. Irene joined him. She pointed to the ceiling. "There was a bunch of, I don't know, goop dripping from there. You can still see where it was wet, but I put towels on the end of the mop and wiped it up as best I could."

"Goop or shit? Don't tell me the upstairs bathroom is leaking down here. That's all I need," Bruce said.

Afraid Bruce was getting upset again, Irene said, "No, it couldn't be a leak. It was right over the drain, almost like it shot straight up from the drain. No wonder there was so much more of a mess than usual."

"But how could it shoot up with a force like that? Anyway, it's quiet now, and I'm done with it for the night. The damn thing will still be here tomorrow, right?" he said, grabbing Irene around the waist and pulling her closer to him.

Irene answered, "Unfortunately, yes."

After cleaning themselves up, they snuck into their own bed like thieves, each one creeping in on either side of Will, careful not to awaken him. As they lay in silence that night, Irene and Bruce both couldn't help wondering if what their kids said was true.

Worried about the Fellers, Helen had a fitful sleep. She thought of angry outbursts she had seen from Bruce and hoped he didn't take it out on his family. Even though she didn't find Bruce to be a bad guy, the thought nagged her. Whatever was going on, the Fellers did their best to hide it, much like Helen hid her life away.

She thought of how she and her father hid their grief from the townspeople after her mother had disappeared. It was a burden, especially since they felt such anguish already. But at least they had had each other. After he was gone, the burden was all hers.

So much solitary time gave Helen too much time to replay that horrible day of her dad's death. An awful image was seared into her mind—that of her father's fragile old body lying dead on the tiled bathroom floor. He was facedown, and blood pooled around him. She could still picture the way the blood flowed into the drain as it mixed with the running water.

His eyes had remained open and fixed, a look of terror frozen on his face. Strangely, the cover had been removed from their oversized drain opening, and her father's left hand had been submerged in it. Helen had turned off the water and pulled her father clear of the drain. Odd zigzag-patterned lacerations ran the length of his left arm. She had been startled by a hand reaching up from the drain and had been even more stunned when the hand grasped her father's wedding band, slid it from his finger, then disappeared back down the drain with it.

Helen had sat in shock next to her father's dead body, for how long, she couldn't say. She had been too terrified to scream, too scared to try and find help, and had felt frozen in time. A noise had come from the drain that had snapped her out of her paralysis. It was a grinding, metal-on-metal sound. Shrieks sounded intermittently. She had peered over the drain and had been horrified to see a writhing, snakelike black thing moving from below. Whatever it was, it had hollowed out a place for itself in the drain system. She couldn't make sense of any of it. She had been too afraid to keep looking and backed away just in time before a blast of water and black sludge shot straight up from the drain, then stopped as suddenly as it had begun. It had repeated a few times, and all Helen had been able to do was curl up in the far corner of her bathroom, afraid to move.

She kept thinking of her dad's missing ring. Something was living underground, and it wanted metal. So she had unhooked the silver-plated wristwatch she had worn for years, crept to the drain, and dropped it in. To her utter horror, the black, sludge-covered hand had slowly reached up from the drain, palm open and upward. Helen had torn the delicate gold necklace she wore from her neck, placed it in the palm, and backed away, causing the hand to retreat yet again.

Before it had a chance to return, Helen had raced to her garage to grab a box full of nuts, bolts, and screws. She had brought it to the bathroom and dumped its contents down the drain. It hadn't returned that day. The noises had ceased, and she had replaced the drain cover, trembling.

She had only called the ambulance for her father after dealing with whatever this thing wanted. She knew it had been far too late to help him. He had been dead long before she had even arrived home that day. Before the ambulance had arrived, she had pulled his body from the shower and had dragged it into the hallway. She had dried the body with a dirty towel, because what did it really matter anymore? Then she had covered him with a blanket. She had thought about how no one would ever believe a story like this, especially not coming from her of all people. She couldn't even make herself believe what she had seen.

Helen covered her eyes and took deep breaths. "Stop. Just stop," she told herself. She couldn't keep questioning the choices she had made that night. It did no good second-guessing herself after so much time had passed. She reminded herself that she had reacted out of shock and fear. No one would have known what to do.

The thought of how the police had questioned her relentlessly still made her stomach turn. They had managed to make her feel as though she was somehow guilty of her father's death.

Enough. Helen forced the thoughts away. She sat silently in her living room, meditating, clearing those toxic memories from her mind. She always ended her meditations by dropping more metal down her drain, so she retrieved a fresh box of nails from her garage, brought it to the bathroom, and flushed a handful of nails down the toilet. She lifted the drain lid to throw another handful down. Whatever was down there, metal kept it quiet, and the ritual gave Helen as much peace of mind as she possibly could over such a bizarre thing.

She knew she could never tell anyone about it. The townspeople already thought she was crazy. The way the cops had questioned and treated her that night left her with the sense that they would be no help to her. She feared they would institutionalize her, so she fed this monster in solitude and hid it to survive.

Although she questioned whether anything was really there at all, she still fed it every day, keeping it at bay. If it were there, she wondered what the thing did when she was out. Did it wait for her? She constantly worried that if she didn't give it enough metal every day, one day when she returned home, it would be waiting for her and would kill her.

As Helen lay tucked in her bed, she thought about the Fellers, wondering what had happened to bring them home early that night. She thought about the secrets people kept, like the ones she kept herself. She laughed, considering she and the Fellers had more in common in that regard than they probably realized.

CHAPTER 8

Bruce awoke Sunday morning to no hangover. It didn't feel bad, but it didn't feel right. It irritated him to have been cheated out of his well-earned Saturday night session.

Bruce reached for his cigarettes on the bedside table, tipped the pack upside down, and tapped the end of the box, dislodging the loosest packed cigarette. Bruce always chose the one that slid out easiest. He had been taken aback when Bernice fetched a cigarette for him in the exact same way. She was about six years old at the time and asked, "Daddy, can I pick the cigarette for you?" Bruce knew it wasn't right letting her do it, but he had to admit it was flattering to know Bernice had picked up such a nuance by watching him. Yet the fact that she was watching him so closely at such a young age made him uneasy. He couldn't hide much from her.

Bruce lay in bed, taking long drags from his cigarette. He puffed O's of smoke into the air. He thought about last night and wondered what really happened to his kids. He thought of having to spend another day cleaning up downstairs. He dreaded getting out of bed and took his time doing so. The most he could hope for was to procrastinate his responsibilities for just a little while longer.

There was no leisurely morning for Irene. She had gotten up early with Will and was busy preparing Sunday breakfast: pancakes, sausage, hash browns, and eggs—all Bruce's favorites. This plus strong coffee equaled a happier Bruce on his moody, hungover Sunday mornings.

Bernice could smell the coffee and the familiar mix of breakfast scents wafting all the way to her bedroom. She had been awake for a while but was leery about approaching her mother that morning after how they had left things. Bernice knew that when she walked into the kitchen, Irene would act as though nothing had happened, ignoring the problem to avoid conflict. But the silent treatment always left Bernice confused, not knowing what to say or do, and blaming herself. She would rather be screamed at and get it over with rather than endure the silence, never knowing how long it was going to last.

The enticing smells of breakfast lured her out of bed. As Bernice left her bedroom, she saw that her dad was still lying in bed. A cigarette dangled from the corner of his mouth, and a trail of smoke swirled up toward the ceiling. She was relieved to face him first before having to face Irene. Bernice peeked her head around the door, eyes puffy from too much crying the night before, and said, "Morning. Getting up now?"

"Yup, in a minute," Bruce said, making no immediate attempt to get out of bed, much to Bernice's dismay.

Bernice had to kill time, so she escaped to the bathroom. She listened for movement from her father—the sliding of dresser drawers, heavy footsteps down the hallway. Finally, after a few minutes, she heard Bruce walking down the hall. When Bernice heard the sound of a chair being dragged along linoleum, she knew she was safe to join him in the kitchen.

She shot a glance at Irene when she got there and was relieved to find her busy managing three different frying pans at the same time. That familiar robotic, forced smile was on her face. Bernice was used to that look, the one that signaled she was trying to keep the peace but was likely seething inside.

Bernice grabbed a mug and poured herself some coffee. She added milk and way too many spoonfuls of sugar. Irene saw this and commented more for Bruce than for Bernice.

"Uh-huh, a caffeine fiend just like her dad, except with enough sugar to choke a horse." It was a way of talking to Bernice without directly engaging with her. The goal was to get Bruce talking, getting him off on the right foot.

"Her grandma ruined her, not me. I wonder. How little were you when she gave you your first cup of coffee?" Bruce asked, turning to Bernice.

"Don't know. Don't care. I just love it," Bernice answered with a smile, relieved that her father was there to talk to.

Breaking himself away from cartoons, Will joined the rest of his family at the kitchen table. Bernice snuck a discreet look at his arm. It was covered in gauze and taped up to his elbow. She quickly turned her attention to the food on the table, taking one of everything Irene had put on the table and eating in silence, hoping they could get through breakfast without talking about what had happened last night.

Everyone was quiet that morning, even Will. Bruce made the occasional swipe at Will's food to make him laugh, but it did little to cut the strain that hung in the air. When everyone had finished eating, Bruce leaned back in his chair and lit his after-breakfast cigarette. Usually, they would hang around at the table and enjoy one another's company for a while, but today prompted Irene to start clearing the table right away.

Bernice got up and began clearing dirty plates as well, doing her best to stay out of Irene's way. She hoped Irene would notice how she was helping without being told. It would be nice to feel her mother acknowledge her effort to help. Instead, that fake smile was frozen in place, but now the frown lines had joined in the party. Bernice understood that the smile, although fake, was meant for Bruce. The furled brow was for Bernice, so she kept her head down and stuck with breakfast cleanup.

After his third cup of coffee, Bruce slammed the mug down and pushed his chair away from the table. "Well, this damn sewer isn't going to take care of itself, is it?" he asked rhetorically.

"I'll help," Bernice offered quickly, scared to go back downstairs but wanting to stay on her father's good side by helping. She was also desperate to get away from her mother and the deafening silence of disapproval.

"You know what? Take a break this morning. Finish helping your mom, and then go find your buddies. You only have a couple of weekends left before school starts. Go on and play. I'll come get you if I need you," Bruce ordered Bernice. It was his way of making up for how tough he had been on her yesterday. He also wanted to be alone with his thoughts.

Bruce headed downstairs, leaving Bernice and Irene alone together. Irene had all she could handle that morning already—tending to Will, making breakfast, being pleasant for Bruce, and now cleaning. She just had nothing left to offer Bernice. Besides, Irene felt that Bernice was old enough, at ten years old, and strong enough to get by on her own without her mom holding her hand every step she took. And Bruce was good at talking to Bernice, and she seemed happy with Bruce's talks. Right now, Irene needed time alone too. "I'll finish from here. Get dressed, and head outside," Irene said to Bernice with all the warmth of a glacier.

Bernice draped her dish towel over the oven handle, then jetted to her room to get dressed. She threw on the first pair of shorts and T-shirt she saw and then bolted out of her house. She sprinted through her backyard, crossing the alleyway into Mandy and Lynne's yard. It was a little early for Bernice to be calling on her friends that Sunday morning, but she needed to escape the drama at home. The gorgeous summer day was made even better when Bernice saw that Lynne was already outside that morning. She was busy helping her dad, James, in their impressive vegetable garden, the stalks of corn and sunflowers both towering well above their heads.

Lynne noticed Bernice and sprang from the garden, her bare feet covered in dirt. "Hey!" she yelled.

"What's goin' on? We hangin' out today?" Bernice asked.

"Dad! Do I have anything going on today?" Lynne shouted to her father, who stood just a few feet away from her.

"First of all, I'm right here. Second, it's Sunday. What do you ever have going on, on a Sunday?" Lynne's dad answered, smirking.

Lynne shrugged off her father's comments. "I guess we're on."

Lynne was the same age as Bernice but twice as carefree. She was brash, spoke too loudly, swore too much, and dared do anything. That was what was great about her. Lynne was the up-for-anything, daredevil kamikaze of the neighborhood, a title well-earned. But she had paid for her recklessness. She had been in more fistfights and had broken more bones in the past few years than anyone would even think possible. No matter what, she always went back for more. Bernice loved that about her and envied her boldness but not her broken bones, bruises, and scars.

Mandy, Lynne's older sister, couldn't have been more different from her sister. She was equally as strong but was quiet and self-controlled. Where Lynne was excitable, Mandy was calm. When Lynne was loud, Mandy was subdued.

"Jeez, could you talk a little louder?" Mandy said in a monotone voice as she came out of her house to join the girls.

"What? This is how I talk. Get used to it," Lynne answered.

"As if we have a choice," Mandy teased.

The three girls headed to the park across the street from Mandy and Lynne's house. Mandy looked down at Lynne's feet as they walked and couldn't help but remark, "You're going without shoes? And why are your feet so dirty?"

"Piss off, Mandy!" Lynne fired back.

"Jesus, Lynne. I was just going to say that there could be broken glass on the street or at the park, that's all. But never mind. I'll just 'piss off,' at your request," Mandy said as she walked over to the merry-go-round and plopped herself down.

Bernice was used to this kind of exchange between the two sisters. It was annoying at times, but she welcomed it today. It felt normal, and that was what she needed.

Bernice and Lynne joined Mandy on the merry-go-round. The girls lazily pushed the ground away, sending the trio into a gentle spin. The arid summer breeze wrapped itself around them as they twirled. Bernice was unaware that Lynne had been studying her face.

"Damn. Your eyes are puffy," Lynne remarked.

Bernice didn't like for anyone to know that she cried, especially Lynne. "Allergies or something." Bernice hesitated in answering, and Lynne caught it.

"Bullshit! What's wrong? You were crying, weren't you?" Lynne prodded Bernice for answers.

Bernice knew she was caught. Mandy knew it too and had a way of being subtle that put Lynne and her boldness in check. She shot Lynne a tired look, like she was exhausted from having to be Lynne's calm counterpart all the time. Lynne knew this look meant that she should shut up.

"Everything okay?" Mandy asked Bernice, much more delicately than Lynn had.

"I don't know. It was a weird day yesterday," Bernice began. "Our sewer backed up again, and I had to help clean up all day. Then something…something else happened later on. I…I don't want to talk about it."

"Aw, come on! You can't just say that and then not tell us what happened," Lynne goaded, totally ignoring the obvious strain in Bernice's voice.

"Lynne, cork it! Go on, Bernice," Mandy said.

"No, that's okay. I really don't want to talk about it anyway. You wouldn't believe it if I told you."

"Really? How can you leave us hanging?" Lynne begged.

Bernice couldn't tell them, though she desperately wanted to. Mandy would listen, but Bernice was afraid of what she might think of her. She looked up to Mandy and didn't want to tarnish the good imagine Mandy had of her.

"Well? You gonna tell us or not?" Lynne begged.

"Not," Bernice said. "At least not right now. I just need to forget it for a while. Drop it, all right?"

Lynne slumped dramatically, then threw her head back and shouted to the sky, "Fine! Then what are we doing today?"

Both Bernice and Mandy were relieved that Lynne was letting it go, at least for the time being. The girls threw suggestions at one another about how they would spend their time together that Sunday. They thought about having a water balloon fight, biking around town, or going to the town pool. Bernice didn't feel up to any of those things. They had been doing those same things all summer.

Mandy said, "Hey, the chokecherries are ripe in the alley. Let's go pick some."

"Wow, what an idea, picking chokecherries, Ms. Excitement," Lynne said with heavy sarcasm.

Bernice got up from the merry-go-round without saying a word and walked toward the alley. It really wasn't what she wanted to do, but it would take her mind off things for a while.

The three girls crossed the street and walked up the alley that ran in between each of their properties. Mandy grabbed an empty plastic ice cream bucket from her yard, and they got to plucking the tiny deep-purple berries from the bush. They weren't the kind of berries you would want to eat a handful of. At first, they were delicious and sweet, but they quickly turned on you, becoming unbearably tart and making your mouth so dry that it felt like your cheeks would shrivel up and implode on themselves.

Even so, the girls couldn't resist popping the occasional one into their mouths knowing it was like a little form of torture. Before the sugary flesh of the berry was even dissolved on their tongues, they would be hit by intense bitterness, forcing them to spit the little stone out quickly. It always made them laugh when they got to this point because their mouths felt too dry to make enough spit to get the stone out. But the chokecherries made delicious jams and syrups, so they gladly picked them for their moms to make something out of.

Bernice popped the first chokecherry into her mouth. When the bitterness hit her, she forgot about her troubles and couldn't help but laugh. She let the stony little pit fall from her tongue, leaving a purple trail as it slid down her chin. *It feels so good to laugh,* Bernice thought. It felt so good, in fact, that she decided to grab a handful of chokecherries and shoved about twenty of the tart little devils into her mouth all at once knowing she would get a hysterical response from her friends.

Mandy and Lynne doubled over with laughter as they watched Bernice try her best to chew with her mouth closed for as long as possible. Bernice's eyes bugged out of her head until, finally, she opened her mouth and let a slimy clump of stones slide from her mouth. Tears of both pain and laughter sprang to Bernice's eyes as she waited desperately for the saliva to come back to her mouth. She coughed and gasped dramatically.

Lynne and Mandy were disgusted and completely amused by Bernice's struggle. They were happy she was back to herself, back to going the extra mile to make them laugh.

Bernice tried to ask for water, but her mouth was too dry to speak, so she pointed furiously at her mouth, her tongue hanging out like a panting dog. Lynne grabbed Bernice's wrist and pulled her toward the back of Bernice's house and toward the water spigot. Mandy found the end of the garden hose and passed it to Bernice as Lynne cranked the water full blast. A spray of water gushed into Bernice's face, causing another round of uproarious laughter among the giggly friends.

Their raucous laughter was brought to a halt by the sound of Bruce's angry voice roaring from the downstairs window. "Turn off the goddamn water!"

"Oh, shit! I forgot he's working on the drain!" Bernice said, grasping the spigot and cranking it shut as quickly as she could.

Lynne and Mandy were taken aback by how quickly Bernice's mood had changed from joy to fear. They knew of Bruce's moodiness. Some days, he would joke with the girls and be a ball of laughs. Other days, he was a quiet, brooding shadow of himself. So they followed Bernice's lead and kept quiet and steered clear of him. It had always scared Mandy and Lynne when he was quiet like that. They weren't quite sure why, but the fact that his personality seemed to change so dramatically made them uneasy. They wondered if it was the reason why Bernice's eyes were so red and swollen that morning, but they didn't dare ask.

Bernice yelled loudly through the basement window, "Sorry, Dad!" Then the girls retreated back to the alley, feeling safer there. Bernice cracked a smile again as she realized she was drenched and had chokecherry pits stuck to her shirt. "I must look like a lunatic."

Lynne and Mandy tried to flick the little stones off Bernice's shirt with their index fingers. Giggles crept up on them again. Lynne was distracted by something over Bernice's shoulder. "Speaking of lunatics, don't look now, but guess who's out talking to her rhubarb plants," Lynne said in an uncharacteristically low voice.

"Is she really talking to them?" Bernice whispered back.

"I can't really see her mouth, but she's just bending over the leaves."

Mandy repositioned herself subtly so she could get a better look at Helen. "What the hell? She's just staring at the damn things. Her lips aren't moving. What could be so interesting about those plants?" Mandy remarked.

Bernice couldn't help but giggle and joked, "Maybe I should go ask her to help me get the pits off my shirt."

Keeping the momentum of fun rolling, Lynne dared Bernice to actually do it. They laughed at the thought of Bernice walking up to Helen, bent over her rhubarb, and interrupting her to ask for help taking pits off Bernice's shirt. They pictured Helen's possible reaction, striking them as so funny that they laughed until their cheeks ached.

"Oh, shit! Too late. She's going back to the front of her house," Lynne said. "Hey, let's go spy on her!"

The fun had to continue, so they watched. The girls knew it was wrong. They knew Helen was all alone, and they knew the reputation surrounding her. But the guilt didn't stop them from spying on her. Helen had always been an enigma, and it scared the girls just a little. That was what made spying on her irresistible.

The girls hustled over to the lilac bushes that ran along the backyard of Helen's property. They crouched down and peered between the fragrant flowers to the front of Helen's house. They saw Helen removing a folding aluminum chair from the side of her garage. They watched intently as she opened it up on her front lawn, just in front of her house by the front steps. Then she sat, resting a canvas bag that she had been carrying with her on her lap.

"Have you ever seen her do that, just sit outside and do nothing?" Lynne whispered.

"I'm sure she's done it before," Mandy said. "I bet she heard us and wants to listen in on what we're saying, so keep it down."

Helen turned her head to the left and stared off into the same direction. The girls watched, waiting for something to happen.

Bernice said, "She knows we're here."

"No, she doesn't! How could she?" Lynne countered.

"She's not stupid. Why else would she keep her head turned that way? I don't think she's looking at anything at all. She's pointing her ear this way. She definitely knows we're here," Bernice said.

59

"Yeah, and it's not like we moved over here like ninjas. More like stampeding bulls," Mandy added, making all three of them muffle their giggles.

"I wonder what's in the bag," Mandy said.

"It's a sack full of door knockers," Lynne said, sending the girls spiraling into another fit of laughter, desperately trying to keep it quiet.

"You smart-ass," Bernice said. "That was good. She'd want to have a bag full of door knockers. Her knuckles must be like steel from all that knocking she does."

"If she got a dime for every time she knocked on her door, she'd be a fucking millionaire by now," Mandy added, cracking everyone up.

After the laughter had died down, Lynne suggested that they really find out what was in the bag. Summer break was quickly coming to a close, and the girls were feeling restless and bold. They wanted to do something that would make a mark on the summer. And who knew? Maybe they would find out Helen carried something in that bag that would give them enough fuel to keep them going all year until next summer. It was worth a shot.

They tossed around ideas about how they would get a look inside the bag. Should one of them or all of them walk all the way around the alley to the front and just act like they were casually walking and then strike up a conversation with Helen? Too obvious, they decided. Maybe only one of them should do it. Without warning, Bernice stood up and walked toward Helen, leaving the other girls whispering, "Oh my God, Bernice! What the hell are you doing?"

After what Bernice had seen last night, Helen didn't scare her. In a split second, she had decided she would try the direct approach and just march right up to Helen and start talking to her. She would start with a cheery, "Hey, Helen. How are you today?" But Bernice was stopped cold before she could think of anything else to say.

"Hi, Bernice," Helen surprised her by greeting her and using her name before Bernice could speak. Bernice immediately felt like a fool and knew that Helen had been aware of the girls spying on her all along. "Cat got your tongue?"

Bernice said, "No, no. Just wanted to come say hello."

"And what about your friends? Or are they just going to stay hidden in my lilacs?"

Helen's voice was surprisingly gentle yet firm. She didn't sound annoyed as she asked questions that made it crystal clear that she knew she was being spied on. She knew these three girls and had watched them grow over the years. They were harmless and kind girls at heart, she knew. She couldn't blame them for their curiosity. She never intended on becoming the neighborhood Boo Radley.

"Who, them?" Bernice pointed over at Lynne and Mandy. "Oh, they aren't hiding. They're...they're looking for...their cat. We thought we saw it run into your lilac bushes. It's, uh, white with orange spots on it. Have you seen it?"

Lynne and Mandy couldn't hear what Bernice and Helen were talking about, and when Lynne saw Bernice pointing in their direction, she thought they were being ratted out by her. "Is she blowing our cover?"

"Shut up!" Mandy warned.

"Lost their cat, huh? You should really try yelling for it by its name." Helen enjoyed being in the catbird seat. She contentedly sat looking straight ahead with a satisfied grin frozen on her face.

Bernice knew without a doubt that Helen was on to them. Humiliation rose up within her. She shifted anxiously from one foot to the other. She didn't bother going any further with her foolish tale. Lying always sat in Bernice's stomach like a boulder. She couldn't bear it, so she confessed. "I'm sorry, Helen. I lied. There's no cat. We were just, well, we were spying on you, really. Sorry," Bernice admitted, feeling both mortified and relieved to be free of the lie.

Helen turned her head, so her eyes met Bernice's. This was the closest proximity Bernice had been to Helen, and she was struck by her dark-brown eyes, much like her own. She couldn't help but notice her flawless pale-white skin, thinking she looked much younger than her actual age. *She is actually quite pretty,* Bernice thought.

"I'd prefer to be asked questions rather than spied on. I don't bite, you know. But I do speak." What Bernice didn't know was that Helen was just realizing at that moment that she was able to talk to someone without anxiety. She was speaking her mind with ease in a way she couldn't with adults. She didn't know if it was Bernice's honesty that made her feel comfortable or if it was something else. Either way, Helen was experiencing a close encounter of her own, just like Bernice was. Helen, very uncharacteristically, took control of the conversation and said, "Tell you what. Why don't you ask me any question you want? If you're satisfied with my answer, then I get to ask you a question."

Lynne and Mandy couldn't believe Bernice was still right next to Helen and was actually talking to her. And stranger still, it seemed like she was enjoying it and had forgotten all about them lurking like a couple of tits among the bushes. As the two girls looked on, Bernice took a few seconds to think about what she really wanted to ask Helen. It felt like she may never have this chance again. She appreciated this chance Helen was giving her, and what she asked was not out of nosiness but out of true curiosity.

"Helen, why do you always stare at your house and knock on your door so long before going in? Are you afraid of something?"

Helen figured the question would have something to do with one of her peculiarities, but she didn't want to get in too deep right away with questions and answers. "Okay, that's more than one question, but I'll answer as best I can." Helen sat quietly in contemplation for what seemed like forever to Bernice. The truth was that Helen knew what she was afraid of. It was that metal-hungry thing in the drain and the uncertainty of it. What she didn't know was why she had developed such a long process in reentering her house, a process that was, she admitted to herself, probably not doing her any good. Bernice asking her the question was the first time Helen had to try and put her process into words. It made her uneasy, but she made good on her offer and answered. "I guess it makes me feel safe. I live alone, so yeah, it makes me feel safe. There, how's that?"

"Makes sense," Bernice said. She was dying to hear an answer for her second question but knew it wouldn't happen right now and that she shouldn't be rude and push it. Truthfully, she was a little deflated by Helen's answer. The reason for her tedious routine couldn't be for feelings of just safety alone, could it? "You got a question for me?"

Bernice asked Helen, wondering what Helen could possibly want to know about her.

Helen used her question wisely as well and boldly went to what she was truly concerned about. "Bernice, did something happen at your home last night? I noticed your parents came home quickly and that your father brought the babysitter home soon after she had just gotten there. I'm just wondering if everything is all right," Helen asked with genuine concern. She had noticed Bernice's puffy eyes as well.

Taken aback, Bernice reeled back to what had happened last night. In that moment, she desperately wanted to tell Helen the truth. Something inside her told her that she could confide in Helen, but she just couldn't make herself do it no matter how much she wanted to. "Hey, that's more than one question," Bernice said jokingly but then answered reluctantly, "Something did happen last night. It was...scary. My brother...he got hurt—"

Helen interrupted. "My goodness! Is he all right?"

Trying to keep the mood light, Bernice said, "That's three questions. Not fair, Helen. Not fair."

Sensing that something serious had happened, Helen wouldn't let Bernice stray from the subject. She urged Bernice to go on with her story about what had happened. It looked like Bernice was about to tell her when they heard Irene yelling Bernice's name. Irene's shouting startled Lynne and Mandy, and they immediately sprinted to their house. This made both Bernice and Helen laugh. "Bernice!" Irene shouted louder.

"Sorry, Helen, gotta go. It was nice talking to you," Bernice said as she ran to her house. She was truly sad to have left the conversation.

Helen shouted, "Anytime, Bernice." She meant it.

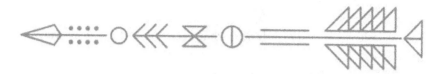

CHAPTER 9

"Goddamn it! She knows I'm down here working on this fuckin' thing! How many times have I told her not to run water when I'm working down here?" Bruce ranted to Irene. When the girls had turned on the spigot, more water and sludge had spurted from the drain, flooding the basement again, causing Bruce to erupt.

"Yelling at me isn't going to help! Maybe Mandy or Lynne did it. How would they know what's going on down here? It was a mistake," Irene said, hoping her words would subdue Bruce's wrath.

"It's not just the spigot, Irene. It's her bullshit story about last night. What the hell was she thinking? I mean, a hand coming up from the drain? It's just pissing me off. In fact, you know what? Call her in now. This shit is going to be settled once and for all." He kicked the pile of dirty towels and punched the paneled wall.

"Why don't you wait until—" Irene was about to suggest that Bruce cool down before talking to Bernice, but he cut her off.

"I said call her in," Bruce demanded.

Irene hated being ordered around like a child. When Bruce acted like this, like a spoiled child, her mind would go blank. Her focus became making Bruce happy again, doing whatever she had to do so that he wouldn't blow his top. Irene loathed herself for her inability to break this cycle, but she wasn't one to rock the boat. Irene stomped up the stairs, Bruce shouting after her, "And if she thinks she's getting out of here before she tells me the whole goddamn truth, she's sorely mistaken!"

Bernice ran from Helen's yard toward home after hearing Irene call her name a couple of times. She knew better than to let her mother have to yell for her too many times. Approaching home, Bernice saw Will sitting on a flower bed covered in dirt and shoving handfuls of soil into his mouth. "Did you know Will's out front eating dirt?"

Irene heard what Bernice said but was distracted by her soaking wet, purple-stained T-shirt. Irene scanned Bernice from head to toe, a flabbergasted look on her face. "I don't even want to know how that happened, Bernice. You don't have time to tell me anyway. Your dad wants to see you downstairs. Now." As Bernice tried to get past Irene in the doorway, Irene grabbed her forearm and warned, "He's going to ask you about last night. He's in a mood, so I suggest you cut the shit."

Irene found Will sitting happily in the garden, eating fistfuls of soil just as Bernice said he was. He had also removed the bandage on his arm and had rubbed dirt into the wound. Irene scolded Will and led him into the house by his elbow, a mangled garden spade dropping from his little hand, looking like a dog had chewed on it. Irene only gave it a quick glance but got on with forcing Will into the house. She also wanted to get in quickly to listen in on Bruce and Bernice in case she needed to step in.

Irene's warning to Bernice about Bruce's sour mood was enough to make her stomach acids burn like they would eat a hole straight through her gut. Bernice walked down the steps with all the braveness she could muster. As afraid as she was to approach her father, she was even more afraid to go anywhere near the drain again. She was also worried about her parents working so close to it. But how could she voice her concern or warn them if they didn't believe her?

Bernice looked down at the state of her soaking, stained clothes and regretted that she had to approach Bruce looking like a fool. She tried to preempt his questioning by taking initiative, hoping it would deter the conversation. "Hey, Dad. I'll grab some towels and help," she said as she purposely skirted far away from the drain, watching it out of the corner of her eye.

Bruce noticed her avoidance of the drain. He also noticed that Bernice looked like she had just poured grape jelly down her shirt. He couldn't help but crack the slightest of smiles. "I guess I know why the water was running. Chokecherries? That T-shirt is as good as ruined."

Bernice thought she was in the clear and started telling Bruce about how she had made Lynne and Mandy laugh by stuffing handfuls of chokecherries into her mouth.

After Irene washed up Will, she left him upstairs watching cartoons before rejoining Bruce and Bernice downstairs. Bernice was in the middle of telling Bruce the chokecherry story when she arrived. She was relieved to hear some laughter from the two. Bernice had a knack for getting Bruce out of his bad moods, sometimes anyway. She would never admit it, but sometimes, Irene was a little jealous of Bruce's relationship with Bernice. They had a special connection that Irene wasn't a part of. Maybe she should have been happy for it, but it stung her.

With the palpable change in the atmosphere, Irene joined Bruce and Bernice. The sounds of the drain continued in the background. Bruce upended an empty plastic gallon bucket and slapped the bottom with the meaty palm of his hand. He looked at Bernice and head-pointed toward it, and she took a seat, scooting the bucket a little farther away from the drain.

Bruce squatted down to eye level in front of her. The anger was gone for now. Bernice could see some tenderness back in his dark eyes along with exhaustion. She sensed what was coming, and she desperately wanted to please him, but she also knew she couldn't lie about what she had seen. Bruce knew his daughter was too scared of him to lie, which was why this story was so hard to believe and infuriating to him.

"Bernice, you know your mom and I love you. There's nothing you could ever do that would change that. Whatever happened yesterday, I need the truth right now. I don't care if it was you that hurt your brother. I just need the truth. Of course we'd be damn mad, but we'd get over it. But I won't tolerate you lying to me. You have never pulled any story like that before, so I don't know why you're trying now."

Bernice began to shake a little and felt tears welling up in her eyes again. She absolutely could not lie to him. "Because what I told you is true. I swear to you," Bernice managed to say through her trembling lips. Bruce fought to remain calm. He had promised him-

66

self he wouldn't raise his voice, which proved exceedingly more difficult than he had thought. He took a deep breath and scratched at his stubbly chin. "I'd never hurt Will. And you saw how upset Marie was. I know what I saw, and it was a hand that came out of that drain. I don't even think we should be near it."

Struggling to regulate the fury building in his voice, Bruce said, "Yes, I did notice how upset Marie was. She was shaking and just stared out her window the whole drive home. Didn't say a word. In fact, when I told her we'd see her next week, she just got out and ran to her front door as fast as she could." Bruce thought for a second, then said to Irene, "I'm surprised we haven't already gotten a call from her mom this morning. Maybe you should give a call and check in, huh?"

Irene nodded. "I did. No answer." Bernice continued with the same story she had told her parents yesterday. She hadn't had the chance to tell them about how the water spewed all the way up to the ceiling. She was pointing to the wet area right above the drain. Irene said, "Bruce, the ceiling was soaked, especially right in that spot."

Bruce laughed in frustration. He just couldn't believe any of this, but he also couldn't make himself believe that Bernice would lie like this. "You understand why this is pretty damn hard to believe, don't you? I mean, it's crazy."

Engrossed in conversation, the three of them hadn't realized that the drain was growing much louder and more active. A suctioning sound came from deep within the drain. Water mixed with a glistening mud-like substance spurted into the air. Unsure of what to do, Bruce grabbed a few towels and threw them on top of the spurting water thinking it would stop the watery mud from spraying. The towels quickly turned black, saturated with sludge. A gurgling, forceful suctioning noise came from deep down in the drain followed by the towels being violently sucked down.

"What in the hell?" Bruce said, moving toward the drain.

"No, Dad! Stay away!" Bernice warned.

He ignored his daughter's warning and reached his hand down the drain to see if he could retrieve a towel. Something inside grabbed Bruce's arm and pulled him down violently. He grimaced in pain as his head hit the concrete floor, his shoulder stuck on top of the drain. Bruce tried in vain to get up, but he was pinned to the ground by whatever had a hold of him underneath the floor.

As Irene and Bernice went to help Bruce get up, he began to rise slowly from the drain, but not voluntarily. As Bruce's arm emerged from the drain, they were horrified to see what looked like a human arm attached to something that looked like a thick snake at the arm-pit giving the arm extra length to lift Bruce high into the air before slamming him down to the floor with such force it crushed Bruce's skull, leaving the skin of his face and head grossly misshapen. His eyes remained open. Teeth had been knocked out of his gums and lay next to his bloodied face.

Then the horrible thing shoved Bruce's limp body away from the drain. On its way back down the drain, the creature plucked a couple of Bruce's silver-filled teeth off the floor before retreating back down into whatever type of hell it had come from.

Oblivious to the hell that was going on in the Fellers' basement at that very moment, Helen sat outside enjoying the sun's rays on her face, thinking about the lovely exchange she had just had with Bernice. She pondered the possibilities of having a friend. Not since her school days had she called someone a friend. Helen's brief encounter with Bernice awoke feelings of yearning for camaraderie.

Sitting outside on a Sunday morning wasn't completely out of Helen's character, but having a conversation with someone was. Usually, she would dart straight for her front door if it looked like someone may walk by or try to approach her. Today's encounter was a small change, but it was the first time Helen allowed herself to even consider that she could make some changes to her old, tired routine. *Change can be good,* she thought. She was tired of living in dread.

Had she been inside her house at that moment, she would have heard the thing in her own bathroom drain becoming active as it churned and clunked from underneath her bathroom floor. If she had heard it, maybe she could have tossed some metal down the drain to satiate it for a while. Maybe she could have saved Bruce Feller. But she didn't know they were being visited by that devil.

Recently, Helen had noticed more activity and noise coming from the drain. She wasn't sure why but decided it would be best to throw in more metal from now on. It truly was her beast of burden, having to keep it a secret yet give it sustenance. She didn't know how she had kept the secret for so long.

She thought of how she had changed her personal habits in order to keep the haunting creature a secret and to keep herself safe. Since Helen only had one bathroom, she made her trips infrequently and quickly, being sure to always supply the monster with metal before doing anything else. Her daily showers had ceased and had been replaced by quick and infrequent ones. It took her an entire month before she dared shower after her father's death, resorting to washing herself with a washcloth and a bar soap at her kitchen sink.

Helen's extra-long time outside that Sunday morning had irked the beast. Helen felt drunk on pleasant thoughts, allowing them to whirl through her worried mind and calm it for the first time since she could remember. But with her attention turned completely inward, the thing retaliated with a vengeance and was taking it out on the Fellers.

Helen couldn't have known that while she sat so content and self-satisfied, Bruce Feller was being thrashed to death by that beast in his basement as his wife and daughter looked on. As Helen felt a possible rebirth of her social self, Bruce was coming to the end of his.

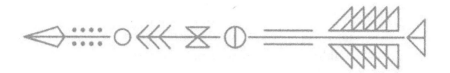

CHAPTER 10

Irene and Bernice huddled together in the far corner of the room. Bruce's body lay facedown just a feet away from them, unmistakably dead. Their nerves were frazzled by the shock of what they had just witnessed.

They heard light footsteps pitter-pattering down the stairs. Irene sprang up, desperate to stop Will before he had to witness this grisly scene or before he was hurt again by the monster if it reemerged. But Will made it to the doorway before Irene could get to him. Her blood ran cold when she saw the look on Will's face as he looked at his father's gory, damaged corpse. He appeared completely unmoved by the sight. No tears welled in his eyes. He didn't scream. In fact, his eyes looked dead, like he was bored by the entire scene. He gave a cool glance to the two heaps of despair that were his mother and sister before approaching Bruce's body.

"Will, honey, you're in shock. Come to Mommy," Irene said, perplexed by her son's reaction and trying to coax him over to her.

Will ignored her. He casually lifted Bruce's slashed and bloodied arm, examining it. Irene and Bernice watched in disbelief as Will smiled when he noticed the same zigzag pattern wound that matched his own. He slid his little hand down to Bruce's wrist where his watch had been attached just minutes before but was now gone. Will's hand found his father's ring finger and was delighted to find Bruce's gold wedding band. He slipped it off and clenched it in his small fist. He released Bruce's limp arm, letting it land hard, then crouched down so his face was just inches away from Bruce's busted face. Irene and Bernice watched in horror as Will stood back up and then popped the wedding band into his mouth, swallowing hard. He relished it as though it were a buttery piece of toffee. He turned on his heels and gingerly walked back to the door.

Reflexively, Irene scolded him. "Spit that out at once!"

The air of amusement on Will's face as he turned to face his mother made Irene feel silly and powerless. Her mind was a tangle of chaos. She forced herself to at least look like she was standing her ground by putting her hands on her hips and forcing a look of disappointment to her face. But her reaction was too delayed, and Will saw right through the act, exposing her weakness. The dead stare he gave Irene sent chills up her spine. *This couldn't be my son,* she thought.

"Here you go, Mommy," Will said sweetly. But it was artificial, tinged with sarcasm. Will put his hands over his stomach and dry-heaved. Sweat sprang to his forehead. His face flushed, and his eyes opened wide. His mouth spewed forth a stream of slimy, bile-infused mud. It struck Irene with force. She fell to the ground and screamed. Will let out a sinister laugh and raced back up the stairs. Irene and Bernice could hear his short strides above them as he ran upstairs.

"My God, Mom, you're bleeding!"

Irene looked down at her body to find nails and bits of shrapnel embedded in her skin. Blood seeped out of the tiny nicks and cuts in her skin. She and Bernice tried to pull a few pieces out, but it proved futile as both of their hands were shaking so badly from the amount of adrenaline flowing through their veins.

"That was not Will," Irene said, her voice strained. A door slammed upstairs, and the footsteps ceased. "He left the house!" Irene said.

"I'm going after him."

"Bernice, no! That was not Will." Irene began to crack. "That was not my Will! Where is he?" she screamed and began to cry.

"Mom, it was Will! I have to see what's going on. What if he hurts someone or gets hurt himself?"

"And what if you get hurt, Bernice? Then what? My God, what the hell is going on?" Irene exclaimed in exasperation, looking back at Bruce's body.

"I'm going. Move away from the drain, Mom," Bernice ordered Irene before bolting up the stairs and out the front door. Irene's desperate plea for Bernice to come back faded into the distance as Bernice ran outside, leaving her mother alone with her husband's fresh corpse.

Bernice spotted a trail of small, muddy footprints. She followed them through the grass and to the sidewalk, keeping her eyes open for any sign of her brother. As she moved farther up the sidewalk, Bernice heard the sound of knocking against glass. She was right in front of Helen's house. She looked up and saw Helen standing by her picture window, a look of concern on her face. She beckoned Bernice to come, but Bernice shook her head and mouthed, "I can't." Helen gave another firm rap on the window and then pointed her index finger down, indicating someone or something was there.

Bernice broke into a run toward Helen's front door. She busted in, not waiting for Helen to open it for her, and there she found Will. He sat contentedly on Helen's sofa, muddying the fabric, a menacing smile on his face. Bernice's mind raced. Then it hit her that she was standing in Helen's house. She didn't know what to say to Helen. How could she explain what was going on? She didn't realize that she really didn't have to. Helen already knew by the state Will was in that this had something to do with the monster in the drain.

Helen's eyebrows buckled. Her gaze darted between Will and Bernice, waiting for one of them to break the silence. She was involved now, whether she wanted to be or not. Bernice thought of her father, dead in their basement, and wondered if she should tell Helen about that at least.

"Talk to me, Bernice. What's going on?" Helen asked.

Bernice looked at Helen. Tears spilled down her cheeks. Finally, she admitted, "Something awful has happened. You won't believe it. But I can prove it's true. I don't know why Will came to you. Something's wrong with him. Something happened to him last night."

"What?" Helen coaxed Bernice on.

Helen saw the familiar zigzag cut on Will's arm. It was the same laceration her father had when she found him dead. She never knew for sure that the monster had made those marks on him, but now, seeing Will's marks, she knew the evil being had everything to do with it.

Bernice abandoned all second thoughts and blurted out, "You'll probably think I'm nuts, but a hand reached out of our drain last night and grabbed Will. It got my dad today, but he got worse than a scratch." Bernice choked on her words. She couldn't make herself say it. She could only cry.

Cruelly, Will let out a sinister snicker in response to his sister's tears. He slid from the couch and onto the floor. He slipped past Helen and ran down the hall and into her bathroom, slamming the door and locking it behind him. Helen went after him and wiggled the door handle. She pounded on the door, demanding Will to open up, but he just chortled at her requests.

"At least we know where he is," Helen said.

With a resolve she hadn't felt in years, Helen took control of the situation. She saw herself in Bernice. Helen would give Bernice what she herself had desperately needed for so many years but hadn't received. She took Bernice by the shoulders, bent down to eye level, and looked her in the eyes.

"Bernice, I'll believe whatever you tell me. Do you hear me? I've seen the hand too. In fact, I've seen it for years. But who would have believed me?"

Bernice wrapped her arms around Helen's waist and hugged her with all her might, surprising Helen. Tears welled in her eyes as she felt the warmth of a hug for the first time in many years. She wished she could indulge in this feeling longer, but a feeling of urgency told her she needed to do something. She unwrapped Bernice's arms from her waist and held her hands.

"We need to figure this out and fast. Whatever that thing is, I know it is calmed by giving it metal. I've been giving it metal through my drain a few times a day to keep it at bay for years. Have you been doing the same?"

"No! I only saw it for the first time last night. But you've seen it? You've known, and you didn't tell anyone? Why didn't you ever say anything? My dad is dead! You could have stopped it!" Bernice cried out.

"What? Your father is dead?" Bernice nodded. "Oh my God, Bernice. Oh my God. It killed my father too. I was all alone, Bernice. I had no one then, and I have no one now. I thought I was the only one who knew about this thing. Please, blame me later if you have to, but right now, we must think fast. Wait, where's your mom?"

"Home. She's hurt, but she's okay."

"How is she hurt? Did it grab her too?"

"No. Just Will and Dad. Will seemed fine last night, but he's acting strange today, like it's not him at all."

Helen's mind was reeling, but she focused on what they could do now to hopefully calm the beast. "Bernice, look at me. I need you to run home as quickly as possible. Go to your garage and find as many pieces of metal as you can. Throw them in a big bucket or something and bring it back here quickly. And make your mom come back here with you. She shouldn't be left alone in that house."

"Should we go get her?" Lynne asked Mandy.

From their own yard, the girls had been keeping an eye on what was going on at Helen's house after Bernice heeded Irene's call. The view wasn't nearly as good as it was from Helen's lilac bushes, but they could see Helen folding up her chair, leaning it against her garage, then retreating into her house. The girls kept watch until they were surprised by movement in the back window. The lace curtain pushed aside, and Helen gave a quick glance to her audience. Mandy thought quickly and ran to a soccer ball a few feet away, kicking it at Lynne, who was still staring dumbly at Helen's window.

"Quick! Kick it back. Act like we don't see her," Mandy urged Lynne even though she knew it was already too late. They had been caught. By the time Lynne retrieved the ball, Helen had already drawn back the curtains and was gone. Lynne kicked the ball back to Mandy. She stopped it and held her foot on top of it.

"Well, kick it back," Lynne whined.

"Never mind," Mandy said, rolling her eyes.

"Come on! Just kick it. It's something to do until Bernice comes back," Lynne suggested.

Five minutes turned to ten as the girls lobbed the ball back and forth, shooting glances at Bernice's house in between turns.

"You think she had to help clean up again?" Mandy asked.

Lynne shrugged. "Should we go knock on their door, see if she'll be able to come back out? Or you think she's in trouble? What do you think she did?"

Mandy knew how her sister worked. Lynne was a chronic questioner. If you kept answering her questions, she would keep asking. So instead of answering, she simply shrugged her shoulders. It worked like magic. Lynne's questions stopped. They batted the ball between them a few more times, all the while eyeing the Fellers' house.

"Hey! There's Will! Will!" Lynne hollered to him as he ran out from the front of the Fellers'. It was impossible not to hear Lynne when she yelled, but Will hadn't. He just kept running. Both girls called his name, but he didn't respond. They couldn't believe their eyes when they saw Will turn from the sidewalk and head straight toward Helen's front door. "Holy shit! Why's he going there?" Lynne exclaimed, dumbfounded.

"And no one's going after him," Mandy said as she started walking tentatively toward Helen's house, unsure if she should take it upon herself to fetch Will.

Lynne followed Mandy toward Helen's, but they both stopped when they saw Bernice bolt out of her front door, looking frazzled and scared, startling them both. They were stunned to see Bernice going to Helen's as well. Lynne was about to call after her, but Mandy put her hand firmly over Lynne's mouth and whispered for her to be quiet. They were now in Bernice's backyard, and Mandy was getting a sickening feeling she couldn't explain. Lynne didn't struggle. She sensed something was wrong, and when Mandy felt this way too, Lynne fell into step.

The girls crept toward the front of the Fellers' house and peeked around just enough to confirm what their eyes had seen—that Bernice had, in fact, gone to Helen's house. Mandy and Lynne looked at each other, baffled. They spoke to each other in whispers.

"What the hell?" Lynne exclaimed.

"I know. And why is Bernice's house so quiet? Why aren't her parents looking for them?" Mandy wondered.

They couldn't see into Helen's house from where they stood, but they knew for sure that Bernice and Will had gone inside. Were they staying there? Voluntarily? Mandy saw Will's little footprints on the ground. Looking closer, she noticed they were made of a slimy, muddy substance with some streaks of red swirling throughout.

Lynne peered down at the footsteps and asked the question Mandy was thinking. "Is that paint or blood?"

Mandy acted like she didn't hear. She was pretty sure it was blood. Thinking of how Bernice had looked when she ran to Helen's house and thinking back to earlier that morning and how Bernice had shown up with eyes red and swollen from crying over something, Mandy was sure there had to be a connection.

"Should we knock?" Mandy asked. She had already intended to, but saying it out loud to Lynne gave her a little more courage to do it. Lynne shrugged and nodded in agreement.

Mandy knocked on the door. No response. She pounded with the meat of her balled up fist, and still nothing. Both the truck and the car were in the driveway, so the girls knew someone had to be home. Mandy twisted the doorknob and gently shoved the door open. They listened before they decided to cross the threshold into the house. They had been taught to never enter someone else's home without being invited first, but instinct pushed them to override their manners. The girls tiptoed through the upstairs living room and kitchen, hearing nothing until they reached the top of the stairs leading to the basement. They heard whimpering coming from the basement.

Fear gripped the girls. They didn't have to speak to each other to know what the other was thinking. The first thought they had was that Bruce had snapped and that they were walking in on something that was none of their business, and they wished they had never ventured into the house. Mandy and Lynne stood at the top of the steps, still as stones, trying to calm their racing hearts and imaginations.

Through the whimpering, they heard Irene's voice rise from the basement, not in a yell but in a sad plea. "Oh God, somebody, help!" The girls' fear of Bruce was replaced with concern for Irene. Mandy cautiously descended the steps with Lynne close behind.

Hearing the footsteps, Irene called out. "Bernice, did you find…" She trailed off, mortified, as she locked eyes with the neighbor girls standing in front of her. The girls covered their mouths, muffling the screams that escaped deep from their diaphragms at the sight of Irene, still dripping with blood from the metal shards Will had purged at her. Irene struggled to find words to explain, but they wouldn't come. Irene was just as gobsmacked as they were. At least she had managed to step around the door, blocking the girls' view of Bruce's body. They didn't need to see that.

The front door slammed again, breaking the silence. Bernice bounded down the stairs and froze when she saw Mandy and Lynne. "What the hell are you guys doing here? You shouldn't be here right now!" Bernice tried to grab their wrists and force them up the stairs, but they struggled free of her grasp.

Mandy, feeling a surge of adrenaline and anger, demanded from Bernice, "What the hell is going on, Bernice? What happened to your mom? Why is she bleeding? Your dad did it, didn't he?"

"No!" shouted Bernice in defiance. "How dare you even think that!"

"I don't believe you anymore, Bernice," Mandy continued, emboldened. "Where is he? What has he done?"

Bernice was pissed off at the insinuation and defended her father. Without giving it a second thought, she brushed past her friends and turned to face them. "You want to see where my dad is right now? I'll show you! I'll give you a damn good look!" Bernice grabbed Mandy by the elbow and pulled her along, budging past Irene, forcing her to the spot where Bruce's body lay broken and lifeless. Lynne followed, gripping Mandy's other arm. "You guys happy now?" Bernice said through tears of fury.

Lynne and Mandy were sickened with shock and fear. Seeing this, Bernice was struck with guilt at her rash behavior, inadvertently pulling them into the situation. Irene and Bernice expected the girls to scream and run away any second, leaving them to deal with whatever hell came next. Instead, the girls were quiet and still, their eyes transfixed on Bruce. They couldn't believe he was dead. What in God's name had they walked in on?

Mandy squinted her eyes and took a couple of steps closer and bent over to look at Bruce's arm. "Those marks. How did he get them?" Irene and Bernice looked at each other, neither volunteering an answer. Mandy looked at Lynne for a moment before asking her, "Remember his sketches?" Lynne nodded, crossing her arms over her chest and cowering down into a crouch as though it would protect her from things she may not want to hear.

"Bruce's sketches? What are you talking about, Mandy? He didn't sketch," Irene said.

"No, not Bruce. Roy. Roy had sketchbooks," Mandy clarified.

"Yeah, the pictures that got him sent to the ward," Lynne added.

Both Mandy and Lynne had never before considered that the drawings their older brother had made nearly two years ago had anything to do with something real. At the time, it was hard enough to accept that their own brother was turning into another person, breaking down mentally, and would be taken away from them at such a young age. The change in Roy seemed to have happened overnight, very abruptly. Mandy's mind raced. She had to ask no matter what her question made her sound like.

"Is…is Bruce dead because…because of something in…in the drain?"

Bernice said nothing but affirmed with a nod. Mandy moved away from the drain. The images of a snakelike thing with huge black eyes and humanlike arms flashed through her mind. She had seen it so many times in Roy's sketches. She remembered seeing that zigzag pattern over and over again on different pages. Something real had deeply scared Roy. Of course, no one had believed it. It was easier to believe that he was going insane. The realization that it was real and that it wasn't Roy's fault emboldened Mandy but filled her with dread that there was actually some sort of being that lurked in the world beneath them all.

"Roy saw it. Whatever did this, Roy saw it, and all he could do was draw these horrible sketches of it until it just ruined him," Mandy put forth the words as her mind snapped together pieces of this puzzle. It wasn't quite relief she felt in knowing that whatever had caused Roy's psychotic break was something real. Relief would only come with redemption for Roy.

Bernice broke in. "We don't have time to talk about this now. Will's locked himself in Helen's bathroom. She's seen this thing too. We have to get back over there. She's been waiting for me to come back this whole time. She said it's calmed by metal, so we need to grab some metal and get over there right away. We're all in on this now, right?"

No one answered. There was no choice in the matter.

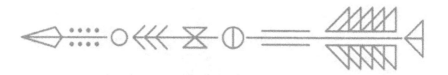

CHAPTER 11

After Bernice had left to retrieve Irene and some metal, Helen focused on getting Will out of her bathroom. She walked down the hallway, stopped at the bathroom door, and stood quietly, listening. She could hear the rustling of paper and what sounded like hard objects being dropped on the floor. Then there was silence. She could see the shadow of Will's feet as he came and stood close to the door. He knew she was there listening to him.

"Will, I need you to unlock this door," Helen ordered calmly. No response. "Will, I said unlock this door. You are not safe in there all by yourself," Helen commanded more forcefully.

Helen heard Will shuffling away from the door. Then the all too familiar noise began, the one she did not want to hear—the grinding, hissing, and burping of the drain. There was no way to unlock the door from the outside. She would have to try and break the door down.

"Stand back, Will," Helen warned before stepping back and slamming her shoulder into the center of the door. It budged a little the first time, so she slammed harder. The wooden frame split. She was almost in. Before ramming her shoulder into the door one last time, Helen noticed there was no longer any light shining from underneath the bathroom door. She looked down at her feet to find them being enveloped by black sludge seeping out from under the door.

"I'm coming, Will!" Helen shouted and threw the full weight of her body onto the door. She gripped the doorknob, bracing herself as her feet slipped on the sludge.

At first, all Helen could see was that her bathroom was dripping from floor to ceiling with the sludge, noticing how it glistened. She turned her head and was met with an unimaginable sight. There was Will, cradled in the arms of a long, thin, snakelike being. Its head nearly touched the ceiling. It was covered in the muddy slime. It looked at Helen out of its huge almond-shaped, jet-black eyes. A single point of red sat in the center of each eye. Although utterly terrified, Helen forced herself to appear calm and to move slowly. She couldn't allow the panic to overtake her if she was going to save Will.

Helen broke her gaze with the beast's hideous eyes and then studied its solid tubelike body. It looked reptilian but with no scales. Its arms looked strangely familiar, human. Her eyes skimmed the length of the arms and rested on where they attached to the body. Helen was revolted to see a thick, bumpy seam where the arms looked as though they had been soldered to the monster's body. She shuddered, thinking this monster had attached human arms to itself.

In order to save Will, Helen forced herself to replace her fear with anger. She used images of her dead father to fuel her anger. She thought of Bruce, dead at the hands of this creature. Now it had Will in its stolen human arms. Helen looked it dead in the eyes and thought of the only thing she knew it craved.

"Hungry?" Helen asked the monster, grabbing the small silver chain that hung around her neck. She tore it away in one tug before tossing it at the adversary. She watched as a mouth emerged from beneath the thick layer of goop. It opened vertically, revealing tiny, sharp, jagged teeth. The length of the mouth was easily the length of Will's entire body.

Helen gasped as the monster dropped Will to the floor so it could use its arms to grasp desperately at the silver chain. But rather than keep it for itself, Helen watched in terrified wonder as Will opened his mouth, and the monster dangled the chain over Will's head before lowering it in with the finesse of a mother offering her child a strand of cooked spaghetti. Will chewed on the chain and swallowed hard. When he opened his mouth, Helen could see that his pearly-white baby teeth were badly chipped, leaving jagged, sharp, piranha-like little nubs.

Helen hoped her instinct was right, that this thing was not going to hurt Will since it had actually fed him. She forced a grin to her face and looked the monstrosity in the eyes. Whether it possessed feelings or not, Helen didn't know. But if it did, she wanted it to see that she was pleased with how it was taking care of Will first before itself. It was the only thing she could think to do in the moment.

With a forced kindness and warmth in her voice, Helen said, "And now something for you." Helen held up her index finger, hoping that the invader would somehow understand that this meant she would be back in a second. Helen sensed that this thing could feel human emotion.

She backed out of the bathroom slowly, but the second she was out of the brute's sight, she raced to her kitchen as fast as she could. She thought of the largest metal objects she had in her house and opened the cabinet where she kept her pots and pans. She grabbed a small but heavy cast-iron skillet and a stainless steel pot before walking back down the hall, putting both pans behind her back before she turned to face the foul fiend. She pasted a smile on her lips and spoke to it like it was a pet.

"I brought you something," Helen advertised in a singsong voice. She flashed the pots from behind her back and held them up for it to see before placing her offerings on the floor. She backed away.

The grimy behemoth reached out its arms to fetch the pots and then deposited them both into its grotesque mouth. Its teeth gnashed against the cast iron and the stainless steel, creating an earsplitting din that reverberated through every cell of Helen's body. It chewed and gulped both pots down with ease and within seconds. Will sat expressionless beside the monster, completely unfazed by the ruckus.

The satiated beast closed its mouth, allowing it to disappear underneath the sludge that clung to its body. The eyes disappeared in the same way, falling under the veil of black ooze. With the mouth and eyes gone, all that remained of the monster was its snakelike body and arms hanging at either side. Helen caught a glimpse of something glowing and red on the monster's body between its arms but couldn't make out what it was.

A deep, low hum began emanating from the beast. The glimmering muck, now nearly covering the entire bathroom, began to swirl in a whirlpool motion, slowly at first but quickly churning with ever-growing speed. The force of the whirlpool sludge pulled at Helen's feet, threatening to take her down. Before trying to escape its pull, Helen lurched toward Will, grabbing at his arm, but she was violently wrenched off her feet by the agitated muck. She crashed hard onto her hip but still managed to pull herself out of it and into her hallway. She escaped in time to see the whirlpool spin faster, humming ever more intensely. The shiny goo was being sucked back down the drain, the opening growing larger as the spinning accelerated, like it was tearing pieces of the drain walls away.

Will sat cross-legged on the bathroom floor, the sludge creeping up to his hips. His body shifted as the ominous mud grabbed hold of him, sending him spinning in the direction of the whirlpool. Helen shouted his name, but Will was completely overtaken. He looked catatonic, completely transfixed by and under the savage's control. The ground rumbled, and the sound of pipes being burst and crushed came from deep in the belly of the drain. The creature disappeared down into the whirlpool, taking Will along with it.

"No! Will!" Helen cried helplessly. Helen couldn't take her eyes off the constantly churning cesspool that had taken over her bathroom. She listened for screams from Will or for any noise that would indicate that he was still there and still alive. But the constant hum of the relentless whirlpool drowned out any sound that may have been fighting to be heard from below. The only other noise she heard was the sound of her front door swinging open.

"Will!" Irene hollered, barging into Helen's home. Bernice, Mandy, and Lynne followed. She stumbled around, wild-eyed, searching for Helen's bathroom where she was told Will had locked himself away. She saw the obviously flustered Helen sitting on her floor in the hallway.

"Where's Will?" Helen didn't know how to answer Irene, who was approaching her now, clearly agitated. "Answer me, Helen. Where is he?" Irene asked Helen, her tone laden with blame.

Helen pointed toward her bathroom. *Irene has to see it for herself,* Helen thought. Bernice, Mandy, and Lynne watched Irene go toward the bathroom door. They saw Irene's jaw drop as she peered inside.

Bernice crept toward her mother. "Mom, what is it?"

Irene put her hand out and gave Bernice a weak "Stay back." Of course Bernice didn't heed the warning. She bolted to her mom's side and stood agog as she beheld the whirling vortex that was now Helen's bathroom floor. Mandy and Lynne joined them and looked on in fright. Helen rose to her feet to offer the girls support at the sight even though she felt as though she needed the support herself.

The group looked on as the whirlpool began spinning with greater velocity, a great suctioning noise emanating from the vortex. Within seconds, the sludge was completely sucked down, leaving traces of itself in slimy, muddy puddles around the bathroom. The humming ceased. In the monster's wake, a large opening the size of three manholes now marked the spot where the small drain had been. The walls of the freshly made culvert dripped with the glittery ooze. An aroma of motor oil, heated metal, and sewage saturated the air.

Irene's terror turned to wrath. She took it out on Helen. "Where the hell is my son?"

Taken aback by Irene's apparent blame, Helen answered directly. "It took Will down with it."

"What the fuck do you mean, Helen? What are you talking about?"

Bernice understood her mom's fury but was embarrassed at how she was taking it out on Helen. Bernice, trying to aid Helen, explained to Irene. "It's the same thing that got Dad."

"If you saw it, then why the hell didn't you stop it from taking my son?" Irene screamed at Helen.

"Mom! Helen didn't do it! Stop talking to her like—" Irene's hand slapped the rest of the words right out of Bernice's mouth. Bernice held her cheek and looked at Irene, shocked by the strike.

Irene's slap awoke a maternal instinct in Helen. She stepped in front of Bernice and faced Irene. Mandy and Lynne stood on either side of Bernice as though they were protecting her as well. Helen said nothing but locked gazes with Irene, sending a silent plea that she should come to her senses and realize they were all on the same side. Helen felt as though she was dealing with a wild animal who had gone mad looking for its wayward young.

Irene stared back at Helen, unable to calm her frayed nerves. Her pent-up anxiety and anger had to go somewhere. She stood as tall as possible, ridiculously trying to meet Helen's six-foot frame with all five foot two of herself. Her nerves wracked her body, making her twitch as she tried to control herself. She peered around Helen's frame and directed her words toward Bernice.

"So you're on this lunatic's side now? Just yesterday, you and your dad stood in the window and watched her, mocking her. Now he's dead, and your brother's gone missing on her watch, and you run to her side? She's obviously known about this thing for a long time and didn't think it was a good idea to say anything to anyone. Why the hell else had she been so goddamn afraid to go into her own house for years that she feels the need to stare at it and knock on her own door like a damn fool?"

Helen stepped closer to Irene and stared down into Irene's hate-filled face. She didn't feel the need to defend herself to this woman. Everyone already thought Helen was crazy. She was angry at Irene, but not for having accused her of knowing about the beast or for being called a lunatic. She was angry about the way Irene aimed at Bernice's self-esteem by using this moment and all its uncertainty to make her question herself and what she had actually seen. Helen couldn't stand for that.

"Irene, accuse me of whatever you like. The fact is that this monster, which I've only just seen in its entirety today, still has your son. I don't know if he's dead or alive. And we aren't going to find out as long as you stand here and focus on who's to blame. We need to get to Will. We need to focus our energy on that. You can berate me all you want afterward."

Irene relented for the time being. She showed no remorse for her behavior toward Helen. Anger was still apparent in Irene's eyes over what Helen had said. But for now, Irene resigned herself to work with the group just long enough to find Will.

Even though Irene had seen the hand with her own eyes and had watched it thrash her husband to the ground until he was dead, she still felt the need to hold someone accountable, someone she could see right now. Irene was so well-trained in the art of denial that she actually started to make herself believe that she hadn't really seen the hand. It was far too difficult to explain. *It would be easier to lie, to block that part out,* she thought. The ramifications of just having to relay such an outlandish story to anyone was more than she could bear. It didn't matter to her that her own daughter could back up her story or that three others could now do the same. She just couldn't stand the thought of even one townsperson not believing her story and that she may be looked upon as crazy. She couldn't have that. She had worked on her untarnished reputation her whole life, and she wasn't about to let this monster ruin it. And she wasn't going to let Bernice ruin it for her either. *Bernice could never just let things be,* Irene thought.

Irene pictured her husband lying dead in the basement and had the twisted, harsh thought that maybe now Bernice would feel guilty about ever questioning how much Bruce drank and would finally drop it now that he was dead. Irene had been poisoned with codependency for years but was blind to it. It had clouded her judgment for so long that it was automatic for her to find someone else to blame for her husband's faults. Many times, it fell onto Bernice.

"We need to call the cops," Irene announced.

"Not yet. We don't have time," Helen countered.

"It's my son down there, and I say we call them now," Irene insisted.

"And say what, Irene? How do we explain this? Do you really think they're going to believe it? We'd waste too much time trying to convince them, and we need to use our time to get Will back," Helen said, hoping her reasoning would get through to Irene.

"Well, at least the sanity of the cops can be trusted," Irene snidely remarked, peeved at Helen's control of the situation as her son's life hung in the balance.

Catching the passive-aggressive dig, Helen said, "Well, you make a good point. The fact that I'm involved would give our little group a lot less credibility with the cops, wouldn't it?"

"Who says you would be the one saying anything at all? It's my son and my husband, and I'll do the talking," Irene declared.

"But we're all involved in this, Irene. We're all affected. I can't just let you do the talking while the rest of us sit in silence," Helen fought back.

"*Let* me? I don't need your permission to do anything," Irene snarled as she began walking down the hall in search of Helen's telephone. The girls begged Irene to wait. Helen got to the phone first and stood in front of it, blocking Irene. The noon whistle sounded from outside. Bernice knew what that meant for Mandy and Lynne.

"We've got five minutes to get home for lunch, or Mom will be out looking for us. What do we tell her?" Mandy asked Helen.

"Tell your parents nothing. Can you get through lunch without saying anything? We need to think before we act on this," Helen answered.

"No, Helen! There's nothing to think about. We don't need to waste any more time. Now get out of the way," Irene argued as she tried pushing past Helen.

Helen pushed Irene away with such strength that it knocked Irene back, her feet backpedaling too slowly to catch the weight of her falling torso, causing her to collapse onto her backside. Helen hadn't meant to push Irene so forcibly and was startled by her own might.

"Go home, and don't come back," Helen ordered Mandy and Lynne. "You can tell your parents the truth later, but not right this second. Now go!"

The girls rushed out of Helen's front door and ran for home as quickly as their legs would carry them, leaving Helen, Bernice, and Irene behind, hoping they would be able to figure a way out of this mess and quickly, however bleak the situation seemed.

Irene fumed as she stared up at Helen from the floor. She supported herself up on Helen's coffee table, her eyes darting between Helen and Bernice. "You know how stupid that was, right?" Irene asked Bernice. Bernice didn't respond but watched as her mother slinked back toward Helen. "Stupid because Helen here doesn't know that Lynne can't hold her piss. She'll probably spill her guts before she crosses the threshold of her front door. But that works in my favor, so thanks, Helen. If the cops won't show up soon, Lynne's parents will," Irene said with the satisfaction of an asp spewing venom on its prey.

Helen was fed up with Irene's combative attitude. Even so, she managed to keep her anger at bay. She had to focus on what to do next and could give Irene no more consideration than a pesky fly buzzing around her face.

Bernice couldn't stand the tension between her mother and Helen. She couldn't help but take Helen's side but struggled with the inherent guilt of going against her own mother. Subconsciously, Bernice sensed where this was going. Even though both Helen and Irene knew something was prowling underground, Helen knew it had to be faced head-on. Irene, on the other hand, was busy creating more drama to distract from the inconvenient, awful truth.

After some silence, Helen proposed, "Either one of us goes down there, or we try and lure it back out."

Irene cackled over the suggestion. She was completely stuck in her own fight-to-win, egocentric mind. Irene would consider no other option except contacting the police. Helen and Bernice tried to ignore her. "I'm the smallest, so I should go down there," Bernice offered.

Irene didn't protest, but Helen did, saying, "I can't let you go down there. It may not be an option for any of us, but I definitely wouldn't allow you to go."

"Why don't you go down there?" Irene asked Helen, her voice flat and monotone. "After all, Will went missing while he was with you in your house. You've managed to turn my own daughter against me. It seems it's the least you could do."

Irene's spiteful words were met with silence from Helen and Bernice. Bernice looked to Helen for a sign of what to say or how she should react. Helen's warm look back at her told Bernice to keep quiet. It was a silent agreement between the two that they would not respond to Irene's cruel insinuations. Getting Will back had to remain the priority even if his own mother was blind to it. Something evil and ugly had come over Irene.

"Bernice, there's some rope hanging on a hook in my garage. You'll see cardboard boxes full of old tools and pieces of metal on the floor by the back wall. Bring me the rope and as many pieces of metal as you can carry. We'll try luring the thing out."

Bernice didn't like the idea, but the resolve in Helen's voice implied it was not up for negotiation. Bernice hurried to Helen's garage, leaving Helen alone with Irene. While Bernice gathered the materials, she considered how protective and nurturing Helen was. She was willing to risk her own life for Will, and she wouldn't allow Bernice to risk hers.

Helen and Irene walked back down the hall and stood peering into the now gaping, ominous opening in the bathroom floor. With Bernice out of earshot, Helen had to get something off her chest. "I couldn't help but notice that you didn't protest when Bernice offered to go down there. You showed no concern for her safety, not an ounce."

There was no malice in Helen's remark. Rather, her words were imbued with heartbreak for Bernice. Irene read it loud and clear and couldn't bear the truth in what Helen's words implied. She wouldn't allow this woman to judge her so harshly. This had to stop. She let her anger completely consume her.

Irene grabbed Helen's arm and tried to fling her into the widened drain. Helen's leg slipped from underneath her and slid down into the opening. She was able to hold on to the edge of her medicine cabinet just enough so she wouldn't slide down completely. Irene raised her leg up high to stomp down hard on Helen's arm, but Helen was able to knock her leg away with her other hand, causing Irene to stumble. Helen grabbed Irene's other ankle and tried using it to pull herself from the drain. The suction sound began, and the whirlpool cranked into action once again. Helen's pull sent Irene crashing to the ground, landing her in a pool of the glittering muck. The more Irene struggled, the more fixed in it she became, like quicksand.

Helen managed to escape the sludge quickly, scrambling away on hands and knees into her hallway. She turned to see Irene shrieking in horror as she lost her battle to break free. The drain widened further and swallowed Irene, swiftly and completely.

Bernice struggled to breathe as she hoisted the heavy materials from the garage up Helen's steps and back into the house. She noticed a familiar car drive by the house twice. It went by once while she entered Helen's garage and again as she was making her way back into Helen's house. Bernice knew that station wagon from somewhere with its beige top and wood grain bottom, visible dings in its bumper. It drove by often, she only just realized. She had never paid attention to who drove it. She tried to catch a quick look at the driver this time before she disappeared back into Helen's house, but all she could make out was a woman's profile and a head full of large dirty-blond ringlets that brushed the woman's shoulders. *I'll mention it to Helen,* she thought, *just in case we are being watched.* Maybe Helen would know who it was.

Bernice forgot all about the station wagon as soon as she saw Helen's look of alarm as she sat staring into the bathroom from her hallway. Bernice heard the hum of the whirlpool as she moved closer to Helen. Helen didn't try to stop Bernice as she peered into the bathroom and looked around.

"What is this? Where's my mom?"

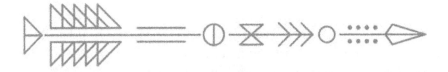

CHAPTER 12

Before stepping into their house for lunch, Mandy grabbed Lynne by both shoulders and spun her around so they stood face-to-face.

"Lynne, we can do this. We have to, okay? Just look down, eat fast, and we're back outside. If they ask if something's wrong, let me do the talking. You got it? Don't blow it!"

They opened the screen door and slipped off their shoes in the entryway. They each took a deep breath before turning the corner and walking into the kitchen. They were surprised to find the kitchen empty. The table was set, but their father wasn't sitting in his usual perch at the head of the table. Their mother, Regina, was also strangely absent. Usually, she was busy puttering around at the stove, fridge, or table, adding the finishing touches to whatever she had made for lunch. In fact, no food had even been prepared.

From the other side of the house, they heard their mother's laments. "And you were the one who signed the papers! You had him committed!"

Mandy and Lynne walked toward the voice and saw Regina standing in the bathroom. James came into sight and wrapped his arms around his wife. Regina buried her face in his chest, muffling her cries against his starchy work shirt. Lynne was the first to notice the familiar sludge that clung to her father's arms and stuck to his stockinged feet.

James saw Mandy and Lynne from his periphery and quickly released the grasp he had on his wife and slammed the door shut. "Go outside until I tell you to come in!" James frantically ordered his daughters.

Mandy pressed her ear to the bathroom door and heard a whirring noise, the same noise she had heard in Helen's bathroom. She gave Lynne a knowing look. Mandy wondered whether she should pound on the door and admit that they knew what was going on inside or whether she and Lynne should take the chance to go back to Helen's house to help find Will.

Lynne broke Mandy's train of thought and banged on the door with her fist, begging for her parents to get out. Mandy grabbed her by the wrist and shushed her. Lynne obviously wanted to stay to protect their parents. *But what could we do?* Mandy thought. She knew her dad wasn't about to open the door for them.

"We're going back outside!" Mandy hollered through the closed door. She forced Lynne away from the door and back to the entryway, ignoring her protests. "He's not going to let us in, Lynne. There's nothing we can do. Will is already gone. We have to use this time to get back over to Helen's and help get him back if we can. We have to," Mandy urged.

Both girls clumsily stuffed their feet back into their shoes and started back across their yard toward Helen's house. They noticed the station wagon slowing in front of Helen's, so they hid behind the Fellers' house and waited for it to pass. They recognized the vehicle as well. It slowly trolled past Helen's house, then came to a dead stop in front of the Fellers'. Lynne peeked around the corner and saw the woman in the driver's seat.

"It's the stalker," Lynne announced.

"She must've seen someone going into Helen's or something. Why else would Patsy slow down in front of her house?" Mandy said. They waited to move toward Helen's until they saw the station wagon roll away and turn the corner.

"Do you think Bernice knows? About Bruce and Patsy, I mean?" Lynne asked her sister.

"I don't know. Everyone else seems to."

Officer Carson dropped the phone back on the receiver. His thick fingers drummed atop his desk as he chewed over the call he just had. He pushed himself away from his desk, the wheels of his chair squeaking as they rolled across the old pine floor of the Ramsey Police Department.

"Burns, finish up. We gotta spin by the Fellers' place up on Eighth Street," Carson ordered his junior partner.

With his mouth packed full of roast beef sandwich, Officer Burns asked, "Bruce's place? What's going on? Who called?"

Bits of meat and bread ejected from his jabbering gob. Burns took a swig from his bottle of root beer to wash the sandwich down, grimacing hard as he gulped down the vigorous carbonation as it mixed with the soggy sandwich and slid down his throat like a fizzy sponge. He let out a robust belch and then fastened his holster, put on his hat, and raced to the door. The eagerness of his junior partner amused Carson.

"Whoa, Burns. It's just a wellness check, not a murder," Carson said.

"Hey, how often do we have something to do on a Sunday?" Burns said, slowing himself a little to wait for Carson.

Burns had only been on the force for about a year. He had hoped for more action, but a small-town precinct didn't offer the excitement he had anticipated. For now, it was the only job opening within the county, and Burns wanted to stay in the area he had grown up in.

It had taken Burns a while to settle in. Carson had his work cut out for himself having to be the one responsible for breaking Burns of his bad habit of being a little too overzealous in his dealings with minor traffic offenses or with the juveniles who broke curfew.

About two months into his service, Burns had rashly decided to pin fifteen-year-old Kyle Lambert against a chain-link fence by his neck, all because he had climbed over the fence to retrieve his football, either ignoring or not seeing the No Trespassing sign. Young Officer Burns had pinched Kyle's neck a bit too firmly with one hand while he scolded him about how he shouldn't ignore those No Trespassing signs, that they were there for a reason, and that he shouldn't be rooting around on private property no matter what.

Carson had been watching the scene unfold from the patrol car and raced to intervene immediately the second he saw Burns go for Kyle's throat. It was the first time Carson had allowed Burns to approach a situation alone, much to his regret. Carson raced to the scene. Kyle, though young, looked more confused than scared as Burns overreacted to his offense. "Burns, that's enough. What's going on?" Carson asked.

Carson listened to Burns sternly explain that it was a trespassing situation. Burns's intense seriousness as he explained the ridiculous details was absurd. It reminded him of Barney Fife, the blundering, simpleton sheriff from *The Andy Griffith Show*. That coupled with the confusion on Kyle's face almost set Carson on a fit of laughter. But the thought of how Burns had held Kyle by the neck quickly shot down the anger.

"All right, Burns," Carson said, turning to Kyle. "No worries, kid. Just make sure you pay more attention to posted signs. Is your neck okay?" Kyle nodded. "All right. Go on home," Carson ordered.

When Kyle was out of earshot, Carson got in Burns's face. "Just what in the hell did you think you were doing? You think that was a situation worthy of a choke hold? He's a kid, and it was only trespassing! And by the way, since when do we grip the neck with our hands? Saw that in a movie or something? I never want to see that shit again, hear me?"

It was the first of many tongue-lashings about how Burns's interventions were usually way too over-the-top for the situation. Aside from Burns's overblown antics, Carson genuinely liked the kid and knew he would be able to make a good cop out of him someday. But for now, he needed to be kept on a short leash.

"Bruce Feller's place, eh?" Burns said as he slid into the passenger's side of the patrol car.

Carson cranked the ignition and said, "Yup, your old pal Bruce. That was Patsy Jensen on the phone. Said she drove past the Fellers' this morning—surprise, surprise—and saw Mr. Critic's daughter running back and forth from their house to Helen's. Said she saw the wife do the same thing."

"Helen? Paranoid, crazy Helen? I didn't think anyone ever talked to her, let alone visit her."

"Cut her some slack. She's had a tough life." Carson defended Helen even though he only knew her through town gossip. He had never spoken to her in person. "But you're right. As far as I know, she doesn't mix with anyone in town. Never has visitors or anything. That's probably another reason why Patsy was concerned. That, plus she said Bruce's wife and daughter looked pretty rattled. She said it looked like the missus was bleeding."

"I'll give you two guesses who did that. That arrogant prick! I always suspected he was beatin' her. The guy's a walking time bomb with that temper. Must've finally gone off," Burns concluded.

"You know you can't assume shit like that. And you can't let your own history with Feller cloud your judgment, all right? That stays between you and him."

"Yeah, I know," Burns said. "But you gotta admit. The fact that Patsy called it in makes you wonder, don't it?"

"Burns, we don't know if those rumors are true either," Carson warned.

"But of all people, Patsy. Just seems like quite a coincidence to me that it was her that just happened to be driving by at the right time to see Irene coming from her house, and bleeding no less. Who knows? Maybe they got in a fight over Patsy." Burns couldn't help but make assumptions.

"Point taken, Burns, but just keep that in your back pocket for now, all right? Besides, even if you're right, why the hell would they be going to Helen's?" It was Carson's time to push for information. "Anyways, what was the cause of that row between you and Feller that time?"

"I thought you said it was just between me and him," Burns said, annoyed.

"You seem to be in the talking mood, so spill it."

"I overheard Feller talkin' to his buddies about my old man when I was on duty at the county fair last year. Feller said something about how there ain't no way a son of Joe Burns could be in law enforcement. Then he told 'em, 'The best part of that boy slid down his mother's leg.' Well, they all laughed, and I lost it. You know what happened next," Burns said, looking out the passenger's window.

"You lost your cool, dropped your weapon, and got your ass kicked. How could I forget? And not as much as a slap on the wrist for Bruce. That's the power of reputation in a small town, boy. That's why you gotta learn to keep your cool. You talk about Feller's temper. You gotta keep a lid on your own," Carson advised Burns.

Burns rested his head on his hand, his elbow propped against the ledge of the car door. The look of embarrassment and defeat on his face made Carson regret bringing up the subject. To lighten the mood, Carson screwed his face into a look of disgust and went for some good-intentioned ribbing of his partner.

"Best part of you ran down your mother's leg, huh? Whew, that's harsh! Pretty good, though. I gotta remember that one," he said, nudging Burns on his shoulder.

"Fuck off," Burns fired back with a smile, playfully slapping Carson's arm away.

The patrol car rolled to a stop in front of the Feller home. Carson turned off the ignition. "Let's sit tight for a while."

With Patsy's station wagon out of sight, Mandy and Lynne made a mad dash from the Fellers' backyard to Helen's house.

"Lookie here. We got some runners," Burns said, watching the two girls sprint toward Helen's house. Their interest piqued when the girls bounded up Helen's front steps. They stopped suddenly but didn't knock.

"Mandy, stop," Lynne whispered as they reached the top step. Mandy saw Lynne motion toward the cop car stopped in front of the Fellers' house. All Mandy could think to do was to knock on the door, hoping the cops wouldn't think anything suspicious was going on. *But someone had obviously called the police. Why else would they be stopped in front of the Fellers'?* Mandy thought.

Mandy's hopes of avoiding the cops' suspicions were dashed by the fact that Bernice appeared in the doorway to let them in rather than Helen. If the cops weren't suspicious of how Lynne and Mandy had run to Helen's, they would surely be suspicious now if they saw Bernice answer. The small-town cops knew Helen's sad story. They would surely know something was amiss now that a bunch of kids were at her house.

The girls heard the patrol car doors open. Panicked, they dove into Helen's house, slamming the door and locking it behind them.

"Who called?" Bernice asked, annoyed, pointing her head toward the patrol car.

"Wasn't us, Bernice. We don't know," Lynne answered.

"Is it the girls?" Helen inquired from the hallway.

"Yeah, and the cops are outside. They saw them come in," Bernice said.

Helen got up and approached the girls, asking Bernice, "Any sign of that station wagon again?"

"No, not again," Bernice answered.

"We saw it," Lynne spoke up. "It was Patsy." Lynne looked at Bernice for signs of recognition but detected nothing.

"Huh" was Helen's response. Of course she had already known who was driving the station wagon the minute Bernice told her about it, but she couldn't let on that she knew. Helen had notebooks full of documentation on the regularities of the neighborhood, and Patsy's frequent drive-bys had become a large section of a certain notebook.

Bernice peeked at the cops through the window and reported, "They aren't coming. They're standing outside the car looking at my house."

"Well, they could come here any minute. You girls say you didn't call the police? You didn't tell your parents anything?" Helen asked Mandy and Lynne, who answered by shaking their heads no in unison.

"But we didn't have to tell them. That thing is in our bathroom now. My parents are stuck there with it."

"How can that be? And why did you leave them?" Helen asked.

"Dad told us to get back outside. He didn't think we saw anything. We saw the muck on the bathroom floor," Mandy reported, trying not to break down as she thought of the danger her parents could be in.

Helen, surprising herself, hugged the two girls. She had no words to offer them. She couldn't tell them everything would be all right. She gave in to a dormant maternal need to protect and soothe them even though she was terrified of what was happening.

Bernice walked down the hall to the bathroom and watched the whirlpool sludge. Helen hadn't yet told her what had happened to Irene while she was fetching items from the garage, but Bernice already knew something had happened. She could feel it. Bernice's inquiring eyes looked to Helen for an answer. Helen affirmed with a head shake, and she was shocked by Bernice's sudden fury.

"How, Helen? How the hell did it happen?" she yelled as she charged toward her.

"You pushed her, didn't you? I saw how you were looking at each other! You had me go into the garage so you could push her in, right?" Bernice accused Helen.

Mandy and Lynne were a mess of tears. Helen left them and blocked Bernice's charge, grabbing ahold of her shoulders as she bent down to eye level. "No, Bernice. It was just the opposite. Do you hear me? She pushed me, but I caught hold of the cabinet. She was about to stomp on my arms to send me down, but I was able to knock her away. She slipped, and it just took her. I didn't mean for that to happen. It was too strong, and it happened so quickly. I'm so sorry, Bernice."

Bernice stared blankly into Helen's eyes, those eyes that hadn't lied or betrayed her since this whole thing started, those eyes that had seen the iciness in Irene's interactions with Bernice and had understood the pain it caused her. She wanted to believe Helen but felt terribly conflicted. It still was, after all, her mother on the other side of the coin. Even though she knew how Irene could be, it still felt awful to go against her. And now with her father gone, her mom was all she had.

Meanwhile, Lynne had been stealing glances at the cops from the window and announced, "They're walking up to your house, Bernice! They just knocked!"

"Oh my God. What if they go in?" Bernice asked Helen, thinking of the mayhem it would cause should the cops discover Bruce's body in the basement.

"Holy shit! I can't believe it. Irene just answered!" Lynne exclaimed.

"How can that be?" Helen asked, bustling over to the window and nudging Lynne to the side. She had to see Irene to believe it.

Carson and Burns approached the Fellers' front door and rang the doorbell a few times with no answer. They knocked repeatedly, each knock becoming more urgent. Burns yelled, "We're coming in!" He took a few steps back, preparing to bust the door down.

Carson stepped in front of Burns, halting him with outstretched arms and palms out. Rather than raising his voice, Carson let his raised eyebrows imbue emphasis on his words. "Calm down. No need to break down doors just yet."

Burns relaxed his shoulders and relented, disappointed. As Carson reached for the door handle, they were surprised by Irene opening the door from the inside. They were startled by the state of her appearance as she stood there looking like she had been rolling around in a pig sty and then tried washing herself off with motor oil and glitter. It looked like she had at least tried to clean her face.

Irene acted surprised to see them, exclaiming, "Oh, Officers, what a surprise! What brings you by? I hope you weren't here long. I was working in the basement. Our sewer is giving us trouble, a lot of trouble obviously," Irene said, looking down at her soiled clothes.

Carson sensed phoniness. "Mrs. Feller, sorry to bother you when you're obviously busy. Sewer, huh? What kind of junk you have flowing through your pipes? Never seen anything like that," Carson asked Irene as he eyed the strange sludge dripping from her body. He tried to keep his voice light and devoid of insinuation.

Irene shot back, "If we knew that, maybe we could fix it once and for all. Now what can I help you with?"

"Well, we got a call from a concerned neighbor and thought we'd check on you," Carson said.

Irene let out a sarcastic chuckle, "A concerned neighbor? Concerned about what? I know all my neighbors, and they'd come to me first if they were concerned. So who really called? Or was there no call, and maybe you're just nosing about? It isn't nice to be harassed on a Sunday afternoon, Officers."

The smug change in Irene's demeanor was menacing. Carson felt taunted by her and knew that Burns with his hot-button defensiveness was feeling it too. He needed to diffuse the tension yet stand his ground. Something was amiss, and Carson needed to keep Irene talking.

"We're not here to harass you. I think you know that. We're here because someone you know was concerned about you," Carson said, wishing he hadn't let out the "someone you know" part.

Irene acquiesced a little. She eyed the officers up and down, scanning their guns in their holsters, the rings of keys attached to their belt buckles, and their badges pinned to their uniforms.

Burns blurted out, "Yeah, Patsy called because she saw you and your daughter going to Helen's. She thought you looked upset." Burns knew he had fucked up. He never should have mentioned Patsy. Carson's reddened face and narrowed eyes said it all. Burns's cheeks burned hot as he wished his careless admission away.

"Well, you coming in?" Irene asked, stepping aside to make room for the officers to enter before adding, "We wouldn't want to upset Patsy, would we?"

Irene was speaking with an artificial June Cleaver sweetness that sickened Carson. He was being patronized, but he acted like he wasn't aware of it. Burns didn't know Irene and hadn't caught the inconsistencies in her behavior. Besides, he was far too preoccupied with his own act of portraying a good cop. Carson took off his hat before he stepped inside, and Burns followed suit.

"We'll make it quick, Irene. Really, we're sorry to impose," Carson said reassuringly. He and Burns scanned the kitchen and dining areas. Carson pointed toward the hallway and asked, "Mind if I have a look?"

"It's bedrooms and a bathroom. Knock yourself out."

Burns stood awkwardly in the kitchen with Irene. He couldn't help but think of the fight he had had with her husband, and he knew she was aware of it. The silence was crushing. "Sewer problems, huh? That's the worst. Funny, though. You're covered in it, and I don't smell, well, what you'd usually smell in association with sewage," Burns said, hating the words coming from his mouth and feeling like a horse's ass.

Irene pounced on his insecurities with sarcasm. She had Burns where she wanted him, anxious and humiliated. "What a nice compliment! I don't smell like shit. Thank you, Officer!"

Carson emerged from the hall and announced, "All seems well. But I would like to take a look in the basement. I assume that's where Bruce is hiding out, working on that sewer, huh? His truck's here, so I assume he's home?"

Irene thought of Bruce's body and moved quickly down the steps before calling up, "Of course. Just give me a second to mop up a little so you won't slip."

Carson gave Burns a whispered tongue-lashing while they waited for Irene's okay. Meanwhile, Irene feverishly tried to slide Bruce's corpse into the enlarged drain. Rigor mortis had set in, making it impossible to bend the body. She settled for the pile of dirty towels that had accumulated during the cleanup and haphazardly draped them over Bruce's body, flinging the last one on as she heard the officers make their way downstairs.

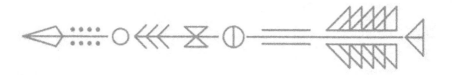

CHAPTER 13

"We have to go back to my house," Bernice urged.

"Quiet," Helen ordered the girls. "Did anyone hear that?" She crept down the hall toward the bathroom. "There it is again!" The girls heard nothing. "It sounded like Will's voice," Helen said. Bernice joined Helen at the door of the bathroom. They saw nothing but the void of the drain. They listened quietly but still heard nothing. Bernice gave Helen a look of disappointment. "Will's alive, Bernice. I know I heard him," Helen said with conviction.

Mandy was looking out the window from over Lynne's shoulder. Her attention was divided between whatever it was that Helen and Bernice were listening to and to what was happening at the Fellers'. "They've been in there awhile," Mandy reported.

"I can't stand this! We can't just stay holed up in here, waiting for something to happen. We need to do something!" Bernice said, her aggravation apparent.

Lynne agreed. "I say we get out of here too. Staying in here isn't going to help my parents either."

As Helen listened to the girls team up in what felt like a mutiny, the agoraphobia began to rear its familiar head. The stress was getting to her. Her old habit of hiding away until it passed wasn't an option right now, she knew. Her heart raced as she fought internally to keep that old habit from resurfacing. The thought of abruptly leaving her house without preparing mentally as she used to do every time she left her home had triggered a quasi-panic attack. Bernice sensed Helen's struggle but stood firm in her resolve.

"Helen, we're leaving. We need to go to our own homes. It's not like we're any safer here," Bernice reasoned with Helen. Bernice looked at Mandy and Lynne, thought for a second, and then asked

Helen, "Please come with us. We need you." The girls were genuinely concerned about Helen's safety and wanted to get her out of her home. But they were also terrified to return to their own homes alone, and Helen was the only adult available.

"Fine. Let's go. Just...don't...don't talk. Let's just go," Helen forced from her anxiety-laden throat.

The girls surrounded Helen as she knelt by her front door to slip on her shoes. Her hands trembled, and a tear splattered onto her shoe. Bernice placed a hand on Helen's shoulder in comfort and coaxed her on. "You'll be okay out there, Helen. It's a lot scarier in here right now than it is out there, right?"

Helen stayed crouched, tears falling from her face. Her sniffling subsided, and her breathing slowed. She breathed deep, meditative breaths. She stood abruptly and unlocked the door. "Let's just go," Helen said, walking out the door first and leaving the three girls to follow, closing the door behind them.

Helen ignored the urge to go back and lock her door. She couldn't remember the last time she had just left her house without compulsively preparing to the nth degree. *It isn't all that distressing now that I'm out,* she thought. In fact, she felt rather empowered even though the change had been forced. She needed that feeling of empowerment so she could lead this pack of girls. She had a much bigger problem to worry about right now.

Helen led the girls toward Bernice's house first. She glanced up and down the streets and over her shoulders, hoping no one was watching them. The empty patrol car parked in front of the Fellers' was ominous. It had been sitting empty for too long now.

"Maybe we should go to our house first," Mandy suggested.

"We have to see what's going on in here," Helen answered, reaching for the Fellers' front door.

"But what do we say to them? How are we—" Bernice's questioning was interrupted by Helen.

"There's nothing left to say except the truth."

Helen slowly pushed the door open, peeking her head inside. Horrible, familiar sounds arose from the basement. The sounds of metal being scratched and mangled mixed with ear-piercing shrieks emanated up the steps. She motioned to the girls to follow her downstairs and to stay close. They padded down the stairs, the noise intensifying.

They turned the corner and saw two officers lying on the ground, rivers of blood trickling around them. They were more shocked to see Irene sitting there next to the bodies, stripping them of any metal she could find, throwing the pieces into her mouth.

Irene spun her head to find she had a captive audience. She looked crazed, possessed. She placed a badge in her mouth and bit down hard, her teeth actually crumbling as she tore into brass. The noise was excruciating, like amplified nails on a chalkboard.

"Mom?" Bernice uttered, horrified.

Then Helen heard the voice she had just heard moments before at her own house. From the chasm of the enlarged drain came the unmistakable voice of Will, hollering for his mother. Irene grabbed the rest of the metal and disappeared down the enlarged drain. Bernice ran forward and peered into the menacing cesspool but saw nothing but the sludge oozing down the inside walls.

"Mom! Will!" she screamed down into the abyss. She had expected an echo, but her words were absorbed by the thick plasm, like it purposely prevented Bernice's words from reaching their intended recipients.

Carson groaned and rolled onto his back, exposing a gunshot wound to his side. His movement startled the girls, sending them into a cacophony of screams. They had thought he was dead. Helen shushed the petrified girls and then grabbed a folded towel from the stack on the shelf next to her. She brought it to Carson, who took it and held it over the wound before hoisting himself into a sitting position.

"It just grazed my side. It won't kill me. Now what the hell did I just see?" Carson asked Helen and the girls.

"We can't explain either," Helen answered.

"This is nuts! It could be headed to my house again as we speak. I can't stay here. I have to help my parents with or without any of you," Mandy said adamantly.

"Hold on," Carson said, staggering to his feet. "I don't know what the hell is going on, but nobody's going anywhere by themselves. You James and Regina's girl?"

Mandy nodded.

"Me too," Lynne added.

"Okay. You're right across the back alley. We're all going together," Carson directed.

He looked to his left and considered Officer Burns's body. He had been shot once in the face and twice in the abdomen. There was no hope for him, and he was too shocked to register any emotions over the fact that he had just lost his junior partner. *Whatever is going on,* Carson thought, *there is no standard procedure to follow. I just have to make sure the others are safe.*

Carson motioned toward the door, and Mandy and Lynne followed. He turned to see that, rather than follow, Helen and Bernice had both inched closer to the gaping opening in the floor. "Ladies, I can't leave you here by yourselves," Carson said.

Before they could protest, a massive glug of sludge spurted from the chasm, setting the whirlpool in motion once again. Helen and Bernice darted for the door, joining the others. Carson was aghast, witnessing this spectacle for the first time. He observed, defenseless, as the glistening slime swiftly attached itself to Burns's body, dragging it down into the void.

"Burns!" Carson cried out, wincing at the tinge of pain that shot through his wound as he yelled.

Tears of anguish slid down Bernice's cheeks as she mumbled for Will and her mother. The muck shifted and gravitated toward the heap of dirty towels, toppling them and setting them afloat in the swirling goo. Towel after towel tumbled away until Bruce Feller's body was finally revealed. Carson reflexively grabbed ahold of Bruce's leg but was unable to maintain his grasp.

"Daddy!" Bernice yelled in vain as her father's body was yanked down into the abyss.

The vigorous suctioning noise sounded, then ceased. Bewildered, Carson covered his mouth with his hand and breathed hard, his nostrils flaring. Mandy and Lynne had run up the steps and eagerly waited to leave this atrocious sight. Helen had her long arms wrapped around Bernice's shoulders, who repeated almost inaudibly, "They're all gone. They're all gone."

"Officer, I'm sorry about your partner, but we have to get to the girls' house. There's no time to grieve until we know it's over," Helen said to Carson.

"Yeah, you're right. Helen, is it?" Carson said robotically, already knowing full well who she was.

"Let's go. Please!" Lynne called from the top of the steps, coaxing the others up the stairs and out the door. The girls broke into a sprint, racing to their house. Carson moved as quickly as the pain in his gunshot wound allowed him, grimacing in pain with every step.

Helen and Bernice followed Carson. Helen secretly eyed him from behind, wondering if he thought she was crazy like everyone else in town apparently did. She hoped not. Right now, she felt relieved to have another adult in this situation with her, taking the lead away from her for now.

Mandy and Lynne's parents sat at their kitchen table, dazed. A stack of notebooks and shoeboxes were piled in front of them. Like the rest of the group, they were in such a state of shock that they barely reacted to the traumatized and battered crew that entered through their front door. Not even a look of relief came to either of their faces as Mandy and Lynne walked toward them.

Mandy and Lynne recognized the notebooks. Their brother, Roy, had kept a stash of journals for years. This particular set had been taboo to even mention since he was hospitalized because the contents of them were to blame for what had sent him there.

A few of the journals were splayed open, revealing sketches of what looked like some sort of a snakelike monster coming out of the drain in their bathroom. Another picture depicted the monster eating something from a box that Roy had given to it. Seeing their daughters studying the upsetting pictures, James and Regina quickly slammed the notebooks shut.

Carson came forward and asked, "You folks all right? The girls said something's going on over here."

Regina looked up at Carson, saying, "Something's definitely going on, all right."

Regina shoved herself away from the table and grabbed one of the shoeboxes. She walked down the hall toward the bathroom. She pressed her ear against the door and listened for a second. She glanced over her shoulder at Carson and gave a quick tilt of her head, motioning for him to come near. Carson tentatively prodded farther down the hall toward Regina. She slowly turned the knob and inched the door open. She removed the lid from the box and placed it on the floor right at the entrance. Before Carson could see the contents of the box, something from inside the bathroom quickly slid the box inside, startling him.

Regina opened the door a little wider and told Carson, "Look."

Carson's heart pounded like a sledgehammer as he approached the door. He craned his neck and stretched his upper body over to get a look, keeping his lower body positioned so that he could run away quickly if he needed to. There inside Regina's bathroom sat the enormous snakelike creature. Irene and Will Feller lounged on the floor next to the thing, leisurely as though they were enjoying a spring picnic. Instead of macaroni salad and sandwiches, they snacked on the contents of the shoebox. Carson was transfixed, amazed by the motley trio as they snatched random bits of metal from the box and tossed them into their mouths.

Carson backed away and shut the door. He took Regina by the arm and led her back to the kitchen. With a sweep of his arm, he motioned to everyone to go out the front door, ordering James and Regina to gather the notebooks and bring them along. By default, Carson took the lead, but this was an entirely different situation. He didn't know what else to do. He didn't know what he was dealing with or how to go about finding out. Right now, he just needed to get everyone out of the house and keep them together.

Once outside, Regina noticed Carson's gunshot wound, exclaiming, "My God, who did that to you? We need to get you to the hospital."

"Not yet. I'm all right for now," Carson said, grabbing at his side.

James asked, "What next, Officer?"

Carson wished he had an answer for them. Lucky for him, Helen did.

"Those notebooks." Helen addressed Regina. "Do they have information that would help us figure out what this monster is?"

Regina affirmed with a nod and handed a journal to Helen. The group drew in close to Helen as she leafed through the notebook of Roy's drawings and notes. Her brows gathered together as she concentrated on its contents. She handed the notebook to Carson and grabbed for another. About halfway through the second notebook, Helen slapped it shut, held it to her chest, and looked down at the ground. She took a deep breath before she admitted what she must.

"I've been dealing with this thing since my father died. I have notes of my own." She knew what was coming. She closed her eyes and didn't have to wait long before the onslaught.

"You've known about this thing, and you never said anything? What the hell is wrong with you? You might have been able to save lives, Helen!" Regina berated her.

"I'd never actually seen it until today, but I knew there was something. My reputation kept me in silence. Is that so hard to understand? Who would have believed me, huh? You and James? The Fellers? The cops? Not likely," Helen explained.

We can't waste time on blame and who knew what and when, Carson thought. "Helen has a point. Look, no one is to blame. This monster is. Helen, you said you have your own notes. Could you get them so we can compare the information with Roy's information? The more we know, the better."

"I'll grab them," Helen said, all too happy to walk away from the group even for a small while.

James heard Bernice's sniffles and thought about Irene and Will in his bathroom, sitting with the monster. "Bernice, where's your dad?" James asked.

Bernice couldn't make herself say the words, but her pained silence gave James an awful feeling of foreboding.

Regina stammered, "Is…is he okay, Bernice? What happened?"

Bernice turned on her heels and ran after Helen, unable to face the reality of her father's death.

When Bernice was out of earshot, Lynne told her parents, "Bruce is dead. That thing killed him."

"Jesus Christ. If it killed Bruce, it could kill Irene and Will. Hell, it could kill all of us! We gotta move, figure out what this bastard wants," James said as he stacked the journals on the picnic table next to their garden. He told the rest of the group to gather round and then passed a notebook to each person.

"Flip through, and let's see if we can learn anything about this thing. Maybe Roy knew something about it that could help us get rid of it if that's even possible."

Carson watched Helen and Bernice walk away. He rejected taking a notebook from James for the time being, explaining, "The kid shouldn't be going in with her. I'll go in with Helen and send Bernice back."

Helen heard quick footsteps and heavy breathing approaching her and Bernice from behind. She was relieved when she turned to see Carson coming their way.

"Bernice, you head back and start looking through the notebooks. I'll make sure Helen gets in and out of her place all right. Now go," Carson said through gritted teeth, straining from the pain he felt in his side.

Helen preempted Bernice's protest, saying, "Listen to the officer. Please. It's safer for you. We'll be right back."

"I'm not leaving Helen's side," Bernice boldly retorted. After what she had been through within the last few hours, Bernice had no fear of disobeying a cop's authority. She walked purposefully toward Helen and gripped her hand tightly. There was no time to argue, and both Helen and Carson recognized it would have been a losing battle anyway.

The three of them went into Helen's home and watched as she methodically pulled out her stash of journals from a storage box underneath her coffee table. Self-consciously, she opened the storage box lid to reveal the anal retentiveness in which she had ordered and labeled the journals. Her cheeks flushed as she realized Carson and Bernice gawked at her private stash of carefully noted neighborhood secrets.

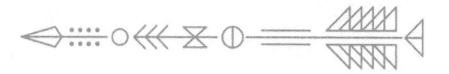

CHAPTER 14

Irene's thoughts were murky, like waking up from being under anesthesia. Her body felt weighed down. Her limbs were heavy, covered in mud, heavy as sandbags. Just trying to lift her arm was exhausting. Irene's eyes came into focus, and she gasped when she perceived the thick, glittering ooze that covered her body. She managed to raise her right arm and beheld some chevron-shaped wounds, the blood from them mixing with the muddy substance.

Her attention was hijacked by the sound of her son's voice calling her name. She looked up to see the grotesque, snakelike being cradling Will, quite content in the devilish fiend's arms. Irene was terror-stricken. She noticed her son's arm possessed the same zigzag wounds she had. Will's little hands were clenched around a bundle of nails and screws, prompting Irene to remember what had happened earlier when Will had thrown metal into his mouth back in their basement. But Irene was hazy on what had happened after that.

Irene gazed at the ooze-covered behemoth as it cradled her son. Then it hit her. This thing had gotten control of her completely, but she didn't understand how. It still had control of her son, so although she was beyond terrified, she thought it best to act like it still had control of her as well. Maybe it would help get her son back.

Irene didn't know where she was. She knew she was in a bathroom, but it was not one she had ever seen before. She saw the gaping hole in the ground, which triggered a memory of her traveling inside it with the beast.

Irene felt the monster's eyes upon her. She was careful not to show that she was out of the trance it had had on her. Irene grabbed for the shoebox of metal and pulled a couple of washers from it and popped them into her mouth and pretended to chew. It was then that she noticed that her own teeth were badly chipped and cracked with some gone altogether.

Irene fought to keep from panicking, praying that this thing still believed she was under its power. It seemed to be working. She forced herself to swallow a washer and nearly choked, causing the beast to reach out an arm and wrap it around Irene's shoulder in an almost maternal caress. Irene saw that the arm was in fact a human arm. She shuddered.

Suddenly, the sludge began to swirl under her feet, and she couldn't help but shriek, remembering that it would whirlpool back into the drain, taking them all back down with it. Her body automatically tried to fight its way out of the slime, giving the monster the information it needed to understand that Irene was no longer under its control. Irene knew she would suffocate and die if she were sucked under the goo right now. She could only survive underground if she was under the beast's spell. She didn't know how to go back into that trance and was too scared to do it again even if she did.

By the skin of her teeth, Irene escaped the adversary's embrace and lunged for the door, grasping the handle as it slipped clumsily from her greasy hands. She flipped her back against the door and saw Will, still under the beast's control.

"Will!" she yelled, hoping it would wake him from the trance. She was devastated to see no change in her son's expression even as the monster wrapped its arms around him and took him underneath once again.

Irene, dazed and breathless, closed her eyes and tried to remember what had happened in her own basement, but the memories wouldn't come. She opened her eyes and was once again struck by the fact that she was in someone else's bathroom. She stood up and fumbled with the door handle and was able to get out this time. She peered out the door, then slowly crept down the hallway. She recognized pictures of Mandy, Lynne, and Roy framed on the paneled walls and figured out where she was.

Irene had never been inside James and Regina's home. She was overcome with anxiety trying to remember how she had gotten there. The thought that she had been seen by people in the state she was in made her nauseous. It was even more sickening to know that the house was now empty and that the beast may have gotten to this family as well or, worse, that she may have done something to them while she was under the leviathan's control.

Irene stumbled out the front door where she lurched over and violently vomited up metal fragments, tearing up her mouth and insides as she did. She dropped to the ground after the last heave. She heard screaming and was mortified to look up and see James and his family gathered at their picnic table, all watching her in shock, disgust, and horror.

Irene began mumbling "It's me. It's me" repeatedly. She wanted to speak louder but was unable to. Her vocal cords had been shredded by the metal. She shakily rose to her feet, knowing she looked like something out of a nightmare, and slowly made her way toward the picnic table. James pushed the girls and his wife behind him and told Irene to keep her distance. She stood with her arms reached out to her sides and forced out of her bleeding mouth, "It's me, Irene! Please help!"

Carson, Helen, and Bernice had just rounded the corner back from Helen's house with her notes in hand when they saw Irene standing there in front of the terrified group. Carson instinctively pulled his gun and started walking quickly toward Irene and yelled, "Get on the ground!"

Bernice broke into a run, getting in front of Carson's path, yelling, "No! Mom!"

Carson yelled for Bernice to get out of the way, but she stayed in the path of the gun and sprinted toward Irene. She could see the fear in her mom's face, and she knew it was her mom back in her own mind again. Irene turned toward Bernice and stretched her arms out to her daughter. From behind her, Bernice heard a gunshot, and she dropped to the ground. She saw Irene collapse.

"No!" Bernice screeched. She turned to look behind her and saw that both Carson and Helen were lying on the grass, Carson on his side, groaning in agony. Helen was on her stomach, both hands clasped tightly around the gun that was still in Carson's hand.

Helen yelled, "It didn't hit her!"

Bernice got up and ran to Irene. Irene sobbed as she embraced Bernice with a nurturing she had withheld from her for far too long. Helen tentatively loosened her grip on Carson's gun, giving him a look of bafflement, begging the question why he would pull the gun on Irene.

Carson moved slowly, wincing in pain as he stood up, the gunshot wound spurting fresh blood. He surprised Helen when he began taking quick strides toward Irene and Bernice, aiming the gun in their direction. He held the gun within inches of Irene's head and told Bernice to get away from her. Her protests were ignored. James had stepped in and pulled Bernice away, looping his forearms under her armpits. She fought like hell to pry herself free. Irene dropped to her knees, exhausted and terrified. Carson heard Helen's quick footsteps behind him.

"Stop, Helen. She's the one that shot me and Burns. She killed him. She ain't going anywhere," Carson explained.

Helen froze behind Carson. Irene looked up at him, befuddled. She had no recollection of shooting anyone. In fact, she remembered nothing of what had happened in her basement. She didn't even know she had been there. "I couldn't have...I didn't do that," Irene countered weakly, her voice gravelly and damaged.

Carson could see that Irene really didn't remember anything and that something had changed in her demeanor. She had been a different person when the officers first came into the Fellers' home. But Carson's anger over Burns's death prevented him from letting Irene off the hook so easily.

Irene continued, her voice a quivering mess of nerves. "It had control of me. I'm so sorry! I can't remember! It still has power over Will!" She broke into hysterical tears.

James released Bernice from his grip. She turned and glared at Carson and shot daggers from her eyes at him. She crouched down and faced Irene. "I know it wasn't you, Mom. And that's not Will in there with that thing right now. But you're back. That means we can get Will back too."

Carson lowered his gun knowing what Bernice said was true. But his instinct screamed for him to hold Irene accountable. He was going to have to force himself to transfer the blame onto the beast. Carson helped Irene and Bernice to their feet and led them to the picnic table where the notebooks were scattered from being skimmed through. "Find anything?" Carson asked.

James passed a notebook to Carson, answering, "Have a look. See if you can make any sense of it. Helen, you have your notes?"

She nodded sheepishly, picked them up off the ground where she had flung them before hurling her body onto Carson, and sat at the picnic table, opening her once-secret journals to the outside world. She flipped through its pages as the rest of the group went through Roy's notes.

Besides the sounds of crinkling paper, Carson noticed how eerily quiet the neighborhood was. He looked up from the notebook he had and looked from one house to another. No one else was around. No one peered through their windows. Most troubling was the fact that even after the loud gunshot a few moments earlier, not a single neighbor had come out to investigate.

Irene gasped and covered her eyes, bringing back Carson's attention. On a page of a notebook lying open in front of Irene was a detailed sketch of the beast. Roy's rendition of it was uncanny, from its haunting onyx eyes to its piranha-like metal teeth. Bernice put an arm around Irene and flipped through a journal with her other hand.

"Let's start throwing some information out. Maybe we can build some sort of a picture of this thing or its patterns or something, anything," Carson initiated. "Does it always come up from a bathroom drain?"

Everyone either shrugged or shook their heads no. Mandy added, "Roy fed it metal when it came back. Looks like it would go away for a while after that. Sometimes for hours, sometimes days."

"Did he note how much metal he would give it? See if you can find that," Carson urged.

Helen's throat was tight as she admitted, "I kept notes about the frequency of the feedings. I noted how much I gave it and when and how long it would be before it returned." She hesitated before adding, "I only recorded that information at the very beginning before... before it became...a habit." How had she let this become a mundane, routine event in her life for so long? The absurdity and shame of it overwhelmed her as she admitted it to the group.

Carson regarded Helen's posture—slouched, shoulders hunched, arms folded tightly over her stomach. *She is crumbling,* he thought, and he felt compelled to stop it. "Seems like we're lucky you kept records, Helen. Let's see if we can match any dates with Roy's notes. Maybe we can learn something else," Carson suggested.

Regina squinted as she read out loud from the notebook she held. "Roy's journal entries are always negative on the days it showed up. Anyone else see that?"

Lynne said, "Yeah, he had a lot of bad days."

Carson found an entry in the notebook he had and said, "I got one here. Everyone listen up." Carson read Roy's passage.

> May 8—Dad's work hours were cut again. Mom and Dad keep arguing over money. I got into a fight with Steven at school. Mom grounded me. I'm pissed off. Better get ready for a feeding tonight. Box of drill bits ready.

Tears welled in Regina's eyes as she remembered that day. When Carson read the last line, she covered her face and forced composure. It was all right there in Roy's notebooks, real accounts of what was really happening. The guilt was unbearable as Regina and James realized they had institutionalized Roy for telling the truth. James sensed what Regina had realized because he had too, saying, "No one would have believed it unless they'd seen it, not even us. Now we've seen it."

"Let's keep reading," Carson ordered.

Over an hour had passed, and Patsy still hadn't heard back from the police. Carson said he would call and give her an update after they had checked on the Fellers. She called the station a few times, and no one answered. There was always someone there to answer, especially on a Sunday. It worried Patsy seeing Bruce's daughter looking scared and filthy, running to Helen's house. Like everyone else in town, Patsy knew Helen's history and reputation and wondered what business Bernice had going to her house.

Mostly, Patsy worried that something had happened to Bruce. The guilt over her strong feelings for him sat like lead in her stomach. He had been there for her when no one else was. She couldn't ignore the feelings she had developed for him. The feelings were mutual from Bruce. Knowing this pained her. She ached for him, knowing nothing could ever come of it. She had too much respect for Bruce's family to ever act on any impulse. It was unspoken, but Bruce felt the same way. Patsy knew Irene could feel it but acted unaware.

Nothing had ever happened physically between them, but the emotional connection they had made was far deeper than either of them could have predicted. She wondered if it ever could have been stopped. Neither of them had ever intended on developing any kind of the connection they had. It was torturous for Patsy, especially since she was left alone with her feelings, her husband and son long gone—not dead but they could just as well have been.

For months, Patsy tried to rationalize that she was just hurt and lonely. She tried to tell herself that Bruce's help was just that, help from a considerate friend. Irene was with him most of the time, but when Bruce began showing up unaccompanied by her, she couldn't help but be drawn to his openness and humor. *Maybe I never should have accepted his help,* she thought.

An ugly feeling arose within her as she sat worrying about Bruce. She was helpless against the thought that maybe something had happened to Irene. She felt sick as she realized that she was hoping for just that. When she couldn't stand the guilt of that thought anymore, she turned her intense and confused feelings on Irene. She thought about the ways in which Irene didn't appreciate Bruce. She told herself to stop. She couldn't live like this, driving herself crazy over someone she couldn't have.

After a good cry that felt more like mourning, Patsy decided that since she hadn't heard back from Carson, she would go to the Fellers' to see what was going on. After that, she told herself she would indulge in her yearning for Bruce no more. If it meant she would have to pick up and move away, she would. In fact, she would make her first step today. She decided that when she drove to the Fellers' to check on them one last time, she would put on a happy face and announce to them that she would be moving out of town, and soon.

Maybe she would tell them that a sick relative needed her help and that she had decided to use the opportunity to pack up and start over. She would tell them that she had always thought about doing that anyway and that this was an opportunity to do it. In truth, she never fathomed that she would leave her hometown.

Patsy went to her bathroom and splashed some cold water on her face. She took a minute to dab some concealer under her eyes, brush on some mascara and blush, and swipe some pale-pink gloss over her aging, thinning lips. She ran her fingers through her dirty-blond hair and tied it back with an old metal clip. Her hands were damp, causing her to fidget clumsily with the clip as she tried to snap it into place. Her emotions were running high as was her irritation. She fumbled with the clip, her frustration giving way to tears, which made her angry with herself for putting herself in this impossible situation in the first place.

She looked at herself in the mirror, her face red, frown lines set in deep. She laughed at herself and said out loud, throwing the clip into the sink, "You lunatic. You really know how to pick 'em."

She put her hands on her hips and bowed her head as she remembered the string of failed relationships she had had in her life. She tried to be compassionate with herself as she would be to anyone else in her position. She wanted to believe that she knew no better from the start, that she didn't know what she was getting herself into each time she found herself with someone new. She seemed to attract the ones who would eventually turn on her and abuse her. Or she would attract the ones who were unattainable. She hoped that maybe her realization at that moment would be enough to break that cycle when she finally moved out of town and started fresh somewhere else. She knew it was easier said than done and that it was probably wishful thinking, but it was all she had to go on, and she needed any motivation she could get.

She reached down to retrieve the hair clip from the sink but was disgusted to feel her hand slide into a basin filled with murky sludge, no clip to be found. She drew her hand out quickly and wiped it on a nearby towel. She had had problems with clogged drains ever since she lived in that house, but she had never seen anything like this. Thinking it was just a major clog, she left the bathroom and went into her purse to add Drain-O to her shopping list. She would deal with the drain later. Besides, she would need something to work on to keep her mind off Bruce.

Patsy left her house with a heavy heart yet with a sense of pride in herself. She was going to take control of this and end it. It was the right thing to do. Her intentions were pure, and she knew the next step she was about to make was the first step in turning her life around. She thought about what she had to say to the Fellers, and as she let it sink in, she began to feel empowered.

She pulled up in front of the Fellers' house, ignoring the patrol car still parked out front, and began walking to the Fellers' front door. She was deep in thought about what she would say and how she would say it when she heard women's voices coming from the backyard. They were arguing. She veered toward the voices.

James and Regina couldn't concentrate on the notebooks after realizing their son had been telling them the truth. All they could think about was heading straight to the psychiatric ward to have their son released immediately and told Carson so. Carson reasoned with them. "You know there's a process for the release of a patient, and it's not going to happen immediately. We have to stay here now and think about Will. Your son is fine where he is. Will isn't."

"My son is my priority, not her son," Regina tilted her head toward Irene.

"Of course, but under the circumstances—"

Carson was cut off by Regina. "Under any circumstance, especially this one! Rather than sit here and rifle through these notebooks, we could just go talk to him! He obviously knows more about this thing than all of us combined. Why waste any more time?"

Irene erupted, her voice hoarse, "Staying here for Will is not a waste of time! Do whatever you need to do, but I'm staying here!"

"It's no wonder this thing has been at your house, Irene. We all know it's been one bad day over there for a long time. Now we've all been dragged into it," Regina barked.

"How dare you! It all began at your house months ago," Irene fired back at Regina but then maliciously turned on Helen. "And you, who's been living happily with this thing for years apparently."

Helen begged, "Stop it. Please."

But Irene continued, her words laden with sarcasm as she croaked out of her slashed vocal chords, "The good news is that now we all know the secret behind Helen's hours of knocking on her own door. It did you a lot of good, didn't it? It's done us a lot of good! It nearly killed me, my husband is dead, my son is lost, a cop is dead, and Roy is in a goddamn nuthouse!"

Carson saw the rage building in Helen's face and stepped between her and Irene. Helen matched Irene's sarcasm as she admitted, "Yes, Irene, my happy life with this thing began right after it killed my father! I was so deliriously happy I wanted to keep it all to myself! The crazy reputation I got from everyone was worth it! Living in fear of it, all alone for so long, I'm really going to miss that!"

Just then, the ground lurched under their feet, and James and Regina's entire house rattled violently before it stopped as suddenly as it had begun. An eerie silence enveloped the group. After the ground rumbled beneath their feet, Irene broke the silence that ensued by spewing her wrath for Helen, saying hurtful, vindictive things. She glared at Helen, nostrils flaring. Helen's heart pounded fiercely in her chest. She clutched her notebook hard as though it would stop her from losing her temper completely.

Out of the silence came the slam of a car door. It came from the direction of the Fellers' home. They heard knocking followed by a woman's voice shouting, "Hello?" A woman appeared from the front of the Fellers' home. Whomever it was spied the group and began walking toward them.

As the woman came into view, Irene became visibly more agitated. James and Regina's house began rattling behind them. As the woman got closer, the group recognized that it was Patsy. Her presence sent Irene over the edge, flooding her with feelings of jealousy and anger. The house shook more violently, and the ground rose up from under their feet, shaking them all to the ground. The ground opened up into a great jagged chasm, revealing a massive underground river of glistening black sludge. It churned and flowed furiously.

The crack in the earth continued to open until it went right underneath Patsy, who fell in and was swallowed by it. Over the shrieks and gasps of the horrified group could be heard a maniacal chuckle. It came from Irene, who looked victorious and ecstatic. A thick arm of sludge projected from the flowing river, rising high into the air before wrapping itself firmly around Irene, wrenching her easily back down into the abyss of the underground cesspool.

Another arm of sludge arose. This time, it targeted Regina. James grabbed his wife before it got to her, but it tried to slither its way in between the two. Mandy and Lynne grabbed hold of their father, which caused the slimy phantom to give up on Regina and return to its pit.

A sixth sense of sorts sprang to life inside Helen. She couldn't explain how she had come to understand it now, but she had an epiphany that this monster was drawn to negativity. It wasn't exactly repelled by love, but it stopped its pursuit in the face of it, at least it had this time. She thought of the nasty words she and Irene and Regina had bounced back and forth just moments earlier. Helen forced the anger from that exchange out of her mind, fearing that any grudge she bore could make her the monster's next target or empower it even more.

Carson yelled for everyone to back away from the wide fissure. As they did, the underground river calmed slightly, a dull hum emitting from it. Mandy and Lynne released their grip on James, and James released his wife, all relieved to be all right. They stretched their necks to peer into the black river, looking for any sign of Patsy or Irene, but they saw nothing.

"It has to be what Roy meant," Carson said, "that it becomes active on bad days. And metal calms it? How does this make any sense?"

"You're right, Carson," Helen affirmed. "It's drawn to negativity. Some of my entries confirm it." In her journals, Helen noted arguments she had seen at the Fellers' or at other neighbors' homes and remembered that on those particular days, she would throw more metal into the drain as it seemed to become more active. Prior to this moment, she hadn't put the two together. Maybe it was because she never really had to and was managing, or at least thought she was.

Carson addressed the remainder of the group. "Okay, so if negativity is what it wants, we all have to do our best to block it out." He couldn't help but chuckle to himself after the advice he had just given to the group. With a note of cheery sarcasm, he added, "It'll be easy. Besides, what do we have to be negative about?"

Everyone gave an exhausted smirk, except for Bernice. She looked fixedly at the gaping crevice, hoping to see any sign of her mother or Will. Carson's heart broke for her. "Hey, they both came back once before. Maybe they can do it again," Carson said, trying to rally her spirits even though he felt ridiculous doing it under these unbelievable circumstances.

Bernice cracked the slightest of smiles for Carson, appreciating his concern. She just wondered why her father didn't get to come back like Irene and Will had. Maybe it was a good thing that he hadn't.

Drained of energy and frazzled by the cascade of events they had all encountered in such a short period of time, everyone in the group was thankful that Carson was able to maintain leadership. They followed him blindly, their exhaustion causing utter obedience to him. Carson was aware of all this. He was relieved to know he wouldn't have to fight for leadership, but he was also worried about running out of energy himself. He didn't have answers for how to deal with the beast. One thing he was sure of was that the group needed a leader, and he would be that person for them for as long as he could. Carson stood on one side of the crack in the earth while the rest of the group were stranded on the other.

"Let's walk down toward the Fellers', see how long this crack is. I want to get on the same side, but there's no way in hell I'm jumping it," Carson said, motioning to the others to follow him as he headed toward the Fellers'.

The group had to walk three blocks past the Fellers' in order to find a section of the crack narrow enough to easily step over, reunifying the group. But the crack only narrowed in that particular spot, and it continued on as far as the eye could see.

"Let's just knock on someone's door, anyone's door," Lynne suggested.

Mandy contradicted her. "You think anyone is going to let us in? Look at us!"

Regina sided with Lynne, adding, "Well, Officer Carson's with us. That should help."

Carson had only been half listening to the suggestions. He had been focused on the unnatural silence that hung in the air. For the three blocks they had walked, Carson hadn't seen a single sign of life in the twelve homes they had passed. *Hadn't anyone else in town felt the ground shake?* Carson wondered. Such a ruckus in a small town should have shaken people right out of their homes, spreading stories like wildfire by now. But there was no one. Carson caught James eyeing the homes as well. He couldn't ignore the neighborhood silence either. Carson gave James a discreet nod of understanding, and James shot one back.

Carson started up the walkway of the Jensons' home, pausing a moment before he rang the doorbell. After another couple of rings and some pounding on the door, he gave up. Instead of retreating down the walkway, Carson cut straight across the Jensons' front yard to get to the next house over. The group moved like a timid herd of cattle as they followed Carson from the sidewalk. When there was no answer once again, Carson moved on to the third house. Helen hugged Bernice, and James huddled his family close. They sensed they weren't the only ones affected by the underground devil.

After checking five houses, Carson lugged his aching, tired body back to the group. He bent over and took a few deep breaths, recharging slightly. "I'm going to force my way in to one of the homes," Carson announced.

"You can't go in yourself," Helen said, releasing Bernice and walking toward the home closest to them.

James raced toward her and gripped her shoulder. "I'll go with him. You stick here with—"

Helen wrenched his hand from her shoulder and stated firmly, "This is not up for discussion. You stay here with your family. Bernice, stick with the group."

Bernice's protests against Helen entering the home with Carson were ignored. With her entire family gone and not knowing whether she would ever see them again, she felt closest to Helen and couldn't imagine something happening to her.

Carson caught up to Helen and asked, "You sure about this?"

"I've got no one and not much to lose," Helen said matter-of-factly.

"That makes two of us," Carson confessed, making his way to the front door of the Weber home. He had already rung the doorbell and knocked, so he tried the doorknob and found it unlocked. He pushed the door all the way open, exposing an empty foyer and den. He called out for Mr. and Mrs. Weber to no response. He motioned for Helen to follow him. Carson and Helen stuck close together as they slunk around the old-fashioned, folksy home. Through the kitchen window, they could see out into the garage and saw that the Webers' car was parked inside.

The Webers were a retired old couple, both pushing eighty. It was not likely they had gone out for a walk, and it was too late for church. Maybe an early afternoon nap, Carson hoped, knowing it was likely wishful thinking. He and Helen made their way down the hallway and peeked around the door of the first room on their right. Pictures of the couple, encapsulated in tacky, schmaltzy frames, hung on the walls. A king-size bed dominated the room, and tiny nightstands fought for space on either side under the weight of humidifiers, water glasses, and seas of prescription pill bottles. The bed was made in all its gaudy, floral-print, lace-trimmed glory.

Ugly, Helen thought, but it painted a warm, loving picture of a long-married couple, which was why Helen felt nauseous when she heard the familiar churning and humming coming from down the Webers' hallway. "No, no, no," Helen mumbled, inching closer toward the noise.

Starved for human touch for so long, Helen was shocked by Carson's hand as it groped her forearm. She gasped, then turned to see him holding an index finger up to his lips. The duo slunk down the hallway together, the whirring and churning growing louder and louder. Then the awful shrieks sounded.

"It's in there. Let's bring it what it wants," Helen said to Carson.

They found the kitchen and grabbed silverware from the drying rack, a copper kettle from the stove, and a stainless steel carafe. They carried their offerings to the bathroom door. Helen grasped the handle and pushed the door open.

There it stood, towering over Helen and Carson, its menacing ebony eyes turning to them. The sight of the beast's grotesque, jagged metallic teeth prompted Helen to toss the silverware straight toward its mouth. The creature caught most of it and chomped down hard.

Helen searched for Carson's free hand with hers, intertwining her fingers with his. The metal seemed to satisfy the monster, but Helen thought that holding Carson's hand would give the beast more reason to give up its pursuit of whatever negativity it craved. The fiend looked directly at Carson, a strange feeling of jealousy emanating from it. Carson threw the carafe, the thing catching it, powerfully crushing and chewing it within seconds.

The sludge whirled at a steady pace, humming away. The evil brute set its sights back on Helen. It bored into her with its stare, reaching its arms deep into the sludge as it did. It searched for something underneath the swirling muck. As it searched, Helen and Carson spotted the dead bodies of Mr. and Mrs. Weber, one piled on top of the other, wedged between the toilet and the wall. Helen nearly crushed Carson's hand to stop herself from screaming. They both forced themselves to remain stone-faced, not giving any fuel to this emotional vampire.

As the thing continued searching for whatever it was looking for, its gaze remained fixed on Helen. She forced herself to maintain eye contact. Carson, free from the savage's horrible stare, gave a closer look at the Webers' bodies. A lump formed in his throat when he saw that their hands had been severed completely off, a tangled mess of shredded tendon and muscle dangled from the destroyed wrists. The familiar zigzag pattern was grossly imprinted on their arms.

The monster sensed Carson's revulsion, exciting it, causing the glittering muck to accelerate. Helen could feel that he was about to lose his composure, so she lifted up her other hand and offered the beast the copper kettle she had taken from the stove. It opened its vertical chops and waited for Helen to deposit her treat. Her hands trembled as she drew closer and dropped the kettle into the antici-pating jaws.

The whirlpool stopped suddenly. Whatever the beast had been looking for, it had found it. The arms emerged from the sludge, bringing forth the body of a child, offering it to Helen as though it was a gift to her. Helen's heart beat furiously, rattling her ribs, as she released Carson's hand and lifted her arms up to receive the child. Carson covered his mouth and stepped back as he took in the incred-ible exchange.

Helen recognized the child. It was Will. As the evil entity deposited the body into Helen's awaiting arms, Helen forced a smile, accepting its twisted offering. The beast slowly slid its arms out from underneath the child, giving Helen time to get a good look at them. Something looked strangely familiar about them. The sludge had dripped away, revealing more willowy arms rather than burly ones, unmistakably feminine. The right thumb was missing at the knuckle, and both pinkies were severely crooked, the tips pointing in hard at the top joint.

Helen's blood ran cold. She shook violently as she backed away, still cradling Will in her trembling arms. She couldn't keep herself together any longer, so she simply turned and walked out of the bath-room, Carson following her, leaving the hideous thing to retreat back into its lair. Carson held the front door open, allowing Helen to sail through with Will.

"Oh my God! Will!" Bernice shouted, dashing toward Helen.

Helen collapsed to her knees, landing Will on the ground with an unintended thud onto the Webers' front lawn. She pulled her arms from underneath Will and examined her own hands, staring at her own severely crooked pinkies. She covered her face and sobbed, unable to express her unbearable anguish at what she had just registered moments ago—that the wicked devil had stolen her mother's arms and used them as its own.

As the group stood over Will, trying to discern if he was still alive, Helen sat on the sideline remembering how her father had teased her for inheriting her mother's crooked pinkies. She remembered her mother's story about how she had lost the tip of her thumb as a result of an infection caused by a splinter.

After decades, this was the first sign of Helen's mother since her disappearance. *There is no making sense of this,* Helen thought. She couldn't imagine how or exactly when this had happened, and she was too exhausted at that moment to even fathom what this meant. At least she knew now that her mother hadn't run off with another man. She had never really believed that anyway, but she was sure her father had the thought in the back of his mind constantly after she had disappeared.

Helen's bewildered mind tumbled with questions: Had the monster killed her mom? Or had it found her dead body and took her arms? No, it had to have killed her. It had killed her father. Was it targeting Helen's family? If so, then why hadn't it killed her yet? The uncertainty was cruel, insufferable, and infuriating.

Hate for the behemoth seethed within Helen, swelling into a rage. In response, the crack in the ground came alive once again, widening to reveal the muddy rapids below. This thing was attached to Helen's feelings. She didn't understand why it had chosen her.

The others hadn't noticed Helen stewing and that it had caused the latest tremor. She was relieved that they hadn't noticed. She had to keep this new revelation quiet until she could figure it out for herself. If this beast had some sort of connection with her, maybe that meant she could find a way to control it or, better yet, destroy it.

Helen directed her attention back to the group as they frantically searched for signs of life. Finding none, James began CPR. It was in vain, which Helen already knew but didn't have the heart to be the one to confirm it for Bernice. It was awful seeing the desperate hope in Bernice's eyes as James pumped Will's delicate rib cage. But Helen could say nothing.

James stopped the chest compressions. Bernice pressed her ear onto Will's chest, waiting for the thud of his heart. "I still don't hear anything," she said, her eyes pleading Carson for help.

Carson knew there was no hope for Will, but like Helen, he couldn't bring himself to be the one to extinguish Bernice's hope. He took over for James. He approached Will and rolled him to his side, the black ooze draining from his petite mouth.

"Will!" Carson yelled, shaking the child's body rather violently. He stuck his index finger into Will's mouth to sweep out more of the sludge. He yelped in pain, quickly withdrawing his now wounded, gashed finger. He rolled Will onto his back and pried his lips open, revealing that the boy's teeth were horribly chipped, jagged, and worn down to half their size. He pulled the side of Will's mouth open and saw deep gouges and lacerations on the inside of his cheeks and on his tongue.

Bernice clung to the last ounce of hope she had even after seeing all this and implored Carson to keep going. He removed his jacket and knelt next to Will. He pinched Will's nose closed and began CPR, forcing his own breath into his tiny mouth. After three breaths, Carson placed his sizable palm on Will's tiny sternum and began chest compressions again, this time shattering Will's ribs. Carson pulled away and gave up. Bernice screamed at him to continue.

"He's gone," Helen announced firmly yet gently, relieving Carson from his charade.

"Don't listen to her! Keep going!" Bernice begged Carson.

Carson was about to begin again, but Helen approached him from behind and rested her hands on his broad, sturdy shoulders. "That's enough." Carson sat back on his haunches and hung his head. Bernice slunk over to him and sat next to him.

"You tried," he was thankful to hear Bernice say. The truth was, Bernice had already known Will was long expired by the time she saw him. But she was desperate to have someone, anyone, from her family back again. She had to indulge in her shred of hope that Will could be revived.

Fury percolated inside Helen as she considered that the monster was responsible for Bernice's pain as well as her own. From the soles of her feet, Helen felt the sludge churn more rapidly underground, responding to her anger. She forced the painful thoughts away and breathed slowly and meditatively until she could feel the underground river recede.

Silence was broken by an approaching ambulance bounding over broken ground as it bumped along closer, its siren blaring. James stood up and waved his arms at the driver, prompting the rest of the group to follow suit. The ambulance came to a clumsy halt just short of falling over the ragged edge of the fissure. Bernice recognized the driver.

"Mrs. Becker!" she shouted. It was Marie's mother, dressed in plain, disheveled clothes rather than in her EMT uniform.

Mrs. Becker walked over to the crack and looked down at the river and said, "My God. It's all over town."

"The entire town?" Carson asked.

She nodded and motioned toward the river. "Yeah, and whatever this is, it's destroying homes and property. That's not all, it's..." She trailed off as she saw Will's body lying in the grass. She covered her mouth with the back of her palm and closed her eyes and swallowed hard to keep the tears from coming.

Bernice asked, "Is Marie okay?"

"Yes, she's fine, darling. She's at the hospital, shaken up, but she's okay. After this thing hit us this morning, she told me about what happened at your house last night. I had to come check on you guys as soon as I could. Sorry it took so long. It's been nonstop." Mrs. Becker scanned the members of the group and looked at Bernice, asking, "Where are your parents, honey?" Mrs. Becker received her answer in the form of awkward, anguished glances among those in front of her. No words needed to be spoken.

"Sweetheart, I'm so sorry. Okay, okay," Mrs. Becker said to herself, trying to keep her composure. "So far, the hospital is still safe. Everyone should fit into the back of the ambulance. I'll bring you all there. It's crowded and chaotic, but you'll be able to eat and get some rest."

Helen said to Mrs. Becker, "Officer Carson should sit up front. He's got a gunshot wound."

As Carson hoisted himself into the passenger's seat and Helen shut the door behind him, Mrs. Becker was unaware that she had been overtly staring at Helen. Like everyone else in town, Mrs. Becker knew Helen's reputation but had never formally met her. Even after all she had been through that morning, Mrs. Becker was still a little taken aback that she was actually having an interaction with the town enigma.

Feeling Mrs. Becker's eyes on her, Helen dismissed her outstretched hand ready for introduction. Slightly annoyed, Helen embarrassed Mrs. Becker by saying, "I hope you got your eyes full. No formal introduction necessary. I already know who you are."

James, Regina, and their daughters had already retreated into the back of the ambulance. James was about to collapse the gurney to make more room but stopped when he saw Helen carrying Will's body toward the ambulance. James collected the body from Helen and placed Will's figure on the gurney, securing it with the straps.

Bernice climbed into the ambulance and solemnly stood over her brother's corpse. Her tears were spent, numb from too much trauma and grief. She spotted a soiled white sheet on the ambulance floor and wrestled it from underneath the gurney's locked wheels. She draped it over Will and then plopped herself down hard onto the side bench in the ambulance.

Helen sat on the other narrow, hard bench directly across from Bernice. Bernice stared blankly at Helen, who reached her arm over the tiny body and held her palm open. Bernice took it gratefully and focused on nothing but the small consolation it gave her.

After witnessing similar scenes that morning, Mrs. Becker offered no condolences as she closed the ambulance door from the outside. The group didn't know it, but Mrs. Becker was making an exception by allowing them to bring Will's body into the ambulance.

Mrs. Becker took her seat behind the wheel, joining Carson in the cab. His eyes were closed as he relaxed his head on the seat rest behind him. Mrs. Becker tried not to slam her door shut, not wanting to disturb Carson's repose. But as she buckled her seat belt and shifted the ambulance into gear, Carson spoke. "The bodies of Mr. and Mrs. Weber are inside their home," he said, expecting Mrs. Becker to retrieve them.

"I can't take on any more dead bodies," she said.

"What? Why?" Carson asked, his eyes now open as he watched Mrs. Becker for her response.

"There's no more room for bodies at the hospital. In fact, this is the first transport I've made today where the living outnumber the dead.

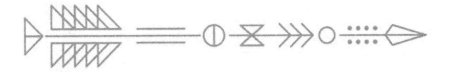

CHAPTER 15

Ramsey Hospital was a mob scene. Overburdened doctors and frazzled nurses barely staved off complete chaos as they struggled to treat more patients than they could handle. The distressed and the weary crowded the waiting rooms and hallways. People who weren't hospital staff did their best to help the already overworked employees. So much had happened in such a short period of time. Everyone was doing whatever they could to help. Patients showed up in various states of shock, presenting injuries from minor cuts and bruises to broken or even severed limbs. The hospital morgue was beyond capacity as they tried to house the corpses brought in.

Mrs. Becker pulled the ambulance up to the hospital. She opened the back, allowing each person to file out one by one. Helen was last to exit. She gripped one side of the gurney and looked at Mrs. Becker, expecting her to take the other side. But Mrs. Becker remained where she was. "They're full of bodies. I've been told not to take in any more," Mrs. Becker said gently to Helen, who ignored her empathy completely.

"Surely there's room for one more. He's small," she stated firmly, reaching over and slapping the other handrail of the gurney, beckoning Mrs. Becker to take hold.

"Helen, I can't."

Since seeing her mother's arms attached to the monster, a boldness and an anger festered inside Helen. She didn't want to misdirect it onto innocent people, like Mrs. Becker. It was a completely new feeling to Helen and strangely empowering. It allowed her to behave in an assertive way she wasn't accustomed to.

Dismissing Mrs. Becker, Helen scooped up Will's shrouded body into her arms and exited the ambulance, bumping past Mrs.

Becker, who made a sorry attempt at blocking her. She couldn't have fought Helen's resolve if she had tried. Seeing Bernice walking alongside Helen as they entered the sanctuary of the hospital, Mrs. Becker knew this was a viable exception.

Mrs. Becker escorted the rest of the group into the hospital. She pointed Carson straight ahead into the emergency room where Helen sat in a chair with Will in her arms, Bernice in a chair at her side. She motioned for the rest of the group to the right toward the waiting room.

Regina remained with Mrs. Becker. "We need to go to the psychiatric ward."

Misinterpreting, Mrs. Becker responded, "Everyone's feeling overwhelmed and stressed. Trust me. This is where you all should stay."

Regina interrupted. "No, my son is there. I need to see him. I need my family to be together."

Mrs. Becker hadn't been on the psychiatric floor that day, but she had heard it was an ugly scene. Even though it was isolated from the rest of the hospital as much as it could possibly be, the residents could feel the chaos and anxiety happening around them. The staff was on edge, nervous, distracted. The psych ward's residents heard whispers from the staff about something going on all over town. They were unable to inspect from the windows as they were barred and purposely set high enough up on the walls so that patients could only see the light of day.

"Word is that the patients are extremely agitated up there today. Not a place for your girls to be," Mrs. Becker warned.

"I think what we've all witnessed outside of these walls is far worse than anything we could experience in that ward," Regina countered.

"Come on. I'll escort you up," Mrs. Becker digressed, leading them to the elevator.

Regina bustled with nervous anticipation over seeing her son. She had kept a notebook with her since they had left the picnic table, foreseeing and hoping that there would be a chance to reunite with her son at some point that day. She clutched the notebook at her chest, believing that the information her son had written and drawn within it were the evidence she needed to not only free him from that ward but also to aid her in apologizing to her son. The guilt of having him admitted to the psychiatric ward nearly two years ago destroyed her inside. She feared, above all else, that he would never forgive her.

As the elevator doors opened to the fifth floor, the change in decibel level was unsettling. Regina and her family had religiously visited Roy in that ward every Sunday afternoon since he had been admitted. Not once in those two years had they been met with such a disquieting and chaotic scene as they encountered now. They heard the psychiatric patients from behind the sturdy doors. They were agitated, yelling, causing a ruckus the secured metal door could barely muffle.

The normally peaceful waiting and meeting areas were teeming with overflow patients from downstairs, mostly those with minor injuries or those who needed a respite from their electrified nerves. Nurses scuttled about, trying to give aid to as many people as they could, all while they worked to stave off panic among everyone at the same time. They were so busy trying to maintain some semblance of order that they didn't notice when the elevator doors opened and more people stepped onto their floor.

Regina saw how busy they all were but still tried to get one of the nurses' attention. She saw Dorothy, Dot as the patients called her. She was busy rearranging some aluminum folding chairs against a wall, announcing to people over her shoulder that there were more places to "take a load off."

Regina hovered close to Dot, waiting for her to break from what she was doing so she could ask about seeing Roy. But Dot went from arranging chairs straight to asking people if they needed water or food. She worked incessantly, like her body was on autopilot.

Regina tried to get her attention, calling out, "Hey, Dot." She called her name a couple more times to no avail.

Annoyed and purposely avoiding eye contact, Dot snapped back, "Yes, I know you're there, Regina. No regular family visiting hours today obviously."

"Well, yes, but—"

"Well, then if you're not hurt, grab a seat like everyone else, or help out if you can," Dot ordered her, abruptly cutting her off midsentence.

James, who had been watching the scene from the hall adjacent to the waiting area, sensed his wife's growing exasperation and intervened. He placed his hand on Regina's shoulder and took the notebook from her hand. He then rifled through a few pages of the notebook until he came upon a clearly sketched, disturbing picture of the creature that was causing all the havoc. James thrust the picture in front of Dot's face. Her reaction was immediate and unanticipated. She stopped what she was doing and covered her mouth with both hands, her eyes filled with alarm at recognizing the figure in the sketch. James had hoped she would recognize it but was surprised by this extreme reaction.

Dot gave James and Regina a look of consternation and then led them through a door at the far corner of the room, a maintenance closet. Dot spoke. "We don't know who has seen this thing out there, but you can't go flashing pictures of it around! Everyone's on edge, and we have to try and keep the peace."

Dot took the notebook from James's hands and gave the sketch a closer look, nodding her head in recognition. She silently contemplated before she made an offer. "You really want to see Roy today?" James and Regina glanced at each other, already knowing they didn't need assurance from each other that seeing Roy was what they needed. They affirmed Dot's question with quick nods. "Meeting room is full of patients, so if you want to see him, you'll have to go back to his room."

"Fine," Regina sounded pleased. "I'll just get the girls before we head down."

Dot stopped her. "No, they shouldn't go. They'll be safer in the waiting area." Dot elaborated. "It's not only that the patients are much more agitated and unpredictable today. Whatever is going on around town today is having a major effect on all of them. It's how they're handling it and the things they've done that make me worried about the girls going in there. They shouldn't see what the patients have done. I don't know if you should either. But this"—she raised the notebook and shook it in the air—"this gives you admission."

Her words were unsettling and enigmatic to James and Regina, but they ignored it and zeroed in on the fact that they would be able to see their son. It would be the first time they could apologize to him, to let him know that they knew the truth, that they knew he wasn't crazy, and that they would be getting him out of there as soon as possible.

Helen and Bernice sat next to each other on the uncomfortable, uncushioned folding chairs that now lined the hallway leading from the main waiting area to the emergency room. The constant bustle around them had turned into white noise for them. They were exhausted, just happy to be sitting. Bernice smiled up at Helen. "He would've liked that," she said.

"What?" Helen asked.

"How you're rocking him."

Helen hadn't realized that she had been gently rocking Will's lifeless body as she cradled him in her arms. She had never really considered having kids of her own, and she had never been around kids since her school days. After that, her life had been consumed—or hijacked, rather—by her mother's disappearance and its aftermath. Supporting her father became her life's priority without a second thought to her own aspirations.

Bernice rested her head on Helen's shoulder. Tears welled in Helen's eyes as she reveled in the maternal instincts Bernice had awakened in her. It reminded her of when she was a child, how her mother had always been there to love and nurture her. Since her disappearance, Helen hadn't allowed herself to remember those times. They were too poignant, caused too much pain. This was the first time she was able to look back and not be overcome with sadness over it. Maybe it was because to Helen, it seemed to pale in comparison to what Bernice was going through.

In Bernice, she saw an innocent, smart, brave girl doing the best she could in the situation she was given. She admired Bernice's extraordinary resiliency and felt a kinship with her. She hoped she could be there for Bernice always. For now, Helen enjoyed the warm feelings radiating through her body as she felt Bernice relax next to her. She continued to sway back and forth, nurturing Will as though he could feel it. After all they had been through together within a matter of hours, this tiny shred of peace, however twisted, was welcomed.

A nurse interrupted the trio, delicately offering, "Why don't you let me take him where he can rest? You both look like you need a rest as well." The nurse was ashamed to have been spying on them from around the corner. She knew Helen and was beyond surprised by the scene and couldn't help but gawk. She was incredibly moved. It was clear to see that the boy was dead, but she wasn't sure if the two were ready to accept that.

Bernice was about to object, but Helen's look of exhaustion when she offered up Will's body to the nurse told her that it was time to let go. She trusted Helen and had faith that she knew the right thing to do. In all the uncertainty that swirled around Bernice's world right now, she needed the certainty of Helen's presence and her words.

"I'll be right back," the nurse assured Helen and Bernice, leaving them alone as she walked through two swinging doors, disappearing with Will.

With her arms freed, Helen wrapped one around Bernice's shoulders and pulled her in, resting her chin on Bernice's gritty, tangled mess of hair. While Helen was becoming aware of the stench emanating from Bernice's head, Bernice was realizing the same thing about Helen. She heard Helen make a grunt of disgust and was grateful for the small moment of comic relief. Bernice laughed and played along. "Jeez! Ever heard of a shower?"

Helen threw her head back and let out a hearty chuckle, retorting, "Is that what that thing was in my bathroom?"

When the quick laughs died down, Bernice confessed. "Helen, I'm sorry if I was ever rude to you. It's embarrassing to admit, but my dad and I actually made a game over how long it took you to get back into your house. Sorry for staring and spying on you."

"A game? About me? Really? I want to hear this." Helen was genuinely amused and intrigued.

"Remember, this was before I really knew you, so please don't be mad. We used to bet on how long it would take you to go back into your house," Bernice said, wrinkling her nose in shame, waiting for Helen's response.

"So you spied on me that much? And what, pray tell, were the stakes of your bet?" Helen asked, folding her arms across her chest and feigning disgust, reminding Bernice of when her dad used to do the same. Bernice knew this game and was thankful to be doing something that felt familiar again even though one player was different.

"Sometimes, we bet money. Other times, it was for dibs on the big TV downstairs or helping around the house." Bernice trailed off, remembering the last bet she had lost and where it had led.

Helen didn't know about this last detail but could feel Bernice slipping off into her own thoughts and tried to keep her in that light moment for a little longer. "You and your dad thought you were pretty clever, huh? Well, I knew you were watching me, how you used to duck below the window or how your dad would pretend to be looking at the clouds. So I watched you too," Helen confessed.

"In fact, I think I can go further than you." Helen couldn't believe she was going to admit this to anyone, but she thought it was only fair. "You know those journals I brought from my house this morning? Well, most of them were notes about what was happening in the neighborhood. But I actually had a special one dedicated to your family. In fact, more than one."

"You didn't! Helen, are you serious?" Bernice's eyes were wide as she waited for Helen to divulge more information. She was tickled to know that Helen took an interest in her just as she had taken an interest in Helen.

"Absolutely serious. What do you think of that?"

Bernice smiled. "I think it's embarrassing and hilarious."

Helen sat back and took in a deep breath through her nose and blew the air out through her mouth. "Thanks for your apology, Bernice."

"I wish I'd talked to you sooner. I guess I was just kind of scared or something too. I know that's silly now. Sorry," Bernice apologized again.

"No need for any more apologies. I think we're even." Helen reached her right hand out to meet Bernice's to shake on it.

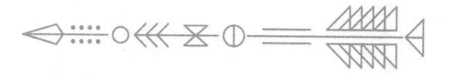

CHAPTER 16

The elevator down the hall from where Helen and Bernice sat had been running incessantly since they sat down. The ding of the opening doors became a background noise they had quickly come to ignore. But this time, Mandy emerged while Lynne pressed the elevator button to keep the doors open. Not spotting them right away, Mandy searched left and right as she called out for Helen and Bernice. Bernice was the first to register Mandy's voice and stood up and waved.

"Dad asked us to bring you up right away," Mandy shouted as she motioned for Helen and Bernice to follow her to the elevator. They both got up and walked toward the open doors.

"Bernice!" someone yelled from farther down the hall. Bernice saw Marie running toward her. Overjoyed to see Marie, Bernice forgot about the elevator and ran to Marie, meeting her halfway. They threw their arms around each other. "I'm so sorry, Bernice! I'm so glad you're okay! I'm so sorry I left you the way I did last night. I was so scared," Marie pleaded for forgiveness.

"Bernice! Lynne's holding the doors. Come on!" Mandy urged.

Helen took control of the situation, saying, "Marie, will you stay here with Bernice while I go upstairs?" Marie was shocked that Helen had addressed her by name as though she had known her for years. She affirmed Helen's question with a nod. Before allowing Lynne to release the button that kept the doors open, Helen asked Bernice, "You're okay?"

"Of course," Bernice assured her, feeling secure that Helen was making sure she was all right even in her absence.

Lynne released the button, and the elevator doors closed, leaving Marie and Bernice to reconnect and leaving Helen alone with

Mandy and Lynne. She read the fear on their faces and asked what was going on. "We aren't really sure. They made us wait in the waiting room while Mom and Dad went in to see Roy. Dad came out after a while and said to get you right away," Mandy explained.

"I hope he didn't want Bernice to come with me. She's been through enough. You all have," Helen said.

Helen perceived the drastic change in the atmosphere as she stepped out of the elevator and onto the fifth floor. A sickening aura of panic stagnated in the air. The girls led Helen to the locked metal door where their father said he would be waiting. Lynne pressed the red button on the side, then she and Mandy turned away and went back to their chairs in the waiting area as they were told.

The door opened a crack, revealing James. A tall male orderly stood directly behind James, holding the heavy door open with one beefy arm. The desperate cries and strained voices of the patients rang out from behind him. James spoke to Helen through the small opening. Helen could see a borderline craze in James's eyes as he spoke to her. "Helen, is it just you? Where's Bernice?" he asked.

"She's safe on the main floor with Marie."

James's wasn't sure who Marie was and didn't care. He just didn't want Bernice to see beyond that point. "Helen, prepare yourself," James warned. The orderly shoved the door open and ushered Helen inside.

Helen walked into a vessel of chaos. She focused on her breath, trying to remain calm. The male orderly was joined by another, equally as tall. They stood like oak trees on either side of Helen and James, hovering beside them protectively as they escorted the two down the looming hallway toward Roy's room.

Roy's room was about fifty feet down the hall, but the walk there felt like an eternity. Helen was on the verge of sensory overload as she heard the agonizing cacophony of shrieks and moans coming from the patients coupled with the pleas of the staff trying to control them. The sight of the highly distressed residents was painful to watch. Some writhed in pain. Others were curled into balls on the floor, in corners, or on beds, sobbing or screaming. Some were forcefully being restrained by the staff, some bellowing and fighting it and some cackling hysterically at their attempts. Other patients wore looks of absolute blankness, staring off into space. Others seemed deep in thought as they sketched furiously on large sheets of paper or on walls.

Then Helen noticed the drawings on the walls. Horrifying pictures of the monster nearly covered the walls as they walked on further toward Roy's room. Then came the unbearable stench, like rancid sweat mixed with feces. Helen saw a couple of orderlies wearing face masks and rubber gloves, scrubbing the walls with bleach. Some of the patients had drawn the monster with their own excrement. Helen gagged and urgently covered her nose and mouth with her sleeve. Just as the feeling of disgust and chaos were about to take her over, Helen, James, and the orderlies arrived at Roy's door. Regina quickly unlocked the door from inside and let James and Helen slip inside. One of the orderlies pulled the door shut with force, the door locking automatically behind them.

Helen was relieved to find Roy's room clean and to see cans of air freshener at the ready. The smell from the hallway still permeated through her nostrils. She needed a few seconds to recover her own breath. Roy's room was gray and stale but tidy. The bed was made. No pictures hung on the walls. Except for the built-in bookshelf at one wall holding a smattering of books and notebooks, the room maintained its dull, clinical atmosphere. An orderly sat in the corner of the room.

"Wow, Helen in the flesh," came a young man's voice.

Helen looked toward the voice and saw Roy sitting at a compact metal desk. She barely recognized him. It had been a couple of years since she had last seen him, and in that time, he had grown quickly from a childlike thirteen-year-old into a young man. She wanted to comment on how much he had grown and changed, but she thought it would make it obvious that she had spied on Roy's family as well. She also loathed small talk and was thankful there wasn't enough time for it now anyway.

The events of that day had made Helen forget for a moment that she had been known as the neighborhood lunatic, for lack of a better word. When Roy had exclaimed surprise at her presence, she was reminded of her old role. When she saw the look of awe on Roy's face, she couldn't help but retreat into that old character expected of her and play along.

"Boo!" she shouted as she lunged at Roy, making him jerk in his chair. The orderly stood up, not sure if he would need to step in, but when he saw James and Regina crack smiles, he shook his head and sat back down. The four of them laughed, which felt great yet inappropriate under the circumstances. The world as they knew it was swirling in chaos around them, yet they laughed. Helen walked over to Roy and warmly offered her right hand to him and said, "I couldn't resist. Forgive me."

Roy stood up, now slightly taller than Helen's impressive six-foot frame, and clasped both his hands around hers. He looked her in the eyes and spoke sincerely. "I've waited for this for a long time."

Helen wasn't exactly sure what Roy meant by "this" and waited for Roy to make the next move and say what he needed to say. She didn't have to wait long as Roy released her hands and went straight for the bookcase. He grabbed handfuls of notebooks, easily gripping eight with each of his sizable paws, and brought them over to the metal desk. He went back for more, then sat down in a metal chair behind the desk and scooted himself in close.

"Mom and Dad told me you've made notes," Roy said, flipping through his notebooks, appearing to be looking for one in particular.

Feeling a cross-examination coming, Helen answered, "I've kept journals, yes."

Roy was direct, asking, "What notes have you kept about this?" He held open a page of one of his notebooks, revealing a detailed sketch he had made of the creature. Helen's stomach lurched as she saw that Roy had captured the detail of her mom's arms attached to the monster. Roy saw the change in Helen and shocked her by asking, "Is there something about this that you recognize?"

Helen stuttered, "I...I just found out this morning...but... how...how did you...?"

Roy didn't answer but reached for a notebook that rested alone on the top shelf of the bookcase. He turned a few pages until he found what he had been looking for. After a moment of hesitation,

Roy held the page open to reveal a familiar scene, one that had taken place just earlier that day.

Helen drew closer to the notebook, her eyes squinting as she tried to make sense of what she was seeing. Roy had sketched the beast as it held Will's body, the moment it was offering it to Helen. What was most striking was that Roy had captured the moment when Helen realized the monster possessed her mother's arms. Helen was astonished as she looked at Roy's rendition of her in that moment when she forced herself not to react with her body, but the awful realization showed clearly in her eyes.

"I know I caught something in your face here, recognition or something. But I don't understand what it is," Roy said.

"I know how this is going to sound, but those arms on the monster? I recognize them. They're my mother's. I don't know how that thing got them or when or why. God! And I just don't understand how you were able to see this, Roy," Helen said, her voice shaky.

Roy, James, and Regina shuddered over the gruesome news about the monster's arms. Regina interrupted. "That's what we want to know too, Helen, how Roy is able to see what he does. Roy said that if we brought you up here that he would explain it to us all at once."

"Well, I tried to explain it to you for years," Roy said to his parents, not in resentment but in understanding of how unbelievable it all sounded. Regina held back tears as Roy continued addressing her and James. "I didn't understand what I was experiencing, and I think I was too young to even explain it. I don't blame either of you for putting me here. I really don't. If I did, that cruel monster wouldn't allow me to live. Anyway, being in here has given me time to understand what I can do. I needed the time, and I knew I wouldn't be able to explain it until I understood and the time was right. I think that time is now."

Roy opened the notebook to a clean page. Helen, James, and Regina watched in careful anticipation, not knowing what to expect, as Roy picked up a pencil with his right hand and reached into a plastic cup with his left. His hand was balled into a fist as he withdrew it from the cup. He placed his clenched hand on the table to the left of the notebook and squeezed hard. He closed his eyes and took deliberate deep breaths. With his eyes still closed, his right hand sprung into action, furiously sketching on the fresh page in front of him. His right hand and arm moved like mad while the rest of his body sat motionless.

The orderly looked on, appearing bored at what was happening in front of him. He had seen Roy repeat this process many times daily and thought it was just a part of his illness, although he never really knew what Roy's illness was or whether he even had one. He had always seemed out of place in the ward, but the orderly minded his business and did his job. Roy was an easy patient, and he had been lucky enough to be the one to supervise him most of the time. He didn't want to ruin that by mentioning to the staff that maybe Roy didn't belong there.

While the orderly wasn't impressed with Roy's rapid sketching, Helen, James, and Regina were riveted. Their amazement turned to dread as they saw the figures taking shape in this new sketch. The beast was becoming clear. It was surrounded by the blackness of an underground tunnel. Random body parts came into fruition as Roy continued to detail his sketch. These body parts were not attached to their owners and were imbedded into the walls of sludge surrounding the monster. The deformed head of Bruce Feller became recognizable, suspended in the glittering ooze, as did the head and torso of Officer Burns, his police uniform tattered but still clinging to his chest.

Roy squeezed his hand tighter, and sweat formed on his brow, his face remaining calm. His hand flew to the bottom left of the page as he began sketching a person. This person was alive, unconfined by the sludge. Regina was the first to recognize the face and exclaimed, "It's Irene!"

The three of them watched as Roy added more details to the picture. The monster held its hand—the hand of Helen's mom, rather—on top of Irene's head. Her eyes were fixed wide open, and her mouth was twisted into a sneer of hatred. The evil creature bore an intense stare into Irene's eyes.

Roy finally released his left fist, sending a handful of paper clips scattering across the desk, and dropped the pencil with his right. He sat back in his chair and opened his eyes. His breath was slightly quickened as he rubbed his palms up and down his thighs as he came back from wherever he had just been. He held up an index finger, indicating he needed another moment, and surprised the group by picking up a single paper clip and tossing it into his own mouth. Regina was about to protest but was stopped by the sight of Roy revealing his tongue, the paper clip dissolving into it.

The orderly broke in. "Hey, wait a second. I have never seen that before. I thought you were using the clips in your notebooks, not eating them!"

Helen was annoyed at the interruption and gave the orderly a look that made it crystal clear that neither his opinion nor his interruption were welcome. Roy tried to explain. "So it's like I can put myself into a trance ever since, well, ever since I got this." Roy opened his left hand to reveal a scar in the same zigzag pattern they all recognized. He reached his hand closer to Helen and asked her to touch it. She was hesitant, but he reassured her it was safe. Helen placed her fingertips on the scar to find it was scorching, like a baking sheet that had just been pulled out of a hot oven. She reflexively pulled her hand away.

"How are you able to stand that?" she asked.

"I really haven't been able to feel the hand at all since the thing bit me. It only half bit me, really. It only had time to sink one side of teeth in before I pulled away."

James said, hanging his head, "And I'd yelled at you for messing with my saw blades. Jesus Christ!" James ran his fingers through his hair, consumed with regret as he remembered the incident. That day, Roy had desperately tried to tell James the truth about the monster while James accused Roy of tinkering with his tools. He had exploded in anger at Roy, furious at the thought of being lied to. James's exasperation led to weeks of barely saying a word to Roy, stonewalling him into isolation and leaving him to deal with this terrifying problem alone. The silent treatment he had given Roy was cruel punishment, especially considering how innocent Roy was. He had been reaching out for help from the person who was supposed to always be there to help and whom he trusted the most, and James coldly ignored that, bullying Roy into feeling as insignificant as a flea.

Roy could see and feel that his dad was reliving how Roy must have felt during that time and that it was shattering James. "Look at me, Dad." The guilt made it close to impossible for James to look his son in the eyes, but when he did, he saw no anger. Before Roy said a word, James could feel nothing but love and forgiveness from him.

"I'm fine, Dad. I admit I was angry for a long time, but I really did need the time alone in here to figure out my connection with this thing. You never could have accepted my crazy story back then without seeing it for yourself, right? I understand that now, and I really don't blame you or Mom."

James said through tears, "I don't know how you can forgive us."

Roy gave pause before he went deeper into his explanation. This was where he needed to get the words right so that everyone would understand what they were dealing with. "This thing, this monster, I've learned that it feeds off of emotions, negative emotions. When I first got here, I was angry and hurt and vengeful. I could sense that the monster had followed me here but not physically. I couldn't see it, but I could feel its pull emotionally every time I gave in to my anger. That's when I'd notice that when my anger would grow, the cut would heat up, and I'd get a strange urge for metal. If I stayed in that anger, the heat would move up my arm, and I could feel it wanting to take over my entire body and mind."

Regina interrupted. "And did it ever take over?"

"No, but once it almost did. I had a gut feeling that if it took me over completely that I would be gone to it for good." Roy looked back at the sketch he had just drawn moments ago, fixating on Irene.

Helen caught Roy's look and pointedly asked, "Is Irene gone for good?"

"Yes," Roy affirmed. "It's using her body and its former connections to her family in order to feed itself. Irene is nothing more than its pawn. Will, too, I'm afraid."

"I thought it fed on metal," Helen said.

"It does, but first, it needs the energy of people's negative emotions to kind of stir it up. Once it gets enough of that, it has the power to emerge in order to get the metal it feeds on. The metal calms it back down. Kind of a vicious cycle. I only knew about the metal part of it before I came here to the hospital," Roy explained.

"I knew about the metal part too. I…I fed it for years," Helen admitted.

"I know you did," Roy said as he searched for another of his notebooks. Helen saw her name written in black marker on the cover of the notebook. She was surprised and felt a little as though it was karma coming back to her for all the notes she had kept about her neighbors. She was both intrigued and fearful to see what Roy had recorded inside.

Roy opened the notebook to a random page where Helen looked at a drawing of herself inside her own bathroom. He had captured one of the many times she had thrown pieces of metal into her drain. This one showed how she tossed in a mixture of nails, screws, nuts, and bolts from the tattered cardboard box she kept them in.

Roy skipped over a few pages and opened to another very telling sketch. It was an aerial-view photo. In it, Helen stood across the street from her house, looking angrily toward the Fellers' home. Faint figures of two people stood by the Fellers' window. The most striking aspect of the sketch was how Roy had drawn the exact layout of Helen's house with the roof off, revealing the monster rearing its ugly head in her bathroom. It had responded directly to Helen's anger and hurt over being watched like a circus freak.

Roy said, "Your feelings have always been right, Helen. All those times you knocked and knocked and knocked on your door, that fear you held in your gut but couldn't quite name, you could sense something, but you had no way of knowing what it was. You were right all along."

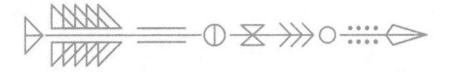

CHAPTER 17

Loaded with pain medication, Carson strode groggily into the hospital cafeteria and took a pea-green melamine tray. He should have received a blood transfusion, but the doctor who stitched him up explained that the hospital's supply of blood had dwindled and that what remained had to be reserved for those in dire need. So instead, the doctor ordered Carson to head straight to the cafeteria and eat something to raise his blood sugar and to get some iron pumping through his veins.

Carson was weak and shaky as he loaded his tray with a baked potato, a slab of meat loaf, and creamed spinach. He brought his tray to the register and fumbled for his wallet. No one was tending the register, and as Carson slipped some bills from his wallet, he heard someone yell, "It's free today, Officer!"

He smashed the bills haphazardly back into his wallet and forced it into his pocket. He laughed at himself for the trouble he was having with these simple tasks, blaming it on exhaustion, low blood sugar, and the pain meds.

"Officer Carson! Hey, over here!"

Carson recognized the voice and scanned the cafeteria for Bernice. He spotted her standing by an empty table, waving her gangly arms to get his attention. Carson had hoped to see Helen along with her, but Bernice was sitting with a teenage girl he didn't recognize. He lazily shuffled over to the table and lowered his body down to the bench as gently as he could, thankful to be sitting. He didn't address the girls and just dove into his food as though he was eating alone.

Bernice and Marie watched, wide-eyed and amused, as Carson shoveled food into his mouth like a ravenous caveman. He guzzled bottled water, letting it escape down his scruffy chin. The girls muffled their giggles as they watched him loudly chomp his food, open-mouthed, and wipe his mouth on his already dirty shirtsleeve. The girls had already finished eating by the time Carson joined them, but they picked at their leftovers so as not to embarrass Carson should he realize they were laughing at him.

After a few minutes of gorging himself, Carson felt more like himself and regained his manners. He realized the girls were stifling giggles as they pretended not to notice how he had devoured his meal like a savage. "All I'm missing is a loud belch, huh?" he remarked, acknowledging how he had eaten with wild abandon and making the girls crack up in the process. Carson noticed clean napkins on Bernice's tray. "May I? I think I know how to use them," Carson joked.

"Are you sure?" Bernice remarked, handing him a wad of napkins.

Carson had to enjoy this a bit longer. He snatched the napkins from Bernice's hand, jutted his chin forward, furrowed his brow, and studied the napkins like he was a Neanderthal seeing a calculator. After he got a good laugh from the girls for his antics, he pulled himself back into character and wiped his face properly. "Ladies, I'm sorry you had to see that. Low blood sugar does crazy things to a person," Carson said, smirking. He turned to the girl seated across from Bernice and introduced himself.

"Yes, I know. Not many cops in town, so I guess you're all kind of famous. I'm Marie. I'm Bernice and Will's—" She stopped and corrected herself, thinking of the awful news Bernice broke to her earlier about Will's death. "I mean, I am…was…Bernice's babysitter."

The mood at the table turned somber instantly. Marie grabbed Bernice's hand. Bernice closed her eyes, angry, questioning how many times she had had to try and force the tears to stop that day. Carson played images from earlier that day in his mind. There was more to do, and he had to act now.

"The doctor patched you up?" Bernice said, pointing at Carson's side.

"Yup, I'm good," Carson answered, abruptly changing the subject. "You and your friend here have eaten and look like you're both doing okay. How about the rest of them?"

Bernice answered, "They're all up on the fifth floor. I haven't seen them in the cafeteria, but maybe they have food up there. I don't know."

"Fifth floor, huh? Helen there too?"

"Yeah, but she joined them later. Mandy and Lynne came down to get her, said their dad asked for her to go up right away."

Carson grew concerned. "Do you know why they needed her?"

Bernice shook her head no. Carson stood up and told the girls to stay together, that he was going to check on things and would be back. He left swiftly, leaving his empty tray behind. The girls watched Carson disappear into the elevator down the hall.

Marie grabbed Carson's empty tray with both hands and spoke as though Carson was still there with them, her voice sarcasm-laden as she said, "Here, let me take that for you, Officer. Don't be silly. It's no trouble at all! I got it, really!" *Thank God I still have Marie,* Bernice thought, *and I still have Helen.* She had to think about what she had rather than all she had lost if she wanted to survive.

Helen's mind was reeling after hearing Roy's explanation. He had vindicated her. She hadn't just been paranoid all those times when she worried that the monster could be lurking around her home. What an absolute relief to know that her gut feeling had been right, freeing her from the pure hell it had been to second-guess her instincts for years.

Helen's thoughts turned dark as she ruminated over the hermit-like existence she had led as a result of the low, evil creature torturing her mentally. The excruciating anxiety that manifested from it all had forced her into isolation, unable to socialize, terrified by the thought of more public scrutiny than she had already had. She used to blame herself for everything that went wrong, from her mother's disappearance to her father's illness and death. Roy said the monster thrived on human pain. Helen thought it must have been feeding on her pain for years, using her, enslaving her.

Roy saw the dark mood sweep over Helen and reminded her, "Whatever anger you're feeling toward it now, try not to feed into it as hard as it is. It's still with us."

But she couldn't contain it. Helen exploded in anger. She grabbed a notebook, ripped pages out, then threw it at the wall as hard as she could. Her outburst startled the orderly, who stood up, ready to intervene. "Damn it! Don't I deserve some retribution? This thing ruined my life! I know it killed my parents, leaving me to deal with it alone. You know what it's like to be branded crazy by everyone around you? You start second-guessing yourself in everything you do, worrying that they're right. I don't know what's worse, worrying that you really are crazy or the ambivalence you start to feel about life after worrying about it for so long."

As Helen ranted, Roy grew nervous as her angry words had caused his scar to heat up. But he knew the anger wouldn't overtake Helen completely as he felt the heat begin to wane once again as she digressed. He was glad he hadn't interrupted her. She needed to get those raw feelings out so they wouldn't fester inside her even if it was just a minute portion of them.

Someone pounded on the door from outside. The orderly went to the door and looked out through the small plate glass window and, recognizing Officer Carson, unlocked the door to allow him inside. Carson shoved his way through the door, relieved to be out of the chaos and away from the putrid smell of the ward. Helen beamed at the unexpected sight of Carson, surprising herself. She couldn't stop from smiling. Her face burned red hot, and everyone else noticed, especially Carson, who had blushed over Helen's unanticipated reaction. He cleared his throat. "Hey, gang. Bernice told me you all were up here, so I wanted to check in."

Roy stood and shook hands with Carson, then immediately sat back down at his desk and flipped through the notebook in front of him in search of another clean page. He grasped a handful of paper clips and found his pencil. He closed his eyes and sat back in his chair. Carson was confused and felt a little ignored by the young man as he stood there watching Roy fumble around his desk. He noticed how the others watched Roy with their undivided attention. Helen snuck up behind Carson and whispered in his ear, sending chills up his spine. "Watch him."

But before beginning another sketch, Roy opened his eyes and flipped to more recent pages in his notebook. When he found the page he had been looking for, he held it up for Carson to see. It was a sketch of Carson lying in the Fellers' basement, Burns dead next to him, Irene pointing his own gun at him. Roy had captured the moment right after Irene had shot Carson. Carson felt a tangle of emotions—revulsion, shock, anger, confusion. Roy flipped to the page he had shown earlier, the one of the beast offering Will's body to Helen.

"What the…how the hell…?" Carson muttered.

"May I?" Helen asked Roy, reaching for another of Roy's notebooks. He nodded, and she brought it over to Carson and stood next to him. She leafed through it slowly, allowing Carson to take in more sketches, sketches showing the dreaded leviathan.

"All right, is someone going to let me in on what the hell is going on?" he snapped, frustrated at not being able to understand all this and what Roy was able to do.

Helen answered, "Roy can connect with it, has been for quite some time."

Through gritted teeth, Carson rebuked Roy. "Connect with it? Then couldn't you have done something about any of this?" Carson pointed at Burns in the picture Roy held in front of him.

Roy had to diffuse the anger now. "No, Officer, I couldn't have. Believe me, I would've if I could. All I can do is sketch what it's doing in the moment."

"What the hell good is that?" Carson shouted.

"Stop it!" James shouted. His outburst was so out of his mild character that his order quieted everyone immediately. He swiped the scattered paper clips into his open hand at the end of the table and dropped them back into the cup. He pushed the cup close to Roy and said, "Show him how you do it."

Helen sat on the corner of Roy's bed and patted the spot next to her for Carson to sit down. He complied reluctantly. Once again, Roy opened to a clean page, clasped a handful of paper clips, and went into deep meditation as he began sketching. Carson was astonished at Roy's ability or gift or curse. Carson didn't know what to call it. While Carson marveled at Roy's feverish sketching, the others were more focused on the actual drawing and what it could reveal.

In the current drawing, the front of the hospital was coming into view. Roy feverishly sketched the figure of a person. It was clear that it was Irene and that she was walking toward the hospital, her face turned to the side so half of her face could be seen. There was a wild look in her eyes, and her lips were pursed tightly. Her arms were held stick straight at her sides, her fingers balled into tight fists. Her clothes were grimy and slovenly, soiled with the rank slime from the monster's lair.

Everyone jumped as Roy released his fist and threw the pencil down. He kept his hands on the desk, his head bowed as he clenched his eyes shut. He then sat back and took a deep breath, opening his eyes. "It's got complete control of her," Roy said, looking at his sketch of Irene. "And it wants Bernice. It's using Irene to get Bernice. No, wait." Roy grabbed the paper clips again and closed his eyes, hoping he would be able to reconnect and see more. He opened his eyes and said with confusion, "It doesn't want Bernice's body. It wants to use her. I don't understand."

"I have to get to Bernice! Let me out," Helen instructed the orderly. The rest of the group followed.

"Hold up! You know I can't let you leave," the orderly said to Roy. "The rest of you can go, but even after what I've seen, I can't just release him. You all know that."

Carson said, "I'll go with Helen. James and Regina, stay here with Roy."

As Helen and Carson walked out the door, Carson told Roy, "Sorry I exploded. If you can keep sketching in the meantime, do it."

Before the door closed, Regina asked Carson, "Please make sure Mandy and Lynne are still in the waiting area and are okay."

Helen and Carson held their breath and moved swiftly to the ward's exit, orderlies flanking either side of them. Upon entering the waiting area, they exhaled forcefully. Mandy and Lynne were still safely waiting where they had been told to. Seeing the state of Helen and Carson as they huffed and puffed after coming out from the ward made them both curious and worried. Lynne couldn't wait on the panting duo to catch their breath any longer. "Is Roy okay? What about my parents? What's going on?"

"Give them a second, will ya?" Mandy scolded.

Carson waved his hand at Mandy, indicating Lynne's question was welcome, and answered, "They're fine. They're fine. They're all safely locked inside Roy's room. An orderly is there with them."

Lynne pushed for more information. "If everything is so fine, then what's wrong with you guys?"

Mandy was annoyed, but Carson smiled at Lynne's precociousness. Helen intervened, saying to Lynne, "Your family is safe. It's the other patients in the ward. There's a reason they won't let you in there. Trust us. You don't want to go in there."

"Come on. We have to get downstairs to Bernice," Carson reminded Helen.

"What's going on with Bernice?" Lynne inquired, worried.

"She's fine. We just want to keep an eye on her," Helen said. "You both stay here in case your parents need you. Have you eaten anything?"

"Not much. A nurse came by and gave us each a granola bar," Mandy answered.

"It'll have to do for now. Just stay here. Please," Helen begged.

Carson and Helen disappeared down the hall and into an elevator. Lynne was tired, hungry, and restless. Mandy hated dealing with her when she was being so rash. "What good are we just sitting here? How long are they gonna make us wait? They're obviously not going to let us into Roy's room or the ward. Nobody's bringing us food, and I'm starving! I've had it," Lynne exclaimed as she stomped down the hall and pushed the down button for the elevator. Mandy protested, but Lynne was too quick and decided to forgo the elevator and slipped inside the doorway leading to the stairwell and nimbly bounded down the steps.

Mandy stood at the top of the steps and yelled down to Lynne, "Get back here! We're supposed to stay here!"

Lynne's bratty voice, becoming fainter with each word as she descended the steps, echoed up to her sister. "Make me, bitch! I'll be in the cafeteria stuffing my face! Have fun waiting!"

"You little shit!" Mandy shouted, slamming her hands down hard on the railing in front of her. She knew how upset her parents would be if they came to the waiting room to find her and her sister gone, but they would also be upset if they knew Mandy had just allowed Lynne to run away and did not try and fetch her. As usual, the choice was made for her by Lynne's impetuous behavior. She glided down the steps after her sister, cursing her under her breath.

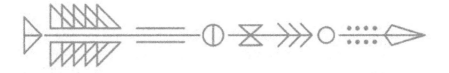

CHAPTER 18

Marie and Bernice rested in the waiting area of the first floor. Bernice looked toward the door where the nurse had taken Will's body earlier. Marie was glad Bernice was looking away because she didn't know if she could bear to look her in the eyes as she apologized to her.

"Bernice, I'm so sorry I left you the way I did last night. I was just so scared. I barely slept. I kept seeing that awful hand over and over again. And I kept thinking of you trying to explain things to your parents and how I wasn't there to help. I wish I'd stayed." Along with her worry over what they had seen in the basement, Marie had also been worried about how Bruce would react to Bernice. She knew he could be awfully hard on her.

"I get it. You don't have to keep apologizing," Bernice said.

"Wonder when your parents will finally get here. Are they still with Will? I mean, with his body? Sorry," Marie said.

Bernice couldn't put off saying the words to Marie any longer, so she let the words fall on Marie like an anvil dropping on her head. "They're dead. All dead."

"Bernice, my God, why are you just telling me this now?" Marie grabbed Bernice and hugged her, thinking how Bernice was all alone, no family left to support or console her. Marie pulled away to see Bernice's face and made a desperate, ridiculous attempt to say something positive, suggesting, "Hey, maybe you can even live with us. Wouldn't that be great?"

Bernice fell into Marie and cried on her shoulder, her arms wrapped around Marie's tiny waist. Marie was facing the automatic sliding glass door to the emergency room. She watched it slide open as she held on to Bernice and was confounded by what she saw. "Oh my God! Bernice, look! It's your mom! She's not dead!"

Bernice spun around to see Irene marching through the sliding doors looking rabid, dirty, and wild-eyed, like she had just finished a couple of rounds of mud wrestling. As Irene came closer, Bernice launched off her chair and ran to her, arms open wide. "Mom!" Bernice cried, lunging to embrace her.

But Irene didn't so much as look in Bernice's direction. Her eyes were fixed on the door in front of her. She violently pried Bernice's arms away from her, treating her as though she were a nuisance. Hurt and confused by Irene's overt rejection, Bernice tried to force her mother's attention again by grabbing her forearm. Irene turned and placed her hands on Bernice's chest and aggressively shoved her to the ground, sneering. "Get the hell away from me! Where's Will?"

Irene continued on through the doors ahead, leaving Bernice on the ground to stew in heartache and fury. Her face blazed crimson, and every cell in her body jumped with nerves. The anguish she felt was quickly transforming into outrage. Utterly confused, Marie stared at Bernice, unable to offer her condolences or to speak.

Bernice faltered as she rose to her feet. Her chest heaved, and it looked like fire could flare from her eyes at any second as she stared down the door Irene had entered. Bernice stomped to the door, propelled by her anger, and pushed it open. Marie didn't know if she should go with her or try to stop her.

The elevator doors opened from the opposite end of the hall, expelling Carson and Helen back onto the first floor. Marie was relieved to see that Carson recognized her immediately and came to her. "Where's Bernice?" Carson asked with urgency.

Marie looked toward the door that Irene and Bernice had gone through and stuttered, "She...they went...she said she was dead... but they both went—"

Helen frantically interrupted. "Who's they? Was it Bernice and Irene?" Marie nodded her head. "Come on!" Helen said, grabbing Marie's wrist and pulling her to her feet. The three of them went through the door where they heard Bernice's hysterical voice coming from the room marked Morgue.

As they approached, they heard Bernice beseeching her mother. "Why don't you give a shit about me? It's always Will! Even when he's dead, you still give him all of your attention. I'm right here, goddamn it! Look at me!"

Carson, Helen, and Marie stood just around the corner of the door. Nurses were coming their way. Carson and Helen knew what was coming and acted fast. "Helen, you can calm her the most. You go in and tell her that it's not her mom, that she's under its control. Bernice has got to calm down!"

"You have to do it," Helen argued. "The last time Irene was under its spell, she went insane with anger when she saw me. It can't be me. You go in, and I'll deal with the nurses. Go!" Helen and Marie both met the nurses before they got to the door, explaining it was a difficult situation and that Officer Carson was taking care of it.

Carson approached Bernice promptly, startling her when he whispered in her ear, "It's not her. The monster is controlling her. It's just her body. This is not your mom." But his words weren't enough. Bernice was livid, totally out of control.

"Stop making excuses for her!" Bernice shouted into Irene's ear, "You can block me out so easily! You've always been great at that!"

Irene was unmoved. Her eyes didn't blink as she stared at Will's body lying on a slab of metal in front of her. She didn't hear Bernice's harsh words. She was there to get what she came for—rather, the cruel beast was getting what it sent Irene for.

Carson knew it was too late. The anger in the air could have been cut with a knife. The ground quaked, causing people on the floor to shriek and then fall silent for a moment. The jolt snapped Bernice out of her fit of anger, but it was too late as she looked down to see that the floor was cracking and splitting open. Carson grabbed her arm and pulled her alongside him as he ran for the door, barely making it out before the floor in the morgue opened up, exposing the enormous, angry black river.

Helen and Marie watched from behind Carson and Bernice. Helen spoke into Bernice's ear as they watched the scene. "Roy told us it gets power from negative emotions. It used your mom knowing you would be hurt and jealous of her going to Will and ignoring you.

That is not your mom. She's gone. The monster made you jealous and angry, not your mother. You must release your anger now, or this thing will keep getting stronger."

Bernice was trying to understand but just couldn't. Her wrath felt cemented into her body. A great cracking noise sounded, and the beast emerged from the pit, larger than before. It hurled out a stream of sludge, grabbing Will's body and taking it down into the trench. The beast hurled another projectile, this time ripping Irene from her feet and yanking her back down into the deep nothing.

The wicked adversary stood tall. It stared back at Bernice. Their eyes locked on each other. Bernice wasn't scared; she was infuriated. Helen could feel that the monster was trying to lure Bernice to it and, in a fit of desperation and courage, ran in front of Bernice and grasped the handle of a metal cart. Helen thrust it forward, straight into the beast. It caught the cart and gnashed into it with its jagged, grotesque teeth, sending an excruciating noise throughout the room.

Helen stood uncomfortably close to the beast, then forced her mind clear, focusing on how she wanted the monster to think the metal cart was intended as a gift. Roy's explanation made Helen understand that the perverse connection she had with this horrible thing was that she could clear her mind and emotionally influence it.

Helen watched as the glittering sludge slowed, and the monster retreated underground. Nurses and patients had gathered behind Carson, Bernice, and Marie and were gobsmacked and terrified at the sight. But they weren't just scared of the creature they saw. They were shaken by how Helen had appeared to control it.

Someone over Carson's shoulder yelled, "Did you see how it went back, and she just stood there? It listened to her!"

Helen stayed in place, her back toward the door. She closed her eyes and listened to the accusations fly. Even as she heard Carson, Bernice, and Marie try and defend her against the newly assembled mob, Helen was disheartened by how quickly she had regained her role as the odd one out, the freak, the villain. She knew these towns-people. She had been defamed by them for so many years, and she wondered if she would ever be able to escape that reputation. But she had spent way too many years worrying about that, and she couldn't do it any longer, especially now. Helen had to resign herself to the task of figuring out how or if her connection to the monster could help to destroy it.

The chatter persisted. Helen heard people saying that she must have known about this thing all along, that it was why she stayed to herself, why she was so strange, why her mother must have left, why rumors remained about the way her father had died. It was clear Helen would never be accepted as a normal member of the community, especially after this if they survived at all. She had never considered leaving town. She was far too scared of the unknown to do that. And she had become far too accustomed to her sad daily routine to break it even though it provided the silk lining to her casket of isolation.

But the prospect that maybe Bernice would remain friends with her should they survive all this gave Helen hope. She feared that Bernice would be ostracized just by associating with her. She would rather die than have Bernice experience any of the isolation and cruelty she had lived with for most of her life. If an association with Helen caused any of that for Bernice, then Bernice would be better off without her.

Mato Watakpe—Running Bear to his family and friends, Mat to his coworkers at the hospital—had been hovering around the action going on in the hospital for most of the day. For the past twenty-two years, Mat had commuted to the hospital from the reservation he had lived on his whole life. Six days a week, he made the fifty-six-mile round trip to and from work, but he didn't mind the drive. Besides the occasional slow-moving tractor on the highway during farming season and besides his dinosaur of a vehicle, the traffic was never a problem. Those solitary hours to and from work afforded him a joyful peace.

Sometimes, Mat broke the silence listening to local talk radio from the reservation. Other times, he would listen to the sixties and seventies music he used to listen to with his dad. When Three Dog

Night or Jerry Lee Lewis would come on, it felt like his dad was still right there with him. Mat pictured his father sitting next to him in his rusty old red Chevy Impala, the window rolled down so his right elbow could rest on the door while his left hand used the dashboard as a piano.

Those days when Mat kept the radio off, he would roll his window down and perch his left elbow on the ledge, steering with his right hand resting on top of the wheel, imitating his father's driving style. Simply assuming that style was enough for Mat to easily replicate the contentedness his father always seemed to possess when behind the wheel. Some of Mat's earliest memories were of him and his father sitting together in the cab of his dad's pickup truck on the way to a fishing trip. Mat's father would sing along with the radio, loud but surprisingly in tune. He would become so consumed with the music and singing that Mat often wondered if his dad even remembered he was sitting there with him. But Mat didn't mind being the fly on the wall. He loved just being present in his father's little moments of pure joy. Mat felt that same joy on his own solitary drives, slowing down to either enjoy the crisp morning air as he drove to work or appreciating the darkening sky as he returned to the reservation after.

But this Sunday morning, as Mat awoke and swung his legs over the side of his bed, he could feel something wasn't right. He hated this nagging feeling in his gut. He had felt it many times before. His grandmother had always told him it was a gift and that he should pay attention to that feeling, that it was the universe speaking without words.

Mat tried to take his grandmother's advice, but the truth was that it was a terribly unsettling feeling, one he didn't like to indulge. He had done it before when he was twelve and had been horrified to learn that the churning pit of nervousness he had felt in his stomach that day turned out to be that his cousin and best friend Red Elk had been killed in a car accident early that same morning. No one had told Mat the terrible news, and no one in his family knew about it until early that afternoon. He had just sensed it. That feeling had led

Mat toward a crushing heartbreak, so he had learned that it usually signaled trouble.

With this feeling of foreboding in his belly, Mat made his long drive to work. He grew more restless as he got closer to the hospital. He parked in his usual spot, the one that pointed his car north toward the reservation. Mat rolled up his window, then sat in silence in his car for a few minutes. He tried to listen to what his gut was telling him, but the words wouldn't come, just a nagging feeling of dread. Mat got out of his car and stood next to it, his hands resting on the top. Faintly, he could feel the car move, like tremors shook it from the ground.

Joey, the tallest and heaviest orderly at the hospital, was outside on his early morning break when he spotted Mat leaning on his car. He assumed Mat was procrastinating the start of his workday. "Yo, Running Bear! Why ain't you running this morning?" No one called Mat Running Bear at the hospital. He was friendly with this orderly as he was with everyone else he worked with at the hospital, but he didn't like how Running Bear sounded coming out of his mouth.

Mat grinned and shook his head from side to side as he strode toward Joey. Running Bear stuck out his hand and shook Joey's. "Morning, Joey. But please don't call me that here," Mat said firmly yet warmly.

"What, I can't call you Running Bear? You're my buddy! You said that's what your buddies call you," Joey pushed back a little, a hint of snideness tingeing his words.

"Call me that when you come to the rez, buddy, but not here. My real name quickly becomes a joke when it's used off rez."

"You ain't a joke around here, man! You're really going to make me drive all the way to the rez just to call you by your Indian name? Damn! I'll just stick with Mat." It was Joey's half-assed way of apologizing to Mat while still admitting that he was dying to use the name Running Bear.

Mat went into the hospital, leaving Joey alone outside. Mat didn't want to tread down the same tired road as he had with other white men before Joey. It was insulting hearing his Native name come from a white man's mouth, how they would say it so glibly, ignorant of their privilege as they taunted and made a joke of his given name. It had happened so many times before, and it made Mat sad to admit how angry it made him to hear Running Bear coming from a white's lips. Underneath the words, what was conveyed was that Native American names were silly, that Indians were lesser people, that they would always be a joke to the white man. Of course this wasn't true for all of them, but in Mat's experience, it had been true, sadly, for most of them.

With the nagging feeling in his gut along with the annoying exchange he had just had with Joey, Mat clocked in and got to work. He organized his crew, and they got to work cleaning, fixing, and keeping the hospital a well-kept machine. Mat was proud of his work and of his crew, and it was reflected in how well the hospital was maintained. This was a big part of the reason why, on that particular day, when all hell broke loose in Ramsey, the hospital staff was able to reorganize to be able to run well in all the chaos.

As Mat began his workday, frazzled and terrified people began streaming into the hospital at a rate he had never seen. He hated gossip, and even though he was more concerned than curious, Mat would never ask a nurse or a doctor what was going on. His job was to maintain how the hospital was run no matter what, and that was what he aimed to do that day, instructing his crew to keep their heads down and do the same, even as they became alarmed at the incoming throngs of people.

As Mat and his crew worked overtime to supply chairs, cots, blankets, food, water, and anything else requested by the staff, they overheard the people telling their stories about what they had seen. As crazy as it sounded, some sort of giant snakelike monster was coming up from the ground and terrorizing the townspeople. The more details Mat heard, the more familiar it became. And when the people began coming in dripping with what looked like glittering, tar-like mud, Mat realized what was happening.

He had heard the elders tell stories about it many times. His own grandmother had her own stories about it. Mat thought it was just that, a story, another legend told to teach a life lesson. He was seeing with his own eyes now that it wasn't just a legend, and he fought to make himself believe it without letting it overwhelm him with fear. He couldn't tell the nurses or the doctors or even the patients about what they were dealing with. He was afraid it would panic them even further. And even though people were seeing this thing firsthand, he couldn't chance being the person to break this news. He had a strong sense it would end badly for him unless he dealt with this in a covert fashion.

Mat kept working at a steady pace, keeping his ears open to the people around him and listening for the unspoken message his intuition was trying to tell him. He had felt a strong urge to go near the morgue. He dragged a bucket with wheels and his mop with him as he approached a doorway where a number of people stood, some crying, some shouting in anger, some trembling in fear.

Mat tried to stay inconspicuous as he inched closer to the door, trying to get a glimpse inside. He pulled a cloth from his back pocket and dropped it to the floor, acting as though he were rubbing out a stain. He looked through the tangle of legs and beheld the very monster he had heard stories about his entire life.

Try as he might, Mat couldn't tear his eyes away from the glistening creature. When someone pushed a metal cart at it, Mat was astounded as he watched the beast bite clear through it before retreating through a giant crack in the floor. He stood up before getting trampled by the fleeing onlookers. He took his bucket and mop and made his way closer to the doorway. He forgot his vow to keep his head down and to keep mopping when he saw that a woman stood calmly right next to where the monster had escaped.

Officer Carson, whom Mat had seen frequently in the hospital for years, stood in the doorway with two girls. Mat wondered why they hadn't run away. Carson noticed Mat nearby. He saw the mop bucket and warned Mat not to go near the room, that it was beyond repair right now and that it wasn't safe. "I know," Mat said cryptically as he inched closer to the door and took a closer look at what was left of the scene.

Carson watched Mat survey the room and, seeing a flash of recognition in Mat's eyes over what he beheld, asked, "What exactly do you know?" Helen turned to see whom Carson was talking to. Marie and Bernice looked at Mat as well. The fact that these people didn't run away told Mat that he needed to tell them what he knew. His instinct screamed at him to talk to the tall woman standing inside the room, Helen.

"I know what this is," Mat said, pointing to the spot where the creature had emerged. Knowing exactly what he must do, Mat turned to Carson and said, "I'll tell you about it." He looked over at Helen and said, "And I need to tell her about it."

Bernice protested, "But we all need to know! It killed my family! I have a right to know!"

Mat spoke directly to Bernice calmly. "You need to be in control of your emotions before I can tell you. That's not my own rule." Marie held Bernice as she cried. Carson suggested that it would be best for the girls to go back up to the fifth floor waiting room where they could be together with Mandy and Lynne. They went in trembling hesitancy.

"We can't draw attention," Mat said to Carson and Helen. "I'll walk back through the doors and then walk down the hall to the left. After a minute, come down the same way and go into the door marked Boiler Room on the right." Mat casually steered the wheeled bucket with his mop handle, walking nonchalantly out the doors and disappearing.

"You know him?" Helen asked Carson.

"Yeah, he's worked here for years. He drives down from the reservation every day. I've stopped him a few times for speeding but a good guy."

"The reservation, huh?" Helen said, thinking about the single ropelike braid falling to Mat's waist and remembering his dark, reddish complexion and his regal, high cheekbones. He reminded her of the only picture she had ever seen of her maternal grandfather. It was black and white, and he stood next to a barn. He wore a dark button-down work shirt with striped overalls. A straw hat topped his head, scant wisps of long black hair fell to his shoulders. He looked somber yet gentle and handsome. His dark eyes, hooded under heavy eyelids, peered off to the right of the camera so the camera wouldn't rob his soul from his body, at least that was the story Helen's mom had told her.

Helen's mother had never met her own father, that handsome, mysterious man in that picture. Helen's mother was not only conceived out of wedlock but was also the result of an interracial relationship between a white woman and a Native American man. Separately, these things were taboo, but the combination of both was nearly a death sentence in those days.

But Helen's grandmother was lucky that her sister's family took her in where she gave birth to Helen's mother and lived there until her death. Other than telling her own daughter since she had a right to know who her father was, Helen's grandmother never told another living soul that the father of her child was an Indian man. Helen's mother only found out about her Native American father when she was an adult.

Helen's grandfather had worked as a farmhand for a family who were friends with the family of Helen's grandmother. They had fallen in love and met secretly a few times. Helen's mother was the result of one of those secret trysts. A relationship between the two would have been forbidden in those times. Even so, the father of the child wanted to run away with the mother, but it just wasn't possible. So Helen's grandmother went to her only sister and made up the story that she was raped and didn't know who the father was, that she didn't want to try and find who did it because she was scared for her life.

Helen's grandfather remained working on the same farm for the rest of his days, secretly sending money to the mother of his child rarely and ever so discreetly. Helen's grandmother was diligent about retrieving the mail even though many months would pass before she would receive a letter. Her adherence to checking the mail roused her sister's suspicions about what she could be waiting for, but she never asked. She figured her sister was in a hard enough position and resigned herself to help her and not cause more problems.

Each envelope contained cash secured by a white piece of paper with a heart drawn on it. Helen's grandfather could never take the risk of being found out, so he never wrote a return address on the envelopes. He had to make the mailings a rarity, sometimes once every six months. He was barely literate so could never write a letter, which would have been too risky anyway. The only risk Helen's grandfather did take was when he enclosed the photo of himself about eight years after Helen's mother was born. About five years after that, the money stopped coming, and not another word was heard from Helen's grandfather ever again.

Helen's grandmother knew that he had died as he was loyal and honorable and never would have just given up on them. His death was only confirmed much later on when Helen's grandmother was old enough and brave enough to inquire about her friend's farm to find out whatever happened to all the workers when she was really only worried about one worker in particular.

Helen's grandmother had only told her story once, and it was to her daughter. Likewise, Helen's mother had only told Helen the story a single time, not because she didn't want to talk about it but because she didn't have anything else to say about it. It was a short, sad story. The questions Helen's mother may have had went unanswered, so she had nothing further to add, except one thing: The subject of their Native American bloodline should never be discussed.

It made Helen feel exotic to know that she had Indian blood coursing through her veins, but it also made her feel isolated. She was angry that she had to keep it a secret, making her feel ashamed for something she had no control over. It had pained her when her father told her how beautiful she was and commented on her shiny black hair and her high cheekbones, saying she must have inherited it from her mother. She shared everything with her father, and this, such a big part of her, had to remain hidden from him. But she had made a promise to her mother and had kept it.

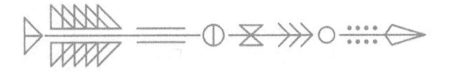

CHAPTER 19

Thinking the boiler room would supply some privacy for him to say what he needed to say to Carson and Helen, Mat was surprised when he walked in to find two girls crouching in the corner behind the boiler. "You two okay?" Mat asked. Mandy and Lynne dug their feet into the floor and slowly pushed themselves to their feet, sliding their backs up against the wall. They bobbled their heads up and down. "You know you shouldn't be in here, right? It's not a safe place for you to be."

Mandy answered rhetorically, "Is there anywhere that's safe right now?"

"You got a point. But why did you come in—" Mat was interrupted by the door slamming shut behind him and a voice shouting.

"Girls! What are you doing in here? Bernice and Marie are on their way up to the fifth floor now where you're supposed to be!" Helen scolded, demanding answers.

Mat stood silently and listened as Mandy ratted on Lynne, that she had run down the stairs to get something to eat so that Mandy had to go after her. Lynne retorted that they were just sitting uselessly upstairs and that she had been starving and that it was obvious they weren't going to be allowed to see their brother.

"But if you were hungry, why the hell did you come in here?" Carson asked, annoyed.

"We heard those noises and saw you guys standing by the door. Everyone else looked panicked, so I guess we panicked too and ran down the hall and picked a door to hide behind," Mandy confessed.

"Well, you can't be running around this hospital by yourselves. You'll have to wait here with us," Helen said.

Mat didn't know the connection between these people. He knew Carson wasn't married, so the tall woman wasn't his wife. He thought maybe he had seen the woman before but couldn't place her. He had seen the girls on the fifth floor a few times in the last couple of years. "You girls know someone on the fifth floor?" Mat inquired.

Lynne answered, "Yeah, our brother, Roy."

"Ah, Roy. Nice kid," Mat said, adding, "My guys told me it's pretty bad up there today. I've been too busy on the main floor to go have a look for myself."

"You know Roy? You ever seen his sketches in his notebooks?" Helen asked Mat.

"I'd never be allowed to look. But I hear from the orderlies that he's some artist."

"It's not the quality of his art. It's what he's drawing that would interest you," Helen said. "In fact, whatever you have to tell us about this thing, Roy should hear it."

Mat was shaking his head no, but before he could argue, Helen sealed her case by telling him, "Roy's been drawing pictures of this creature for years. He has some sort of communication with it, causing him to sketch what he's seeing."

"It has an attachment to him," Mat said gravely. He thought for a moment. "Can anyone else communicate with it?"

"I think I can," Helen admitted with worried trepidation.

Mat paced, deep in thought. He knew what had to be done, eventually. In the meantime, he had to figure out a way to herd this group of people together and make a plan.

"All right. The four of you walk out of here before me and take the stairs to the fifth floor waiting area. Wait there. I'll head up shortly after. Act like you don't know me, and wait for my cues."

"Cues to do what? We need more than that," Carson said.

Mat pushed the door open, peered down the hall, and waved the group out and said to Carson, "You gotta trust me."

It was easy for the foursome to make their way to the fifth floor without raising any sort of suspicion. The first floor was still abuzz with the helter-skelter of patients, nurses, and doctors, especially after the latest incident in the morgue. Doctors and nurses were struggling with the fact that they had to believe the crazy stories the patients had been telling them all day, that there was in fact some sort of monster to contend with. The group reached the fifth floor and reunited with Marie and Bernice.

"Where's that maintenance guy?" Bernice asked.

Helen shushed her, then brought the girls up to speed. "Mat knows what the monster is. He told us to meet you up here and wait. He has some sort of a plan."

"Plan my ass," Carson hissed. "A plan includes steps that you share with a team."

Helen shot Carson a look, replying, "Really? You have a better idea of what to do right now?"

There was no time for questions or further criticism as Mat emerged from the elevator. He didn't look their way but went toward a door marked Personnel Only and took a key ring from his belt and unlocked the door. Before he slipped inside, he gave them a discreet look and raised an index finger meaning that they should wait.

Used to being the lead as an officer of the law, Carson was irritated that he was not in control of the situation. He shifted uncomfortably in his chair and resigned himself to the fact that Mat knew something about this situation that he didn't. He had no choice but to trust in this guy's judgment right now however restless it made him feel. It didn't help that Helen now seemed to be looking to Mat for leadership and answers, which irked Carson more than he could admit.

Mat stepped into the ward's hallway and was overcome with the images of the drawings of the monster on the walls written in excrement. It was his first time in the ward that day, only hearing about the chaos going on in there from his crew. He forced himself to hide his surprise and disgust as he approached Roy's room.

He took out his master key for the fifth floor and told the orderlies by Roy's door, "Hey, guys, I got an emergency situation with the pipes running throughout the hospital. The main pipe runs up along the wall in this room, so I need to get in to access it."

Mat's assumption that the orderlies didn't have a clue about the plumbing system was right. They were clueless and took Mat's word for it, allowing him to enter Roy's room without a second thought. Mat walked into Roy's room to find him furiously scribbling on a page in front of him. Roy's parents looked back and forth between what their son was drawing and at Mat, not necessarily surprised by his arrival. On the other hand, the orderly inside the room, the same orderly who had unwelcomely called him Running Bear that morning, was suspicious.

"Just what do you think you're doing in here, RB?"

RB, Mat thought, annoyed. That was a new one. It was like he was threatening Mat by calling him RB, like the next time he would just come out with Running Bear to let the jokes begin. Mat used his ignorance against him. "Well, Joey, unless you and everyone else in here want to get a nasty steam burn, I suggest we get you all to another room," Mat warned.

Roy stopped sketching when he heard Mat's voice. He looked up and grinned knowingly. Knowing how dense Joey was, Mat walked over to the air-conditioning vent high up on the back wall and pointed to it and explained. "See that? I gotta open it up in order to get through the main drainage pipe for the fifth floor. If I don't release the pressure, well, it will be ugly in here."

Joey looked confused but wasn't about to question Mat about it for fear of looking stupid in front of the others. Mat looked at Roy's parents and said, "Sorry for the interruption. Normally, I'd never do this, but the way things are going today, I gotta take things as they come."

Seeing Roy's look of relief and recognition when Mat entered the room, James and Regina knew to play along; so when Mat suggested that Joey go and find another empty room so the family could be safe and have some privacy, Regina was quick to say, "Oh, we'd appreciate that. Thank you so much."

"You know I'm not supposed to leave 'em unattended. Why don't you go find a room and I'll wait here?" Joey asked.

"They aren't unattended. I'm here. Look, the longer I wait, the worse it could be. I won't start until you get back. Please go find another room. I promise I won't leave these folks unattended. Besides, I don't know if I want to be out there alone with them today." Mat faked having a fear of the other residents.

The appeal to Joey's ego worked. As he unlocked the door to go out, he inflated his own ego even further by making the remark, "Yeah, I suppose there's a reason why I'm in this uniform and you're in that one." Mat didn't care about the ridiculous barb thrown his way. He got what he wanted—Joey left.

"What an asshole," Roy said, causing smirks from all. He then held up the sketch he had just finished for Mat to see and said, "I've been expecting you."

Mat was astounded as he looked at Roy's drawing. It showed Mat leading Roy, James, and Regina out the door. On the other side of the page was a more sinister scene. There it showed Joey walking into a bathroom stall, an arm of sludge reaching up from the toilet just behind the stall door. "We won't have to worry about him anymore," Roy said. He was not happy to say it, but it was one less roadblock for what they had to do.

Mat poked his head around Roy's door and asked the only orderly left in the hallway, "You seen Joey? He was supposed to come right back, and I really have to get to work on this thing."

The orderly, exhausted after the day of chaos in the ward, didn't think twice about leaving his post in the hallway to find Joey, much to the relief of Mat. But they had to move quickly. The orderly turned the corner and out of sight. Mat muscled the door open, allowing James, Regina, and Roy to walk out and move down the hall toward the Personnel Only door. He unlocked it quickly and herded them through, shushing them and keeping them close as he did. They were now in the waiting area where the rest of the group sat.

Mat swiftly moved James, Regina, and Roy into the nearby maintenance room and slipped inside himself for a moment. Mat soon reemerged with a broom. A couple of nurses walked out from the elevator and walked toward the main doors. One spotted Mat, who was sweeping as though he were being watched by a supervisor, and yelled a quick, "Hey, Mat."

Mat gave a nod in response and went back to his work, acting as though he didn't know anyone sitting in the waiting area. He approached Carson and Helen like they were strangers and said, "Excuse me." He dropped to one knee and acted as though he were reaching for something underneath their chairs with the broom. As he knelt on the floor, Mat whispered, "When I go back through the maintenance door, all of you go to the stairwell, and make your way back down to the boiler room. Meet you there with the rest of them ASAP."

Mat got up and briskly walked back to the maintenance door, pressing the elevator button on his way. The group in the waiting area wasted no time and made their way straight to the stairwell. As soon as Mat heard the stairwell door close, he emerged with James, Regina, and Roy and got into the elevator, open and ready to take them to the first floor. Mat pressed and held the 1 button knowing this would bypass all other floors. He positioned himself right in front of where the doors would open and told Roy to stand directly behind him and for James and Regina to go on either side of him.

The doors opened to just a few people waiting to get in. Thankfully, they were all too preoccupied to even notice Roy walking out of the elevator, still wearing the scrub-like seafoam-green outfit worn by fifth floor patients. They made it to the boiler room with no trouble, relieved to find the rest of the group waiting for them as planned.

Mandy and Lynne jumped on Roy and held him tight, overjoyed to see him outside the ward. Their reunion was cut short when Mat tapped Roy on the shoulder and handed him a stack of folded clothes and some blue tennis shoes. "These are mine. Go over there, and put them on quickly," Mat ordered, pointing to a corner on the opposite side of the room by a door leading outside.

Roy flew down the metal stairs and over to the door, gladly tearing off the tired uniform and slipping into Mat's clothes, which were, surprisingly, a little tight on him. As Roy changed, Mat explained. "I know what needs to be done to stop Uncegila."

"Uncegila?" Carson repeated.

"It's the monster. I don't have time to explain now. It has an attachment to Roy and Helen, and I need to take them to the reservation to start the cleansing ritual. The rest of you need to stay here and cover for us as best you can. Officer Carson, I gotta leave those details up to you. Uncegila must be stopped."

Carson agreed, relieved to have regained some control even though it had been given to him by Mat. He hated that Helen had to leave with Mat and Roy, but he really felt he had no choice but to trust in what Mat was doing. James and Regina protested, saying that at least one of them needed to go with Roy. "Too many people make for too many emotions. They're running too high as it is. It has to be this way. Trust me. It's safer for everyone," Mat explained.

"I'm coming with," Bernice said. Before Mat could tell her no, she made her case. "It took my whole family from me. I have no one left, and I want to be with Helen."

Marie interrupted, a bit stung by Bernice's admission. "But you have me, Bernice."

"I know, but you have your mother. You should be with her. I need to be with Helen. That's where I feel safe." Helen took Bernice's hand and led her to the door leading outside and waited for Mat to join them.

"Take care here," Mat said to Carson. "Everyone inside is still distracted by what happened in the morgue and everything else. They probably won't even realize Roy is gone. I'll radio my guys and tell them I had to run out on an emergency and to cover for me."

As Mat raced to the door, Carson shouted, "Do yourself a favor and drive with your hazards on. If you get stopped, drop my name and tell 'em to radio me. Be careful." With that, Mat, Roy, Helen, and Bernice were out the door and into Mat's beat-up Impala, on their way north to the reservation.

On the way out of town, Mat was forced to drive through old back roads in order to avoid the cracks and fissures left in the ground by Uncegila. Ramsey seemed deserted as the foursome passed through town, passing homes that had crumbled and cars that had tipped over ledges of the cracks made in the wake of the raging black underground river. Mat's trusty old Impala bumped and lumbered along until it finally got to the highway leading to the reservation. The path of the monster's destruction stopped at the town line, leaving an undamaged stretch of road as far as the eye could see.

Once Mat was driving at a good clip, he told the group what he knew about the havoc-wreaking, unholy terror. Roy, Helen, and

Bernice hung on his every word as he recounted what he had been told by his grandmother and other elders on the reservation.

"Until I saw it with my own eyes today, I thought it was just a legend. Since I was young, I've heard the stories of the great snakelike monster who was attracted to negative emotions and has a taste for metal. It can sleep and be inactive for centuries, but it can be reawakened through a ritual to curse someone. There is a special ritual that must be followed in order to put it back to rest, but the ritual can only take place if we know who reawakened it in the first place and why. My grandmother is a medicine woman. She and the other elders can help find the source of the latest curse."

"How will they do that? And what if they aren't able to find the source? I mean, who even knows how long this abomination has been awake or even alive?" Helen asked.

"It's been alive since the Creator gave the earth an abundance of energy to create all things. Some of that energy was transformed into an evil spirit. It turned so evil that the Creator was forced to turn it into Uncegila. Sometimes, the elders call it the Great Water Monster. It can never be killed, only put to rest. See, even though it is evil, it is still a living spirit that grew from the seeds of the Creator, and the Creator does not kill life it has created.

"When it is awakened, it lives in a constant state of hunger. It goes through a vicious cycle of hunger for negative emotions and appeasement through consuming metal. That's why the thick mud it moves through glitters. When it digests the metal, it gives Uncegila more power to attract more negative emotions. Now here's what was kind of hard for me to understand as a kid. What it really wants is love but doesn't know how to get it. It senses the bond between people and desires to have that bond and thinks that by destroying them, it will be able to attain love. So it wants love but thinks that stirring up and devouring people with heavy negative emotions toward their loved ones will somehow give it what it needs. When it finds it is not fulfilled, it switches to feeding on metal, which makes it stronger and able to attract and attach itself psychically to one or more people. That's where you, Roy and Helen, come in.

"I remember my grandmother saying that the people who show an attachment to the water monster may be the ones who were involved in its reawakening. That doesn't mean either of you reawakened it yourselves, but there is usually a connection. It can only have been reawakened by the Native American ritual to do so. Do either of you have any connections you can think of?"

Roy sat in the passenger's seat next to Mat, listening intently to his explanation. Roy thought about whether he had some sort of connection to the beast but could think of nothing except for the scar on his hand. "It left this on me a few years back," Roy said, holding his left hand up for Mat to see.

From the back seat, Helen spoke up. "My grandfather was Native American. I assume he was from your reservation because at the time it was the only one within a hundred miles from town. I know he worked on a farm just off the reservation. But I really don't know anything else about him. You see, my grandmother, who was white, was forced to keep the pregnancy and who the father was a secret because—"

"You don't need to explain why," Mat interrupted. It's no secret that the seeds of prejudice still ran deep in the community and throughout the surrounding areas. It was an unspoken ugliness that wouldn't go away, like a wound unable to heal because the scab was continually ripped off. There was an awkward silence in the car.

Even at her young age, Bernice knew what that silence meant. She remembered how her father used to describe Indians—lazy, good-for-nothing drunks. She had always hated it when he spoke like that. She felt pressured to hate them just so her father would accept her, but she knew it wasn't right. Her father's sentiments were shared by most of the people in Ramsey, and they weren't shy about spewing their ignorance and hatred, and Bernice had heard her share of slurs.

Bernice leaned forward and perched her chin on the back of the front seat between Mat and Roy. She watched Mat as he drove. He stared straight ahead into the distance. His lips were pursed together, and the striations of his jaw muscles flexed as he ground his teeth together. She reached over the seat and touched Mat's right shoulder. "People say mean things. You don't seem at all like what they say," Bernice said.

"Yeah? What kinds of things?" Mat inquired.

"Well, that Indians are dirty, mean, lazy, that they drink too much," Bernice admitted, ashamed that the person she had heard that from the most was her own father. She regretted repeating those hateful words because she could see they stung Mat. She also felt like she had betrayed her father because she didn't believe a word of it but still felt like she had a responsibility to defend him. After all, even with his flaws, he was still her dad, and she couldn't think of a better one.

"My dad drank too much. I always wondered why it was okay for him to do it but not Indians. I mean, he wasn't nice all the time either, so there's that." Bernice stopped, fumbling her words, trying to apologize for behavior that wasn't hers.

"I understand. You aren't responsible for other people's ignorance. Sit back now. We'll be at the reservation in about ten minutes," Mat said, forcing the subject to a close, much to Bernice's relief.

Roy fidgeted in the front seat, twiddling his fingers and then drumming them on the dashboard. "I need some paper. You got any in here?" he asked Mat, opening the glove compartment and nosing around inside it before Mat could answer. He found a long receipt and asked Mat if he could write on the back of it.

"If you can find a pen, go ahead," Mat said.

Roy dug deep into the glove compartment and found a pencil. He found a wrench to hold in his left hand. He sat back, closed his eyes, and began sketching. Helen sat forward and watched as Roy's picture became clear. Mat kept his eyes on the road as Helen reported what she saw.

"It's a picture of this car approaching the intersection before the reservation." She paused to watch the other half of the picture develop. "Oh my God, it's on its way toward us! It's moving underground and coming this way! Wait, he's drawing more." Mat stepped on the gas pedal, pushing eighty miles an hour as he awaited the next revelation. "What? No...no...it's the hospital! Half of it's collapsed into the ground!"

Mat floored it.

CHAPTER 20

Mina White Buffalo sat patiently in her front yard. A fire roared in the stone pit in front of her, its flames casting dancing shadows upon her weathered face. Smoke billowed to the darkened sky as she tossed sweetgrass and powdered cedar leaves into the fire. The arrows she had made that day rested safely next to the firepit. She used a large hawk's feather to fan the flames toward the arrows, purifying them before use.

That morning, she awoke with the same foreboding feeling as her grandson had. She had grown accustomed to it over her many decades on earth and was quite acute about deciphering what it was trying to tell her. She lived next door to Running Bear, and as she watched him leave his home that morning, she knew her feelings involved him. The feeling intensified as Mina watched Running Bear's dusty red car fade in the distance.

After he had left that morning, Mina poured herself some strong black coffee and sat at her kitchen table. She lit the three candles that rested on a wooden plank at the center of it. She sat back in her chair, took a few sips of her coffee, then closed her eyes in meditation, breathing deep and clearing her mind to make room for whatever the universe was trying to tell her.

As Mina's own thoughts vacated, she began seeing images of the Great Water Monster, Uncegila. Mina remained calm and still, allowing the images to intensify. She could feel the monster's beating heart, a flashing red crystal within her own chest. As the beast strengthened, the heart pumped and flashed more furiously. The stronger the heart became, the colder it also became, making it impossible to touch with the human hand.

Mina's mind became saturated with details about Uncegila, details she had learned as a child but had long since thought of. She remembered that the crystal heart was the monster's power source and cannot survive without it. In order to take its power, the heart must be removed. In order to remove the heart, the monster had to be put to rest by shooting an arrow straight to the heart. Not only that, the arrow had to be fired by someone whom it had an attachment to. Mina needed to find such a person.

The women in Mina's family had all been the most sought-after and skilled arrow makers, not only on the reservation but also throughout the entire tribe in the surrounding areas. Since she was a child, Mina had made arrows for hunting deer, elk, and buffalo for her father and the other elders in her family. As her skills improved, so did the fruits of the hunt for those who used her arrows. Her superior arrows were attributed to the accuracy and bounty of the kill. Mina carried on the legacy of arrow making throughout her life and knew that the three she would make today needed to be the most precise she had ever constructed.

Mina made only three arrows. The person firing the arrows had only three shots to try and put the hellion to rest. If none of the three arrows hit the water monster, then its skin thickens, making it impenetrable for four days. Only after the four days had passed could three new arrows be shot at the beast to try and put it to rest once again. The more attempts it took, the stronger the brute would become.

The visions Mina saw during her meditation that morning told her that whatever needed to happen would happen that night on the reservation. She focused on her part in what needed to be done and knew that the other elders on the reservation were meditating on their roles. During these times, when one elder felt the foreboding, the others felt the same. No direct communication was needed.

The fire roared as Mina threw the last of her sweetgrass and sage into the flames. She fanned the smoke toward the arrows with great sweeps of the hawk's feather. She heard the rumble of her grandson's old Chevy approaching fast.

Running Bear pulled into his grandmother's driveway rather than his own, threw the car into park, and turned off the ignition. He emerged from the driver's side and hastened toward his grandmother with Roy, Helen, and Bernice close behind him. He knew his grandmother would be ready and was relieved to see the fire roaring and the arrows leaning stoically up against the pit, ready for action.

"This is my grandmother, Mina White Buffalo," Running Bear said, proudly introducing his grandmother.

Mina studied these three strangers' faces. Her eyes met with Helen's and became fixed on them. Helen could feel this woman's eyes almost pulling her closer, so she walked right up to Mina. Mina turned her rickety wooden chair away from the fire and beckoned Helen to stand in front of her, never taking her eyes off her. Mina reached over and grabbed the three arrows, stood up, and handed them over to Helen with both hands. Helen clutched the arrows with trembling hesitancy, not understanding why they were being given to her.

Mina looked at her grandson and announced, "It's her."

Running Bear walked over to Helen, who stood grasping the arrows and looking at them in confusion, and said, "You have to do it."

Helen wanted to protest but couldn't. She had never hunted or killed anything in her life, let alone use a bow and arrow. But the fact remained that she wanted nothing more than to put Uncegila back to rest. "Why me?" Helen asked Mina.

"I can't explain that to you. But someone who can will soon arrive," Mina assured her, then turned her attention to Roy. "You are able to see the water monster in pictures?"

Roy was surprised that Mina knew this about him. He nodded his head yes and thought he should try to explain, but before he could speak, Mina took both of his young, sturdy hands and held them in her wrinkled, feeble ones. She examined his knuckles and fingers. She flipped his hands palm side up and continued scanning them until she found the scar she had been looking for. Mina ran her index finger along its zigzagged edges. "You know, you're the first white man I've ever met that has the mark and hasn't been killed

179

by Uncegila. And you're the first white man I've ever met that can connect with the spirit and not be completely overcome by it." She squeezed Roy's hands as she studied his face.

Roy had known for a long time that he was able to tap into something special because of the scar, but he could never find the right words to explain it as Mina just had. Mina's knowledge about Roy's ability gave him both hope and worry. He hoped that his full understanding would strengthen his ability. But he also worried that by understanding the gift, it could somehow be taken from him.

A beat-up jalopy of a station wagon carrying three people stopped in front of Mina's house. A tall, sturdy man in his late sixties exited the driver's side, grabbing a bow and slinging it onto his back. Mina announced to the group that his name was John Black Elk. A frail old woman struggled her way to her feet from the passenger's side, her old joints taking their time to help her stand erect. Mina introduced her as Rose Leading Cloud.

From the back seat, a woman of about Helen's age swung her legs out the door and stood, holding a metal box with three padlocks attached to it. Mina wasn't sure who the woman was, but she recognized the box. This woman followed Rose Leading Cloud toward Mina's house. John Black Elk stood at Rose's side with his elbow held out to support her. Mina greeted Rose first and then John. She looked at the woman following Rose. She reminded Mina of a little doe, wide-eyed and timid, looking like she would bound away if startled.

"This is June," Rose introduced the woman. "Her grandmother was the last person to perform the reawakening ritual."

June felt all eyes upon her, heavy and questioning. She felt they were holding her responsible for something she had known nothing about and had only just learned of herself from Rose today. "I knew nothing about this. I swear," June said, trying to assuage any possibility of being blamed.

"The box is heavy. Set it over there," Mina said to June, breaking some tension. She pointed to a spot on her front porch where June could place the box. Helen caught June's eye as she lugged the box past her. Helen felt a twinge of anger toward June, but it wasn't aimed directly at her. It was something about her, about who she was connected to, that was making Helen's blood simmer.

The ground began to vibrate ever so slightly underneath their feet. "It's almost here," Rose said.

Mina told everyone to follow her as she led them to a shed just behind her house. She opened the aged, splintered doors of the shed to reveal stacks of metal hubcaps, sheets of rusty scrap metal, old tools, and tubs of aluminum cans. She ordered everyone to take something. Mina pointed to a spot on the far end of her property where an old-fashioned well stood. The base was made of rocks, covered in patches of emerald moss. A wooden bucket hung high above the well opening underneath a roof on the verge of collapse.

"Go throw your metal down the well. It will keep Uncegila satisfied until we're ready."

Mina's orders were followed. Then she led everyone into her house and told them to find a seat in her cramped living room. Being the youngest, Bernice and Roy took spots next to each other on the floor. Mina dragged her rocking chair to the front and center of the room where Rose instinctively took her seat. Mina addressed the group. "Rose Leading Cloud is a respected elder on our reservation. She has the gift to see into the past. Please begin whenever you're ready, Rose."

Even before Rose spoke, Roy could feel his own connection with the elders. It was a powerful yet frightening realization. The realization came in the form of his sensing that intense, heavy news was about to be shared by Rose, news that would impact Helen specifically. Roy scooted closer to Bernice and braced himself for what was to come.

Rose cleared her throat and began, her many-decades-old voice strained as she tried her best to speak loudly enough so everyone could hear: "Today, I saw many visions of our reservation from the past. I saw a white woman talking to an elder, asking questions. This elder was angry over the white woman's presence but pretended to be happy. The elder invited the white woman into her home, then went outside and began digging in her backyard. She removed a metal box from the earth and carried it to her small barn where she kept her medicines and tools for rituals."

Rose paused to take a sip of the tea that Mina handed to her. June could feel her face grow flush as Rose went further into her visions, knowing it was almost her time to fill in the gaps in Rose's visions, dreading the group's reaction.

Rose continued. "The elder retrieved two buffalo bones and a thick deer hide from her shed. She carried them along with the metal box to the street behind her house. Seeing no one in sight, she slid the cover off a manhole in the street. She dropped the two buffalo bones down the hole. She unlocked the three locks on the metal box. She covered her hands with the deer hide and lifted a glowing, pulsating red crystal out of the box. She held it while she closed her eyes, her anger making the crystal glow brighter. When the crystal became too active and cold to handle even with the deer hide covering her hands, she tossed it into the sewer. She walked back to her house quickly, leaving the manhole cover off to the side.

"The elder goes back to her home and asks the white woman to help her. The white woman follows the elder to the manhole. The elder closes her eyes and starts panting. A glowing red light comes up from the hole. The white woman tries to look inside and is pulled down by Uncegila. The elder slides the manhole cover back into place, wipes her hands on her clothes, looks around to make sure no one was watching, and goes home."

Rose turned to June, who sat red-faced and trembling with anxiety, and said, "I saw June's face in my vision and went to her. I told her the visions I had. She knows who the people in my vision are." Rose rested her hands on her bony thighs and waited patiently for June to begin. Roy squeezed Bernice's hand. Helen leaned forward, bracing herself for information she knew must relate to her since she was the one who would have to fire the arrows.

June began. "Again, please believe me when I say that I didn't even believe the Great Water Monster was real until today. I thought it was all legend." She paused before telling her story. "The elder in Rose's vision was my grandmother. She passed away when I was very young. I hardly remember her. Anyway, my mother used to tell me stories about my grandmother, true stories. But there was one story that my mom said Grandma told her herself. Mom said she thought it was made up, that Grandma had told her the story when she was nearing the end of her life.

"My grandmother was a medicine woman. When the white man came to the reservation and built hospitals, she was bitter about how our people chose the white man's medicine over hers. She held quite a grudge, which brings me to why she decided to reawaken Uncegila.

"About thirty years ago, a pretty white lady came to my grandmother's door. She said she was looking for information about her father, that she'd never met him. She said she did some research and found the farm where he'd worked. She asked people on the reservation if they knew of anyone who'd worked on that farm in the past. Someone pointed her in my grandmother's direction, telling her that my grandmother's brother had worked there many years ago."

Helen fought to stay composed. She needed to hear the rest of June's story, but she already knew where it was going.

"My grandmother told the white lady that she was sorry, that she was mistaken, that she never had a brother, and that no one in her family had ever worked for white people. It was a lie. Helen, that white lady was your mother. Your mother had come to the right house. Your grandfather was the brother of my grandmother. My grandmother didn't know that her brother had gotten a white lady pregnant, but it made sense as your mother told her the story. My grandmother had always wondered why her handsome brother never married yet worked so hard on that farm but still never seemed to have enough money for himself. My grandmother had blamed the white farmers for trying to, as my mom told me, "work the Indian out of him and turn him white." She didn't care that her brother was getting paid for the work. In my grandmother's opinion, the little money he earned wasn't enough to label him an employee, that he was more of a slave.

"This is the story my grandmother told my mother. What my grandmother did to your mother was cruel—inviting her into her home, luring her in, hiding her hatred under a fake smile. My grandmother couldn't bear the thought that her brother had a baby with a white woman and that the proof of it was now sitting inside her home. All she could think of was getting rid of any evidence that someone in her family had mixed with the white man. Helen, this was her belief, not mine. I'm sorry that—" June was cut off abruptly by Helen.

"It doesn't matter. Stop apologizing and continue. Time is short," Helen said, unable to hide the disgust in her voice.

Through tears, June went on. "My grandmother initiated the reawakening ceremony while your mom sat in her home. The crystal heart had been kept in the locked box for at least two generations on my grandmother's side. Its powers were entrusted to my family so that the Great Water Monster would never be released again. My grandmother let her hate and anger consume her, so she unleashed this devil."

Helen was gobsmacked, and furious. June didn't know what else to say. She had been oblivious that the story was true up until today. She was still trying to process the fact that her grandmother had basically killed Helen's mother by reawakening Uncegila. Her grandmother was the reason why the beast was alive today. What June did not yet know was the extent of the destruction and death the malevolent creature had caused within the last twenty-four hours in the town of Ramsey.

The tension in the room was heavy, like a saturated storm cloud fit to burst. Running Bear worried that the tension would strengthen Uncegila again before they were ready, but he also needed June to understand how strong the water monster had become and how many it had killed. She must understand what her grandmother had caused. "June, the water monster didn't just kill Helen's mother. It killed her father. Bernice, tell her what happened to your family."

Bernice announced, "It killed my dad, my mom, and my little brother."

Roy added, "It tortured me for years. No one believed I'd seen a monster. And who knows what's happened to my parents and two sisters back in town. It's destroyed half of the hospital where we left my family."

"Stop, please," June muttered, cupping her ears with her palms to block them from hearing any more.

"You remember Officer Carson, right? It killed his partner, Officer Burns," Running Bear told June.

Helen brooded as she realized why her mother had disappeared without a trace so many years ago. She thought about the behemoth's merciless killings within the past day and how it caused half the hospital to collapse, likely killing more people.

June crossed her arms tightly over her stomach and leaned forward, feeling nauseous over the havoc her grandmother had caused by her actions so many years ago. She was horrified and ashamed of her grandmother. June looked almost green, so sickened was she to know that people had been killed and terrorized as a result of her grandmother's hateful, vengeful actions.

Helen read June's body language and grasped that June really hadn't known anything and that it was only the beginning of June's realization. Helen's urge to blame her diminished as she watched June suffer for the sins of her grandmother. June would have to live with it for the rest of her life, knowing that her own blood had caused such horror. But, Helen realized, she shared that same blood.

The ground rumbled underneath the house, causing Rose to announce, "Calm yourselves. It's getting too much to feed on too soon, and we aren't yet ready for it to emerge. Block your emotions. You will be able to unleash your hurt and anger very soon."

John Black Elk rose to his feet and grabbed his bow and a deerskin satchel of arrows and slung them over his shoulder. "You ever shot a bow and arrow?" he asked Helen.

"Of course not. Never."

"You'll learn now. Come on," John said as he walked toward the back door. Helen, confused and desperate to get out of the crash course hunting lesson sprung on her, looked to Running Bear for help.

"It has to be you who shoots the arrows," Running Bear told her.

Helen gave a delirious smile. The thought of her as a hunter was absurd. A chuckle escaped her, which grew into great heaves of convulsive laughter, a catharsis she had no control over. The image of Helen hunting made Bernice crack as well, joining Helen in the hysterics, rolling onto her back and cackling up into the air. Roy wanted to join in but could only manage a smirk as he watched Helen and Bernice take a small break from reality. The thought of his parents and Mandy and Lynne weighed heavily on his mind, wondering if they were all right and if he would ever see them again.

John, straight-faced and serious, opened the back door and held it open for Helen, saying, "Stop wasting time." The sternness of John's manner caused Helen to recant her laughter and to obey like a scolded schoolgirl.

Bernice stifled the laughter that remained dancing around in her belly until Helen had walked out the door. She then rolled to her side and curled up in a fetal position, allowing the laughs to wrack her body for a little while longer. When Bernice finally calmed down and sat up, tears were streaming down her face, and her cheeks were flush with pink. Her hair was a knotted, scraggly mess. Her clothes were filthy. Roy gave Bernice a look and couldn't help but grimace and let out a giggle. "God! You're a complete disaster!"

Running Bear took a seat next to Rose and asked for everyone's attention. "While John is preparing Helen, we need to talk about what we need to do to help. Helen is the only one that can shoot the arrows, but we need to help her by luring Uncegila out of the ground so she'll have a clear shot. She'll only get three chances. After that, new arrows would have to be made and purified, and they can't be fired until four days after the first attempt. We need to get it this time. Look what it's done in a day alone. Imagine what it could do in four. Roy, pay attention," Running Bear said, noticing Roy looking up at the ceiling, his eyes completely zoned out of the discussion.

"Sorry. I can't stop thinking of the hospital. Can we try calling? Do you think the phone lines are still down? I need to know if my family is okay."

Running Bear's grandmother went to her phone, lifted the receiver, and shook her head. Running Bear went into the kitchen and found a pencil and some clean paper in a drawer and brought it to Roy. "I'll need a piece of metal," Roy requested.

Bernice saw an old metal ashtray on the side table next to her and handed it to Roy. Everyone sat quietly and watched Roy go into his trancelike state. As he began sketching, the two elders in the room were in awe of Roy's gift. June was terrified, especially since she began to recognize what Roy was sketching. She stood and hovered over Roy as he added detail after detail. Running Bear stuck his arm out in front of June, making sure she wouldn't interrupt. Roy's face was twisted in frustration. His frown lines stood prominently between his eyebrows. He dropped the pencil and the ashtray in frustration.

"I can't see the hospital. Damn it! I need to know what the hell is going on!" Roy's pleas were ignored completely as Running Bear, his grandmother, Rose, and June studied Roy's latest sketch.

"It's the reservation," Running Bear said. The sketch showed Uncegila lurking underground, beneath the homes on the reservation.

June reached down and pointed to a house on the far side of the page. "That's mine. My husband is home with my son! Oh my God, we have to stop this now!"

Running Bear ran out the back door. He watched Helen aim an arrow at a target pinned to a tree. She hit the tree but missed the target altogether.

"Damn," Helen uttered under her breath.

"We need to do this now," Running Bear said.

"She's barely shot ten arrows and has only hit the target twice," John argued.

"It's better than nothing, and it'll have to do. Roy just did a sketch. The water monster is making its way through the reservation. We have to attract it to us before it does to the reservation what it did to Ramsey." Running Bear led John and Helen back inside to the living room where they found June in hysterics. Rose was holding June's arm, trying to calm her. "No! Let her get upset," Running Bear yelled. "In fact, everyone, get damned mad right now," Running Bear ordered them all. The elders grabbed one another's hands and summoned the others to join them.

"Helen, get the three arrows and go out back toward the well. Get close enough so you can throw these in one by one." Running Bear had stuffed his pockets with metal washers and handed them to Helen. "As you throw them in, think about—"

"I know what to think about," Helen assured Running Bear.

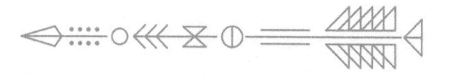

CHAPTER 21

After the collapse of Ramsey Hospital's south wing, things grew deathly quiet. After the initial panic, everyone who had survived quickly became detached, wooden, indifferent. They had lost their will to fight this thing, for it was far too strong. They were apathetic, had lost feeling, given up.

Carson had been knocked unconscious upon the first upheaval. The ground had lurched underneath him, lifting him off the ground and leaving him to fall to the ground, his head cracking hard against a waiting room chair on his way down. He didn't know how long he had been out, but when he awoke, he was stuck in the same strange state of apathy everyone else was experiencing.

He staggered to his feet, noticing there were others lying either unconscious or dead around him. He shuffled his feet lazily over to Mandy and Lynne, who were on the ground a few feet away from where he had been. Their eyes were closed. Carson prodded them with the tip of his dirty work shoe as though they were just a curiosity. He really didn't care whether they were dead or just unconscious. His feelings were blunted. He knew the monster had caused all this. He knew he had been knocked out. He remembered the people he had been with at the hospital and that only two members of that group remained with him now.

There was no sense of urgency or concern whatsoever, but Carson was unable to realize this. He just knew something was off and that he was cut off from his feelings. His logical mind told him he should find the other members of his group, but he couldn't understand why. There didn't seem to be a reason for anything.

He looked at Mandy and Lynne. He recognized them but didn't care about them one way or the other. He remembered their brother,

Roy, and how he had helped him escape with Running Bear, Bernice, and…and…there was someone else. He couldn't come up with an image or a name, but someone else had left an imprint on him that couldn't be erased. He just couldn't think of who it was at that moment. The monster had tried to block this person out of Carson's mind completely.

Mandy stirred on the ground next to Lynne. She rubbed her eyes with her fingertips before sitting up and taking in the scene around her. She looked up and saw Carson, registering who he was and not caring that they were both still alive. She looked over to her sister and gave her a weak shove with her elbow. The shove worked as Lynne awoke to being as dead-eyed and emotionless as Carson and Mandy.

A nurse had been lying on the ground a few feet away from the girls. She awoke, walked over to Carson, and looked at the bandage on his side that had soaked through with blood. She knew she should care and do something. She was a nurse after all. But she felt no rush to help, no urgency. She would do it, but it was purely out of habit. The nurse turned her attention to the girls. She saw an egg swelling above Lynne's left ear where she must have received a solid thud. Blood steadily flowed from it. The nurse stood up and said in a monotone voice, "I'll get some bandages." She then disappeared down the hall, stepping carelessly over two bodies on her way to the supply room.

Carson, Mandy, and Lynne sat emotionally numb, waiting for the nurse to return. All they could feel was confusion. They couldn't communicate their feelings to one another, for that sharing would create a bond. Uncegila couldn't have that, so it tried to render any inclinations to do so absent. The three sat numb and in silence. The nurse reemerged and mechanically tended to their wounds.

"We should find Mom and Dad," Lynne said flatly.

One floor up from them sat James and Regina. James repeatedly thought of Roy but couldn't make himself feel the worry that he knew he should. Regina was having the same thoughts as James about all her kids. She thought of the word *depression* and remembered the words to describe it but couldn't remember the actual feelings of hopelessness, unbearable sadness, or apathy. But now there was nothing, and she didn't know what to call this. Why bother naming such a feeling of void?

One by one, Helen tossed the washers into the well. With each washer, she thought of all the horrors she had lived through that day and throughout her life. Helen could hear the cries from people inside the house, their pain becoming amplified and palpable. The ground shook, and piercing screams came from the house. Helen turned to the well and threw the remaining washers in. She placed one of the purified arrows into the bow and stepped back. She summoned every ounce of anger she could, unleashing it with a scream like she had never screamed before.

The ground swelled underneath Helen and split open between her and the well. The familiar churning river of sludge ran rapidly within the opening. Helen saw the head emerge, its eyes just barely making it up through the sludge. In her rage, she impulsively fired the first arrow, hitting Uncegila in its right eye. Agonizing groans came from the monster, and gel-like blood ran from the wound.

Running Bear ran out to Helen, making the others stay inside at the door. "Focus your rage on the target! You only have two arrows left. You must direct your anger," Running Bear warned Helen as she loaded the second arrow. With Running Bear at Helen's side, the jealous knave boiled with rage over the bond of friendship between the two. The beast reared up, fueled by the jealousy over the emotional connection it desperately coveted but could never attain.

Bernice panicked at the sight of Uncegila towering over Helen and Running Bear and rushed out the door, shouting for Helen and grabbing at her waist. Bernice's grab caused Helen to release the second arrow wildly into the air, missing its mark completely. Vexed with Bernice over the blunder, Helen ripped her arms away from her waist. "Get back into the house, and stay there like you were told!" Helen scolded Bernice with an anger she hadn't shown her before.

The spiteful being grew even taller, strengthened by the anger it sensed from Helen toward Bernice. It enjoyed the possibility of a rift growing between them. It didn't understand that a short burst of anger didn't always grow into a grudge or didn't always build into a relationship-crushing event. But that was when it had learned to strike—while they were vulnerable.

Helen loaded her final arrow and aimed it directly at the monster's chest, right between where her mother's arms were attached. In a final act of desperation and cruelty, the barbarian reached out the arms of Helen's mother toward her, beckoning for her to come in for an embrace. Just as Helen was about to release the arrow, Helen heard a familiar sweet voice she hadn't heard in decades. Coming from the loathsome creature's mouth was the voice of Helen's mother pleading with her. "Please, join me, darling. Oh, how I've missed you, sweetheart. Come. It's time for us to be together, my angel!"

Helen waited for the tears that had welled in her eyes to spill down her cheeks, her vision too blurry to fire the final arrow. She readjusted the arrow and walked so close to the revolting bastard that she could smell its putrid, hot blood. She aimed and fired, hitting the exact spot she intended. The monster writhed in pain. Fearful noises pierced the air as Uncegila bled and sank before their very eyes. As it melted into the black abyss of its home, the heart glowed as it grew white-hot.

Rose stumbled out of the door carrying a swatch of thick buffalo hide. She handed it to Helen and told her to cover her hands with it before removing the crystal heart. Rose saw Helen's hesitation. "You must remove it. Quickly, before it sinks," Rose demanded Helen.

Helen wrapped the buffalo hide around her hands and reached into the already decaying chest cavity as though she were removing a loaf of freshly baked bread from an oven. Helen could feel the iciness of the pulsating heart radiating through the buffalo hide. Within seconds, June was by Helen's side, holding the metal lockbox she had arrived at the house with. She placed it on the ground in front of Helen and opened the lid, exposing its lead-lined walls.

Over the continuing roar of the rushing, roaring black river, Rose said, "Place the heart in the box, throw the buffalo hide into the river, then close the box and fasten all three locks." As Helen let the heart slip from the hide and into the box, she became transfixed by its beauty. "Don't let it trick you. Get rid of the hide and close the box," Rose warned.

Helen tossed the hide into the onyx river that now receded into a weak stream. She snuck one last glance at the crystal heart before slamming the lid shut. As she fastened each lock with a click, the river stopped running altogether.

"It's gone," Rose announced.

Helen pressed her palms on top of the box and began to cry. She cried in relief, in exhaustion, in mourning, in exaltation, and in gratitude. She wanted this day to be done. She needed it to be done. But her thoughts turned to the hospital and the people they had left behind, wondering what had become of them, especially Carson.

Helen looked at the back door of the house to see everyone watching her. Bernice wore a sad smile, tears trailing from her eyes. No doubt she felt relief that wrathful demon was dead, unable to torture them any longer. But now that left her with the horrible reality that she did not have her parents or her brother to go home to or to turn to for solace. It was too much reality all at once. Unconsciously and out of self-preservation, Bernice focused on Helen and rejoiced in her achievement. She had put Uncegila to rest, freeing them all.

The entire group stood in reverence for what Helen had just done. Running Bear could contain his elation no longer and ran to Helen, wrapping his arms around her waist and lifting all six feet of her off the ground. Helen blushed as Running Bear praised her, yelling, "You did it! I'll be damned if you aren't one hell of a sharpshooter!"

"Please put me down," Helen begged, embarrassed and flustered by Running Bear's exhilaration and outpouring of emotion.

"Sorry, sorry," Running Bear said, settling Helen back to the ground. He looked over at John and said, "Not bad for a first-timer, huh?"

Mina asked that everyone gather back inside her house. As they walked back inside, Helen noticed a look of concern on Rose's face.

"Rose, are you feeling all right?" Rose didn't answer but told Helen to pick up the box and carry it inside.

When Helen had the box in her arms and was on her way back to the house, Rose was at her side. "You have some big decisions to make now that the heart is yours."

After a very quick round of hugs and cheers after Helen's slaying of Uncegila, the group got back to business. Bernice had been hovering close to Helen like a bear cub since she walked back through the door. She had hugged her with all her might and apologized for ruining the second shot. Helen told her that she apologized far too much, that she knew her intentions were always good. Besides, she rationalized, maybe she wouldn't have hit her target at all had it not been for the added pressure from losing a shot.

Roy paced, itching to get back to town to find his parents. He rubbed his hands together as he thought about the different scenarios that could be playing out back at the hospital. He realized that the scar on his left hand had vanished. He grabbed the metal ashtray and the pencil and tried to go back into a trance, hoping he could sketch what was going on at the hospital at that moment, but nothing would come. He realized the power had left now that the beast was at rest. He had grown accustomed to it and missed the power. He wished he had it for just one more moment so he could see his family right now.

"I need to speak to Helen privately," Rose announced to the group. Mina and John Black Elk knew the matter the two needed to discuss, so they led the rest of the group through the kitchen and out the front door to the fire that still burned. Bernice reluctantly left Helen's side and lagged behind the rest of the group as they exited the house. Rose smiled at this and assured Bernice that Helen would rejoin her right after their talk. When the front door closed behind Bernice, Rose asked Helen, "Her family is gone? She has no one left?"

Helen answered, "Yes. She's all alone now."

"She seems very fond of you, and you of her. Keep that in mind when you decide what you want to do," Rose said cryptically. Helen had set the metal box on the coffee table. Rose sat down in a chair on one side of the box and motioned for Helen to take the seat opposite her. Rose tapped her knobby, crooked old finger on top of the box and told Helen, "This is your responsibility now. The person who puts Uncegila to rest must also take the heart and keep it locked away and safely out of the hands of others."

The thought of the heavy responsibility of this thing made Helen's head spin. She knew there was no getting out of it, but she couldn't make herself grasp what having this new responsibility would mean for her. "Tell me how to do this. I don't know where to begin. What do I need to know? I'm scared, Rose. I've lived under so much burden in my life. I thought I would be free of burden for once after all this. Now I'm going to be left with an even heavier one. I don't ask for these things. They just seem to find me, I guess," Helen explained, defeated.

"I'll tell you all you need to know. Being the guardian of the heart is more of a gift than a burden. Sure, it will be burdensome knowing you are responsible for keeping it hidden. During your life-time, you will need to decide whom you deem responsible to take over your role as the guardian of the heart."

Helen listened intently, then confessed, "I don't see the gift in all this, Rose."

Rose produced a beat-up leather book from her medicine bag and handed it over to Helen. Helen handled the book with care, studying its binding and cover. A picture of the crystal heart was burned onto the cover as were some symbols, Native American hiero-glyphs, she presumed. "It means that what is written within the pages will aid the guardian of the heart," Rose explained.

Helen carefully turned the book's pages and was deflated to see that the entire book was written in the unfamiliar symbols, wonder-ing how it would do her any good if she couldn't understand how to interpret it. Rose instructed Helen to set the book down on top of the box and to open to the first page. She took Helen's hand and placed it palm down on the text and told her to close her eyes and focus her thoughts on the book. With skepticism, Helen closed her eyes and waited and felt nothing.

"You aren't focusing. Give yourself permission to believe in it," Rose instructed Helen.

Helen released her skepticism and focused in on the book. She felt a slight warmth emanate from the book and move from her hand up to her arm. As the warmth made its way up to her head, Helen was able to understand what was on the page. It wasn't translated into words but into feelings, feelings that would guide her in the decisions she would have to make.

Rose told her to open her eyes and pull back from the text. "You see, I can't tell you everything. As you just felt, some advice and guidance are beyond words and must be felt. But what I can tell you is this: Being the guardian of the heart gives you the power to affect circumstances directly. The powers of the heart are at their strongest right now. If the people in your town can be saved, you must act now. After midnight, you will not be able to gain enough power from the heart to effect major change. You will still have great powers but not on the scale you have right now up until midnight. You can only help the living. There's nothing you can do for the dead."

It had always been the norm for Helen to second-guess herself and her abilities, but it had caused her so much anxiety and had wasted so much time in her life that she decided at that moment that she would break that habit. She would need to trust in her own instinct and knew that she could do that after all that she had gone through. She had a newfound confidence in herself that no one else could have implanted there except herself. Helen thanked Rose. She put the leather book under her arm and picked up the metal box and walked out the front door.

Everyone standing at the fire turned their attention to Helen. "Running Bear, we need to go back to town right now. Bernice and Roy, let's go," Helen said, lugging the box to the car. She opened the passenger's side door and placed the box in the middle of the front seat. She opened the back door for Roy and Bernice and slammed the door swiftly behind them. She looked to Mina, John, Rose, and June and placed both hands over her heart. "Sorry this has to be short, but thank you for your guidance. I'll be back on much better terms soon, I hope."

Helen spoke directly to June. "You aren't responsible for your grandmother's actions. I hold no grudge against you. You helped us put that hateful, ugly thing to rest. It couldn't have been done without your help. Thank you. I hope you won't burden yourself with guilt."

June smiled warmly and said, "You're welcome. Don't forget you have some family here now." June's words made Helen realize what she hadn't had time to register: the fact that June shared her blood, that she was Helen's second cousin.

Running Bear waited in the driver's seat. He revved the engine, signaling Helen to hurry. Helen took her place in the passenger's seat, and the four of them were off again on their way back to Ramsey. Running Bear steered his Impala south on the highway back to town, a drive he had taken so many times before he couldn't count. Under the circumstances, this drive felt like the first one he had ever taken to town in the dark with passengers in tow. He drove a little over the speed limit this time, fighting his urge to floor it. *Getting the heart and everyone else back to town safely has to be my priority,* he thought. What good were they if they had an accident and didn't show up at all? And if they had an accident, what would become of the heart if left without a guardian? The thought kept Running Bear driving at a constant, responsible clip.

Roy bounced his legs up and down and picked at his fingernails as he sat restlessly in the back seat. He wanted to tell Running Bear to drive faster, but he understood that safely transporting the heart kept him from speeding. Bernice was dying to know what Rose told Helen about the heart and what Helen had to do with it. She had hoped Helen would at least discuss some of what she and Rose had talked about, but since their conversation was held in private, Bernice was resigned to think she wouldn't get any answers, not now, at least.

Bernice broke the silence in the car, asking, "Are we all going straight back to the hospital? Is there any sort of plan?"

"I think it's the only place we can go right away. What do you think?" Running Bear said, looking at Helen who sat with her hands atop the leather book resting on her lap.

"What do we have, about twenty minutes until we get back to town?" asked Helen. Running Bear nodded. "I need to ask all of you to be silent for the rest of the time. I need to think about what Rose told me so I can figure out what we need to do. What time is it now?" Running Bear looked at his wristwatch and told her it was almost ten thirty. "We only have until midnight. I can't use this time to explain. I need to think."

Helen opened the leather book on her lap and pressed her palms onto the open pages. She closed her eyes and rested her head on the back of the seat. She sat in meditation like this until Running Bear announced that they were just outside the town limits.

The streetlights lit the streets of Ramsey, exposing streets and homes laid to ruin by Uncegila. Helen opened her eyes and studied the destruction as they drove. Running Bear was about to turn toward the hospital when Helen stopped him. "I need you to drive down Eighth Street before we go to the hospital."

"We're short on time as it is," Running Bear countered but backed down when he saw the look on Helen's face.

Helen explained, "There's something I need to see before I make some important decisions. Please, just go, quickly."

Running Bear drove straight until he came to Eighth Street, then sat idling until Helen directed him to turn left. He didn't know where Helen was guiding him, but Bernice and Roy did. "Turn left. Drive slowly when you get to the second block," Helen said, shifting in her seat so that she faced the driver's side. She reached a hand into the back seat, and Bernice gladly accepted it. Roy turned to look out his window in anticipation.

Running Bear slowed the car to a crawl, and luckily so. There were fissures running through the streets like veins branching out into capillaries. He had to maneuver the car up onto curbs and onto people's properties at times to make his way farther down the street.

A dilapidated home with chipped white paint came into view on their left. When they were directly in front of it, Helen touched Running Bear's shoulder. "Stop for a second. It's my house," she said.

It was a sad scene for Helen. Her ramshackle home reminded her of her old self—sad, broken-down, lonely, and tired. There was the flaking paint, the few missing planks of wood siding, cracked windows, the black paint peeling away on the window frames, the crumbling cement steps leading to the front door, and the garage to the right seeming to almost lean, threatening to collapse at the next strong gust of wind.

Helen wondered in silence if that house was worth salvaging. Could she ever make it into a happy place? Would she ever be able to replace the bad memories with good ones? Would she ever forget the feeling of being stalked by a monster from inside her home?

The outside steps were a reminder of the anxiety that used to well up within her every time she returned home and the agonizingly mundane process she used to perform just to get the courage to reenter. It pained her to think of how much time she had wasted in her life by repeating that ritual. Helen saw what she needed to see for herself and was ready to move on. Helen gave Bernice's hand a squeeze and asked, "You ready?"

Bernice shrugged her shoulders and kept the tight grip on Helen's hand. She leaned forward and braced her head against the back of the seat in front of her. "Drive forward three houses to the yellow house with the cop car out front. Stop there just for a second."

Helen felt Bernice's hand become clammy with sweat and beginning to tremble. Bernice's breath became shallow as she lost her battle to fight back tears, finally emitting a sob that turned into a series of gasps and heaves through a flood of tears. Helen couldn't bear to see Bernice's pain. She told Running Bear to move on and take the next left, explaining that Roy's house was right behind Bernice's.

Roy hadn't seen his home in nearly two years, and the sight of it filled his chest with joy. He felt guilty for his happiness as Bernice sat next to him mourning the loss of her family. He scanned his house and was glad to see that it was as well-maintained as it ever was and that all was the same, except for the large crack in the earth in the front yard, a remnant of the behemoth's wrath.

Helen paid close attention to everyone's reactions and kept them in mind as she directed Running Bear to drive to the hospital. She had needed to see her home, and she needed Bernice and Roy to see theirs so that she could make one of many important choices she had to make before midnight.

Running Bear drove the few short blocks to the hospital with caution, avoiding potholes and breaks in the ground. As they got closer, more people came into view, and there was bustling activity going on all around the hospital. It was a shock to approach the hospital and see it ripped in half, one side doing its best to remain standing while the other side had been reduced to rubble.

Sensing Roy's urgency to get out of the car and run into the hospital to find his family, Running Bear said, "Don't get out until I park. I'll park around back. It looks like my normal entrance is still intact. We have to stay together and be careful. The structure is unsafe, and we don't know where we can go."

Running Bear parked, and then he and Roy got out of the car. Running Bear bent down and peered at Helen, who made no attempts to get out, and said, "Well? Let's go."

"I can't just leave the box here. And there's no way I'm lugging it around the hospital. I'll do what I can from here. Trust me."

Running Bear did trust Helen. In the short time he had known her, he had come to respect her genuine character. Her instincts would serve her well as the guardian of the heart, he was certain. Roy had already made it to the entrance of the hospital and urged Running Bear to hurry. Bernice hadn't budged from the back seat. Her body leaned against the door, and her head rested against the pane of glass. Running Bear took one look at Bernice and knew she wasn't going anywhere. He gave Helen a knowing glance and swung his door shut and raced over to join Roy.

Helen could see Bernice's face in her rearview mirror. Melancholy, grief, sadness, and suffering weighed heavily on her young face. Helen wished, above all else, that she could take away Bernice's suffering. She wished she could make her forget that she ever even had parents and a brother. *Maybe that would be cruel,* she thought. After all, there were wonderfully happy memories that must overshadow the bad. But the endings her family had experienced were all so brutal, and Bernice had witnessed them all. After the initial shock, would she ever be able to cope? Could she ever have a normal life free of the pain she would likely always carry? Would she end up like Helen used to be, crippled by family trauma and reduced to a life of paranoia and isolation? She didn't want that for Bernice. As much as she wanted to remove Bernice's suffering, she also didn't want to erase her memories of her family. That didn't seem fair.

Helen thought about Ramsey and the people who had survived the last twenty-four hours. How would all of them deal with what had happened? Could it ever be explained to the community? Could the hospital and the rest of the town be repaired and rebuilt? If only there was a way to erase this horrid event from everyone's memories, just leaving them with a blank slate like nothing had ever happened.

But Helen didn't want to forget because she felt that it was her duty to remember what had happened so that Uncegila could never be awakened again. She didn't really want Bernice to forget her family. She felt guilty that she wanted Bernice to remember what they had experienced together. She felt guilty because it was her wish to have Bernice to share this experience with because it had happened to both of them, and even though it was a horror beyond words, they had gone through it together, forever connecting them.

Helen really cared about what Bernice thought of her. Through Bernice, who had always accepted her as she was, Helen had learned to accept herself and became strong and confident. She no longer cared what the rest of the community thought of her. Well, maybe she cared about what Carson thought of her more than she wanted to admit.

How wonderful would it be, she thought, *if I could rewrite some of the story?* She was becoming groggy and couldn't stop herself from indulging in these scenarios. She felt a warmth emanating from the book on her lap through her palms, seeming to feed her thoughts and intentions. Helen and Bernice sat in the Impala in silence.

It was 11:45 p.m.

CHAPTER 22

"Mom!" Roy shouted the moment he saw that his mother was alive. But he was confused by her flat, joyless, emotionless response. There was no spark of excitement or relief in his mother's voice when she said, "Roy, you're here. Dad and Mandy and Lynne are alive."

Regina knew that this was the information Roy wanted because everyone around them had been talking about who was dead or alive ever since they had awoken after half of the hospital had crumbled. Roy walked over to Regina and hugged her. She made no effort to reciprocate. Roy pulled away and looked into his mother's eyes. Her pupils were barely larger than a pinpoint. Her face and body language conveyed emotional numbness. Roy watched over Regina's shoulder as his father walked toward them with the same zombielike expression. James simply approached and stopped once he reached his son and wife, no embrace of joy upon the reunion.

"What's going on? What happened to you guys?" Roy asked. Carson appeared from a door on the right, Mandy and Lynne following him, all looking entranced. Roy was relieved to find them all alive but alarmed over the state they were in.

Running Bear came bolting down the hallway toward the group. He looked at the blank stares on each face. "My maintenance crew and the nurses all look the same—what's left of my maintenance crew anyway. I've only found two of my guys so far," Running Bear reported.

"You think there was some sort of a gas leak or something? Could that cause this? They can't all be in the same state of shock," Roy said.

"No, I'm sure this was Uncegila's work. It must have sensed that the ceremony to destroy it had already begun. When it feels its end is near, it can cause great destruction and put curses on people, one that it thinks will destroy the bonds between them."

Upon hearing the name Uncegila, Carson felt a jolt of fear in recognition of that awful name. He felt his heart pump faster, and a gush of adrenaline began flowing through his body. He remembered something and spoke up. "I was knocked out. I think all of us were. When I woke up, there was a faint red haze hanging in the air. I thought it was just my eyesight." Carson's face suddenly became angry, and his muscles began to twitch. He gave a wild-eyed stare at Running Bear. "Helen. Where's Helen? What the hell have you done with her?" Carson erupted with an anger uncharacteristic of him as he suddenly remembered Helen.

Emotions, mostly negative ones, came flooding back to Carson with a vengeance. He couldn't understand why he was so angry with Running Bear. It was like his concern for Helen and any feelings of concern he had for her were morphed into anger.

"She's fine. She's outside waiting in my car," Running Bear answered, hoping the explanation would quell Carson's anger. He was wrong.

"What the hell is she doing in your car? Why didn't you bring her to us, damn it?" Carson shouted, truly confused by his lashing out at Running Bear. Why was he feeling so jealous toward him? It didn't make any sense.

But Running Bear grew keen as to what was going on. The water monster could turn great feelings of love into passionate anger and hatred. Running Bear didn't know if or when Carson and the rest of the people at the hospital would snap out of the trance, so he went along with Carson, answering his questions. "Helen is in the car with Bernice. She didn't think it was safe to bring her inside," Running Bear explained, adding, "And she's anxious to know if you are okay. She's very worried." Whether Helen shared Carson's affections, Running Bear didn't know. But he thought it was better to have Carson believing that she did, especially in the current state of anger and volatility he was in.

The anger building inside Carson was almost too much for him to contain. He pressed his palms to his temples, his face turning bright red. Veins pulsated in his forehead as he tried to control himself and make sense of his reactions. He was beginning to come out of the trance, but the moment he realized it was a trance, he fainted, slumping into a heap onto the floor.

Running Bear and Roy ran to Carson and stretched him out on his back. Running Bear slapped Carson's cheeks, desperately trying to bring him to. "He was coming out of it! Did you see that?" Running Bear asked Roy.

Then a thud was heard, followed by more. Everyone who had been under the trance was passing out. Neither Running Bear nor Roy knew if the fainting was good or bad. Running Bear hoped that it signaled that they were becoming free of the trance, but he couldn't be sure.

Roy was busy rolling his parents onto their backs and stretching out their limbs as he had watched Running Bear do to Carson. Running Bear raced over to Mandy and Lynne and rolled them to their backs as well. Running Bear stood up. Everything went black, and then he dropped to the ground unconscious as well, leaving Roy alone and in a panic.

"No, no, no! Oh my God," Roy said, crawling on his hands and knees over to where Running Bear had collapsed. No sooner did Roy get to Running Bear's side when he himself blacked out and lost consciousness as well.

The remaining half of the hospital was as still as a ghost town. In fact, the entire town of Ramsey seemed deserted. The streets were nearly pitch-black besides the few remaining streetlights that worked. The waning moon cast a faint light over the town. Sunday evenings in Ramsey were always quiet, but this haunting silence was menacing.

Helen and Bernice sat in the silence of the car. It had been so dark and quiet and peaceful, in fact, that the two of them had dozed off. Bernice was stretched out in the back while Helen's head rested back on her seat. She had been in deep meditation about what to do, her palms remaining on the book that rested on her lap. Both Helen and Bernice were beyond exhausted after what they had been through that day, and no part of them could resist the sweet pull of deep sleep.

It was 11:55 p.m.

Bernice hadn't stirred an inch from the spot she had fallen asleep in. While Helen slept as still as Bernice, her mind was anything but still. Helen's sleep was flooded with vivid high-speed dreams, one dream coming right after the other. The dreams came at her so quickly that she went into sleep paralysis. In fact, Helen and Bernice slept so soundly that they couldn't hear the increasing whir of the heart spinning from inside the box. They weren't in the least bit roused when the box began to glow red from the ever-active heart inside it.

Midnight.

Helen awoke, hesitant to open her eyes after her deep sleep. She felt incredibly rested, peaceful, and comfortable. In fact, it felt like she was in her own cozy bed. She remembered falling asleep in Running Bear's car but realized she was no longer sleeping in a sitting position. She was stretched out with a light comforter draped across her body. Before she opened her eyes, she recognized the warm, smoky aroma of her favorite candle, the one infused with vanilla and tobacco she kept on her dresser.

Helen opened her eyes. She lay still, staring up at a familiar popcorn ceiling. She scanned the room as she sat up in bed. Everything looked about the same as ever, but some photographs she had had in frames were missing. The one of her parents' wedding was gone as was the one where Helen stood next to her father on a small fishing boat.

Helen slid her long legs over the side of the bed. She was wearing a flannel nightgown, one she had never seen before. Now that she thought about it, she never wore nightgowns to bed. She had always worn ratty old jogging pants and a plain black thermal shirt.

Helen pursed her eyes shut, confused. She thought about her dreams and about what had happened yesterday. Or was it all a dream? If it had happened, did it just happen yesterday? The sleep she had been in felt as though she had slept for months. Her mind was still cloudy. One thing was certain—she was definitely home.

She heard clamoring in her kitchen. Someone was digging through a drawer, searching for something. She didn't know if she should be scared. Maybe someone had broken in? No. Somehow, she knew it was all right for someone to be in the kitchen, but who? She stood up, ready to go find out, but before she opened the door, she noticed something resting on the chair in the corner of her room.

It was the metal box. The worn leather manuscript rested on top of it. Helen crept over to it and rested her hands on top of the book, and she was flooded with everything that had happened. She thought about the things she had made decisions about when she was meditating, things that would be the most helpful to everyone involved in what had happened in Ramsey.

Then she remembered falling asleep while meditating and felt sick to her stomach. She remembered her hands feeling hot in every dream she had had. What exactly did she dream about? She couldn't remember the details, but she remembered the urgency that drove her along.

Helen heard someone humming in the kitchen. It sounded like a female voice. She took a deep breath before opening her bedroom door. When she did, she was struck by how bright and cheery and new her home looked. It was the same layout, the same house, but everything was changed. She remembered dreaming about her house looking like this.

Helen walked down the hall and stopped when she got to her bathroom door. She shuddered as she remembered the last time she had been in there, the repugnant beast rearing up and destroying everything. Helen nudged the door open with her fingertips and was stunned to find it in working order—in fact, in much better than working order. No signs of the beast remained, not even the drain that used to sit menacingly by the shower stall. She had dreamed of this too, black-and-white tiles, art deco-style fixtures and all.

"Finally! She is risen," a girl's voice came from the kitchen. Helen recognized that voice immediately. She came around the corner to find Bernice hovering over her toaster. "Morning. You want toast?" Bernice asked.

Helen found it odd how Bernice addressed her so casually and how she seemed so at home in Helen's kitchen. "Uh, not quite yet, thanks," Helen replied, playing along as she watched Bernice move around her newly modernized kitchen, finding the peanut butter in the cupboard and grabbing the strawberry jam from the usual spot in the right-hand side of the door. She needed a knife and a plate and needed no guidance from Helen as to where she could find them. It was like she had always been there for many mornings before that one.

Helen desperately wanted to ask Bernice if she remembered anything about yesterday or how they had gotten from the car to her home. But Helen knew that what was going on had something to do with her dream. If Bernice didn't remember anything, the last thing Helen wanted to do was to remind her and upset her. "Sleep well?" Helen asked.

"Sure. I guess so," Bernice said, blasé. The toaster popped, and Bernice got busy spreading a thick, gooey layer of peanut butter on her toast.

"Like a little toast with your peanut butter, I see," Helen joked.

Bernice rolled her eyes and retorted like an annoyed teenager, "Really? You still think that's funny? You seriously need to update your mom jokes."

Mom? Had Bernice just called her mom? Or was she just referring to the bad joke?

Through a mouthful of mush, Bernice said, "After I help you with the garden this morning, do you mind if I hang out with Mandy and Lynne?"

"Funny. I don't remember asking you to help in the garden," Helen said, but what she was actually thinking was that she hadn't done any gardening since her mother had disappeared. And now Bernice was talking about it like it was a well-established habit.

"Well, it *is* Sunday. I just assumed that since it's nice out that that's what we'd be doing as usual," Bernice explained.

"Of course, sure. Hey, on second thought, I'll take that toast now," Helen said before she walked back to her room to change clothes.

"Of course you will now that I've already put the bread and the jelly away."

Helen peeked back around the corner. "I didn't say jelly." Bernice smirked at her and dragged the bread back out of the cupboard. As she walked down the hall, Helen added playfully, "Coffee would be great with my toast." Helen's heart was nearly bursting as she approached her room. She closed the door behind her and leaned her back against the door. She laughed and whispered to herself, "This can't be happening."

As she pulled some clothes from her drawers, she remembered a dream she had had. In it, she had wished that Bernice was her daughter, that she wouldn't have to remember how her parents and brother had been killed. But she also didn't want to erase Bernice's memory of her family altogether. Every family had their troubles, and the Fellers had theirs. But the good had outweighed the bad in Helen's estimation.

Helen's feelings of joy for having Bernice in her home were coupled with a nagging guilt over the circumstances. She didn't know if she had had control in all her dreams. And she hadn't realized how powerful the crystal heart was, that it could create change like it has. She looked at the metal box and remembered that it was her responsibility to hide it and make sure no one knows where it is until she had to pass on her guardianship to someone else.

"It's ready!" Bernice yelled from the kitchen.

Helen left the box in her room for the moment and rejoined Bernice back in the kitchen. Bernice turned on the television in the living room. The local news played. Helen thanked Bernice for the coffee and toast as she sat at her new kitchen table. Helen stopped eating, and Bernice froze where she was when they heard the words coming from the news:

"The town of Ramsey is back on the grid this morning after all communications to and from the small town were knocked out yesterday as the result of what's being called a freak earthquake. While earthquakes are nearly unheard of in this area, geologists warn they can happen anywhere at any time. Experts say that this earthquake may have been a result of the underground pressure caused by the upswing in fracking for natural gas in the surrounding areas. However, it's still unclear as to why this earthquake hit just within Ramsey's city limits and why one giant crack made its way north all the way to the Prairie Lake Reservation."

The female journalist's voice was replaced by a deep, familiar male's voice. "We're doing the best we can this morning. Our main concern is for everyone's safety and for getting medical attention for those who need it."

"It's Officer Carson!" Bernice exclaimed with excitement. Helen hurried over to the television and blushed at the sight of Carson on the screen looking rested, strong, and handsome as ever. Helen's reaction didn't go unnoticed by Bernice. Bernice teased, dawning a Southern accent, "Why, control yo'self, Ms. Scarlett! Do I need to find the smellin' salts?"

Helen blushed harder and gave Bernice a robust "Shush!"

Carson continued. "Sadly, we have a lot of casualties to deal with. And the community suffered a lot of damage to their homes and properties. Some streets and homes were untouched, but there will be a lot of rebuilding that needs to take place. The hospital was hit worst with significant structural damage and casualties. Like I said, our main concern right now is for safety and medical attention to those in need. As far as the rebuilding efforts go, it will take a lot of time and funding, but I have no doubt that our resilient community will see it through."

Bernice had been listening intently alongside Helen, but Helen was too taken with the sight of Officer Carson on the screen and with what the news was saying about Ramsey to even consider what

Bernice may have been thinking about what she was seeing and hearing. Bernice nudged Helen with her hip. "Your coffee's getting cold."

The news switched stories, and Helen tore herself away from the television and went back to her breakfast. She was embarrassed at how flustered she had become at the sight of Carson. In fact, she was taken aback by her schoolgirl reaction. She was even more embarrassed that Bernice had noticed it.

Bernice disappeared down the hall, leaving Helen alone with her thoughts. When she came back, she was dressed in a pair of jean shorts and an oversized red sweatshirt that she had bunched up at the sleeves. "Since you're still eating, mind if I go see Mandy and Lynne? I'll be quick. I just want to see if they're okay after all this. I'll be back to help you in the garden afterwards."

After all this. Helen thought of Bernice's use of words. What exactly did Bernice remember, if anything? By "all this" did she mean what was just talked about on the news, or did she remember anything about what really happened? Was she going to Mandy and Lynne's to really find out if they were okay after the earthquake, or was she going there to find out if they remembered the real story?

Before Helen agreed to let Bernice go, she thought about the Fellers' home. It would be in Bernice's sight when she went to her friends' house. Helen couldn't remember if she had dreamed of the Feller home or not, and she didn't know what to expect. She had to find out. More importantly, she had to know Bernice's reaction to seeing her home, if it was still there at all.

"You can stop by quickly, but I'm going to keep an eye on you walking over there. I don't know how much damage there is, and if it's safe after…the earthquake," she forced the lie from her lips, wondering if Bernice knew it was a lie.

Helen walked out of her front door and glanced around before letting Bernice follow her. She was surprised to see that her cement steps were no longer cracked and that the chipped white paint on her house had been replaced with a fresh cheery yellow coat of paint. The splintered black trim around the windows had been replaced with beautiful rustic wood, and there were flower boxes underneath the two front windows. It was exactly what she would have wanted. *Another dream come to fruition,* she thought.

Helen looked down the block and to the roads and saw that the cracks Uncegila had made were no longer as numerous or as prevalent as they were yesterday. She walked down her front steps and held her hand up to Bernice, signaling for her to wait. Helen walked to the sidewalk across the street, then turned and looked at her house from the same vantage point she had viewed it from so many times before that. It nearly took her breath away that her home was utterly transformed from a place that had been crumbling and melancholy into something crisp, fresh, and beautiful. Seeing Bernice stand in her doorway was both exhilarating and excruciating.

Helen casually looked down the street in both directions. It was a show for Bernice so that she would think Helen's main concern was checking for safety so that Bernice could go see her friends. But Helen's main concern sat three houses down to the right. There on the Fellers' property sat a completely different house than the one that the Fellers had lived in. It was a two-story house with gray siding. There were no cars in the driveway. In fact, the house looked brand-new and appeared unlived in. Another dream scenario. Helen waved her arm for Bernice to come down and said, "Go ahead. You have an hour."

Bernice bounded down the steps and jogged around Helen's house through the backyard toward Mandy and Lynne's. Helen watched Bernice for a reaction. She hadn't been watching long when she saw Bernice give a quick glance to her right in the direction of where her home used to sit. She stopped running but continued to walk toward her friends' house, taking a couple more glances toward the new home.

Helen couldn't be sure if Bernice's glance was one of recognition. The fact that she kept on her path to her friends told her that maybe she didn't remember that she had once lived there. Helen both hoped and regretted that if it were the case.

Helen stood admiring her home for a moment. She mused over how many times she had stood staring at her house before but for anxiety-ridden reasons. Helen walked straight up her steps without hesitation and didn't knock before going in.

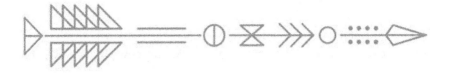

CHAPTER 23

"Mat! Wake up, buddy," someone shouted as they patted Running Bear's cheeks. Running Bear opened his eyes to see an orderly leaning over him, a smile widening across his face. "You look hungover, man. You been here all night?"

Running Bear sat up and realized he had been sleeping on the floor in the first floor waiting room. He blinked hard a few times and took in his surroundings. Something was different. He remembered everything that had happened yesterday at the hospital. And he would never forget the experience with Uncegila. As he searched the faces of people around him—patients, nurses, orderlies, doctors— they didn't seem to carry the trauma that they had yesterday. They seemed concerned, to be sure, but not terrorized.

"Mat, you all right?" the orderly asked.

"Yeah, I'm good. I just feel like I've been in a coma. I guess I must have fallen asleep here with all that was going on."

"Crazy, right? Who'd have thought an earthquake would ever hit Ramsey," the orderly said, confusing Running Bear.

"Earthquake?"

The orderly turned Running Bear's attention to a television in the waiting area and went over to turn up the volume so he could hear the news. Running Bear watched, confused by what the news was reporting. When he saw Officer Carson being interviewed, looking rested and healthy, he was truly perplexed. But something told him that all this was a result of Helen's wishes now that she was the guardian of the heart. He just wasn't certain of all that she had done. So he played along with everyone else just as Helen was doing from her home, unbeknownst to him.

"Damnedest thing, huh?" remarked the orderly, his thick arms crossed over his chest as he stood watching the news report next to Running Bear.

Running Bear listened intently as the reporter spoke about the earthquake leaving a crack that reached all the way to the reservation. He paid close attention when Carson spoke about the fact that there were casualties and a lot of damage to Ramsey with the damage to the hospital being the worst.

"Yeah, the damnedest," Running Bear answered, adding as he walked away from the orderly, "I need to check on things around here—you know, look for my guys and make sure there are no leaks or anything dangerous happening. Catch you later."

Running Bear disappeared through a side door and ran to where he remembered the hospital being torn in two. He was pleasantly surprised to see that this was no longer the case, that there was just some minor damage. The sprinkler system had gone off, and some tiles of dropped ceiling had fallen to the ground. A few chairs and desks were out of place, but it was nothing like the destruction he had witnessed yesterday.

Helen had manifested what was happening, and Running Bear trusted in her judgment even though he had known her for less than a day. He wondered what else the day would have in store. He decided to head up to the fifth floor. Just yesterday, he had helped Roy escape. He wondered if anyone had seen him do it or if anyone even knew Roy was gone. He didn't understand why he still remembered what had really happened and why the orderly didn't.

Much to his surprise, all was quiet as he stepped from the elevator onto the fifth floor. The office staff at the waiting area didn't bat an eye at him as he used his key card to enter the ward. The smell of feces no longer hung in the air, and there were no signs of the Uncegila drawings on the walls. Running Bear walked to Roy's room. He had to know if Roy was back inside.

He took the set of master keys hanging from his belt and said to the orderly on duty, "Hey, I gotta get in here to check a pipe in the dropped ceiling. You okay with that?"

The orderly walked over and held the door open for Running Bear after he had unlocked it. Running Bear was surprised to find the room empty. The bed was freshly made, and the room looked like it was awaiting another patient. The bookshelf lined with Roy's notebooks was gone. The metal desk and chair remained.

"I don't know why you need my permission to go in," the orderly said from behind Running Bear, adding, "It's empty."

"I know. Habit, I guess," Running Bear replied. Running Bear pulled the metal chair over to the wall and stood on it. He moved a piece of dropped ceiling and took his small flashlight from his belt and made like he was inspecting something. He replaced the tile and hopped off the chair. "Looks good" was all Running Bear said, but it was enough to satisfy the orderly, who was completely uninterested in Running Bear's business or findings anyway.

Running Bear went to the front desk to where two nurses sat at admissions. "You ladies made it through the earthquake all right? Your families and homes okay?"

One of the nurses answered, "We're all good at my house, thank God! There's a pretty big hole in the yard across the street from our house, but everything else is good."

The second nurse wasn't as fortunate. "My own family is okay thankfully. My sister is downstairs with a broken leg, but she'll be fine. Could've been so much worse. Did you hear about Laura?"

"Laura…Laura…sorry, you'll have to refresh my memory," Running Bear said.

"Laura Becker the EMT? Head of the ambulatory services?"

"Oh yeah, sorry. Is she the one with the daughter I see around here once in a while?" Running Bear knew full well that Laura was Marie's mom.

"Yes, that Laura." Both nurses sat in silence as they fought back tears before one of them explained. "Both she and her daughter are gone."

"Gone? You mean they left?" Running Bear asked in hopeful denial.

"Gone as in dead. Word is that Laura was going to make a run through town to help anyone she could after the quake. Marie was here, and she insisted on going with. Laura followed the big crack that ran north of town. The police found the ambulance crushed down inside of it."

Running Bear wasn't sure of the connection, but he remembered Bernice being with Laura's daughter at the hospital the day before. His thoughts went back to Roy. He needed to find out if the staff knew Roy was missing or what had happened to him. They didn't seem to know that Running Bear had helped him escape.

"Oh, I wanted to ask you. I just had to check the corner room in the ward. What happened to the kid that was in there before? Um, what was his name again? Roy, I think."

The nurse in front of Running Bear squinted her eyes, saying, "There was never a Roy in that room. The last person in there was that big guy from out west, Keith. You remember him, right?"

Running Bear had no clue who this Keith was, but he faked an, "Oh yeah, him."

The nurse looked back at her coworker and said, "I've been here six years and don't remember a Roy being here. You?" The other nurse shrugged her shoulders and shook her head no.

Running Bear was uneasy not knowing if this information meant that Roy was dead or if the memory of Roy ever being here had been erased. He needed to find out more information. He left the nurses and went back down to the first floor. He found the orderly helping at the emergency room entrance.

"Hey, quick question."

The orderly was a little distracted by the commotion of the emergency room but answered, "Sure, what's up?"

"Were there any other people asleep in the waiting room when you woke me up this morning?"

"Nope, you were all alone, buddy," Joey answered.

"Are you sure? Officer Carson wasn't there? Or were there any patients?"

"Oh, Carson was there, but he woke up when I got here about 4:00 a.m. He told me not to wake you. But there was no one else. Why? You looking for someone?"

"I thought I'd remembered a family being there, a married couple with two or three kids. I was just hoping they were all right."

"Nope, I only saw Carson. But maybe they left before I got in. Sorry I can't help."

Running Bear had to find out what had happened to everyone. Deep down, he felt everyone was fine, but he needed confirmation. He remembered where Helen's house was from the drive last night. He went to the boiler room. He checked the closet where he kept his extra clothes, the ones he had given to Roy to wear yesterday. There was a new set of clothes in the closet, still his but different from the ones he had given Roy.

Running Bear went over to the punch clock and looked at his time card, noticing that his last clock in was yesterday morning with no punch out time. He slipped his card into the machine and checked out for now. His card showed a straight twenty-eight-hour block of work. How would he explain that to his supervisor? He would have to figure that out later.

Running Bear walked out the same door he had used so many times before, but this day felt brighter. After what he had just experienced, he left the hospital feeling grateful that he had his job and his life.

He was relieved to see that the hospital, its property, and the streets weren't nearly as damaged as he had remembered from the night before. Running Bear looked for his Impala, but what was sitting in his parking spot was a fully loaded bright-red Chevy Corvette. No one ever took his parking spot. He walked over to it and found that his pine air freshener hung from the rearview mirror. His work coat and his blue lunch cooler sat on the passenger's side floor. Running Bear dug his hand in his pocket and pulled out his keys and smiled as he saw that he held the key to the Corvette in his hand. He slid into his upgraded ride and got comfortable. He couldn't revel in this for too long. He needed confirmation that Roy and his family had survived before he could fully enjoy this gift. Running Bear roared off toward Helen's.

Bernice smiled as she got closer to her friends' front door. She took a deep breath before ringing the doorbell. She turned to look toward the picnic table and at the front yard. *The same as it ever was,* Bernice thought. Bernice was surprised by Roy answering the door. She waited for him to speak first.

"Jeez! Early enough?" Roy sneered, that old teenage sarcasm back in his voice. But it was a relief to Bernice rather than an annoyance.

"I know, sorry. Are Mandy and Lynne—"

"What? You're not here to see me?" Roy teased. A shoe sailed down the hall and hit him in the head. "Ow! Damn it, Lynne!"

Bernice could hear Regina scold Roy, yelling, "Don't curse at your sister!"

All the familiar voices in their familiar setting. Bernice felt relieved, contented. Lynne ran to the door and pushed Roy out of the way. He was so much bigger than Lynne that it was ridiculous watching his overreaction to being pushed by someone half his size. Lynne's smart-ass personality was back with all its biting, sharp-tongued charm.

"Move it, jackass! No girl is ever gonna come here looking for you." Lynne spewed her snotty little words at Roy as she fumbled to get her canvas shoes on.

Roy smirked as he lay dramatically on the floor with his hand over his heart, saying, "Words hurt, Lynne. Come on. You love your big brother, really."

"Piss off, Roy!" Lynne fired back, causing Bernice to throw her head back in laughter.

"Oh, Jesus. Get up off the floor," Mandy said, stepping over Roy's long limbs that were taking up most of the room in the entry-way. He deliberately tangled Mandy's legs with his, acting like it was an accident. "Seriously? Don't you have anything better to do?" Mandy said, giving Roy a solid, quick kick in his leg before being completely clear of him.

"Losers. You're no fun at all," Roy said as he got to his feet, rubbing his thigh stinging from his sister's wallop. He seemed very pleased with himself, having annoyed his sisters as he intended.

Bernice was amused by it all. When Mandy joined Lynne outside, Roy slammed the door behind them. Mandy rolled her eyes.

Lynne said, "What an asshole."

"He seems back to normal," Bernice said.

The girls looked at Bernice like she had two heads. "What do you mean? He always acts like this," Mandy said.

Bernice tried to explain. "I mean, I thought he was having kind of a hard time for a while, wasn't he? Like, with school and behavior and stuff?"

"That was puberty. I think it's still happening," Lynne offered casually.

"Lynne! What the hell?" Mandy said, giggling.

"What? It's true!" All the girls enjoyed a good laugh.

Bernice noticed that James's tan pickup truck was missing. "Your dad go somewhere?"

"Work. Duh, it's Monday. What the hell is up with you today?" Lynne asked Bernice.

"Oh yeah, Monday. I forgot. See what the summer does to you? You forget what day it is."

Regina knocked on the kitchen window from inside the house and cranked it open, yelling, "Hi, Bernice! Girls, don't go far! Your dad called and said the park is safe and our street is fine, but don't go any farther. The earthquake wrecked a lot of streets and property. Got it?"

"Yeah!" Mandy and Lynne shouted back in unison.

"Race you to the park! Last one there sucks green donkey—"

"Don't say it!" Mandy cut off Lynne abruptly.

The three girls raced to the park. Bernice smiled as she ran, thinking of Lynne's crudeness and feeling a little guilty for how much she enjoyed it and how thrilled she was it hadn't gone away.

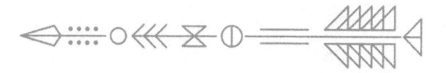

CHAPTER 24

Back inside her house, Helen's thoughts turned to the metal box and to the task of finding a safe hiding spot for it. The words of the elder Rose played in her head as she weighed the heavy responsibility of being the guardian of the heart. She still didn't know if Bernice remembered anything about yesterday, so she figured she better work fast to hide the box while Bernice was out with her friends.

Before Helen could retrieve the box from her bedroom, a car pulled up to the front of her house. Helen turned to see the front of a white car in sight. A car door slammed, and Carson came into view, walking around the nose of the car. Helen's heart skipped a beat, and she warmed all over at the sight of him. She walked closer to the door and watched as Carson strode up her sidewalk and up her cement steps.

His eyes were locked on Helen's, and he couldn't help but smile. Helen was an absolute wreck of bubbling emotions. This feeling was completely foreign to her. She didn't know what to do or what to expect. Her mind was blank to the world except for the man standing at her door. Did he remember her? Obviously, he did. Why else would he be there? Was he going door-to-door everywhere? Her desperate questions were quelled soon enough.

"Helen," Carson said. His voice resonated relief as he said her name. Carson was just as relieved to read the emotion on Helen's face, certain now that she shared his feelings, which made him bold. He removed his hat and asked, "May I come in?"

Helen nodded, and as she held the door open for him, Carson wrapped his arms so tightly around Helen that she gasped. She felt her legs would go out underneath her, especially when Carson whispered into her ear, "My God, I'm glad to see you."

After a long, heavenly embrace, Carson pulled away and held Helen's face in his strong hands and said, "I'm so glad you're all right and that you remember me." He pressed his forehead against Helen's and then passionately kissed her on the mouth.

Helen's legs and the rest of her body did finally give out under the shock of such a lusty gesture. Carson caught her under her armpits and moved her over to her sofa where he had her lie back and put her feet up. He knelt on the floor next to her, holding her hand in his. He brushed her dark hair back from her face.

Helen was embarrassed she had fainted. *How mortifying,* she thought, *that at forty-two years of age, I'd just had my first kiss.* She didn't know what to do with the feeling and was afraid to open her eyes. She had never considered herself attractive and had resigned herself to the belief that the first and only thing people even thought of when they looked at her was strangeness. Her nerves gave way to a cackle that flustered her even more.

"Sorry. That was abrupt, I know. I couldn't help it," Carson said, his voice soft and kind. Laughing, Helen opened her eyes. A tear escaped through a corner of her eye and slid down her temple into her hairline. Carson saw it and said, "Hey, I'm sorry. That's not the reaction I'd intended."

Helen opened her eyes and waved her hands at Carson as he spoke. She gave in to her feelings and spoke freely as she had nothing else to lose. "No, don't apologize. That was…wonderful, great. I just…I never. I can't finish a sentence at the moment, sorry," she said as she giggled in relief.

They both became caught up in the laughter. Helen rolled to her side to face Carson and propped herself up on her elbow. "You remember everything, obviously, right?" Carson nodded yes. "I saw you on the news. So you just went along with this whole earthquake explanation just for show, yeah?" Carson nodded again. "Does that mean that everyone else has kind of been cleared of the real memory of what happened?"

"So far, from what I've seen at the hospital and around town, yes. You're the first person I've talked to that knows. And I knew you had something to do with it. I had some strange lucid dreams of you holding a metal box and a leather book. I kept seeing you close your eyes and rest your hands on the book."

Helen squeezed Carson's hand and kissed it, relieved that he remembered and that he knew to come to her. She only hoped that he had come here of his own volition rather than being here because maybe she had wished him here.

"You know I had something to do with how things have turned out today?"

"Yes, I do," Carson answered and preempted Helen by telling her, "And I was already dying to see you before today. This is real."

This time, Helen kissed Carson, still a little embarrassed when she pulled away. "I'll get used to it. Don't worry," she joked. "Anyways, have you seen Mat?"

Carson said, "The last time I saw him, he was sleeping in the waiting room at the hospital. I didn't want to wake him because I needed to get my own bearings first. When I went back for him later, he wasn't there. Funny. He has a Corvette now." Helen smiled. "No way! Where's mine?" Carson teased.

"Aren't I enough? Or would you rather a Mustang?"

"Can I think about it?"

Helen gave him a playful punch, then changed gears, asking, "You think he'll remember anything? Carson, you wouldn't believe what happened at the reservation, what I had to do, how it all ended. I'll tell you sometime, just not right now."

Carson smiled. "There's no rush. But I do want to hear about it." He looked around at Helen's house, then remarked, "Nice place. Was it always like this, or was it a part of your, uh, renovation plan?"

Helen nodded, adding, "That's not all. Bernice is here. She was here when I woke up. She acts like she's always lived here. I still can't tell if she remembers anything. I can't remember what I dreamed. But that's why she's here. Did you happen to look at where she used to live?"

"Yeah, no sign that the Fellers ever even existed. A new house there and everything," Carson said.

"I dreamed that I'd be the one to take care of her, Carson. I didn't want to erase her memories of her family. That would have been cruel. I only wanted to erase her memories of how they died. But a part of me thinks that that's cruel too. She'd be left with questions about it her entire life. I know what that feels like, and it's hell. I was afraid to bring anything up to her this morning. She seemed so at home and happy here."

"Where is she now?" Carson asked.

"She wanted to go to Mandy and Lynne's. I assume everything is all right. She's been gone about fifteen minutes." Helen's thoughts shot back to the crystal heart. Helen bolted upright and placed her feet on the ground. She put her hands on Carson's shoulders and surprised herself as she boldly planted a quick kiss on his lips once again. "Listen, there's something I need to do and fast. It's something I was told to do by an elder on the reservation. I can't tell you what it is, and I have to do it on my own. All I can say is that it needs to be done so that we'll be safe from that monster, at least for as long as I'm alive. I don't want you to go, believe me, but will you please leave me here, and please, please, please come back later if you have time? I know you'll probably be busy with things around town, so I understand if you can't come back tonight."

"I gotta admit, my curiosity is killing me. But I need to check in at the station and have a lot to do. I'll be back later. Count on that," Carson assured Helen as he embraced her one last time before he got up and went to the front door.

Before he left, Helen said, "I'm sorry about your partner. There was nothing I could do about the dead."

"Well, I don't know if this is a good or a bad thing, but I'm the only one that remembers him. No one at the station has mentioned him. His desk is gone. There's no trace of him."

"Like I said, there's nothing I could have done for him. I'm sorry," Helen said.

"We're all doing our best, aren't we? Don't apologize. I'll see you later," Carson said, winking as he shut the door behind him.

Helen couldn't waste time basking in the glow of requited love. She hurried to her bedroom and grabbed the box and the leather book. She brought them into her garage and placed them on the workbench. She found a few plastic bags and wrapped the leather book inside them securely to protect it. She found her gardening gloves and a spade and brought them out back behind the garage. She found a spot behind her house that was partially hidden by her garage. She gave a quick look around her, making sure Bernice wasn't around or anyone else, dropped down to her knees, and began clearing away dirt. She figured she would bury the box there, deep enough so that it would be hidden and safe, at least for the time being until she could figure out another more secure spot. She dug furiously, and it hadn't taken her more than ten minutes to get to a depth of about three feet.

Helen stuck the spade into the mound of dirt next to her and stood up. She looked for Bernice again and, not seeing any sign of her, went back to her garage to collect the box and book. She peeked outside her garage door before exiting completely and then lowered the box straight into the hole, placing the book wrapped in plastic bags up against the box's side before she began covering it with dirt.

Helen heard the rumble of a car as she reached for the spade. From her knees, she peered around to the front of her house where she saw a red Corvette creeping past her house. The car slowed to a stop as Running Bear caught sight of Helen watching him. Helen knew right away that he had remembered everything. She grabbed the spade and held it up for Running Bear to see, then pointed it down to the ground, knowing that he would understand what she was doing. He had been there for the entire ceremony yesterday. He knew what had to be done better than Helen did.

Running Bear did understand and didn't want to stop Helen from doing what she had to do. He rolled his window down and patted the outside of the driver's side door like it was a baby's bottom and gave Helen a thumbs up in thanks. Helen stuck her chin out at him and yelled playfully, "Show off!"

Running Bear waved and rolled away around the corner, heading toward Roy's house. He drove by the park and saw Bernice with Mandy and Lynne. He rolled by and honked, giving a wave to the girls. Only Bernice waved back, leaving the others to give her an "Ew" look, the type of look that only adolescents could deliver with such pinpoint accuracy and brutal honesty, leaving the recipient feeling raw and exposed.

"Boyfriend?" Lynne teased.

"He's a little old, don't you think?" Mandy added.

"Piss off, both of you," Bernice joked, realizing they both didn't remember him.

The more dirt Helen tossed over the metal box, the more relieved she became.

"What's that? Squirrel coffin or something?" came Bernice's voice from behind Helen, startling her.

Helen dropped her chin to her chest, frozen, not knowing what to say to Bernice. She decided to keep it light. "A squirrel coffin?" Helen asked, smirking. "Is there such a thing?"

Bernice shrugged and smiled. "I don't know." Bernice sat down next to Helen and took the shovel from her hand and began shoveling dirt onto the box. Helen was silent as she watched Bernice methodically dump spadefuls of dirt into the hole. Bernice broke the silence, admitting, "I had some pretty crazy dreams last night. You?"

Leading Bernice into further detail, Helen said, "I'll tell you mine if you tell me yours."

"Sure," Bernice said. "Oh, did you secure the locks?"

She remembers. "Of course I did," Helen answered. "Now about those dreams?"

"Well, you were in all of them. You were holding the book in every one of them." Bernice paused before she went on, afraid to be the first of them to bring it up. "Did you fall asleep in Running Bear's car too?"

Helen said, "Yes, I did. I didn't mean to. I wish I hadn't."

Bernice was confused. Did Helen mean that she didn't like what she saw when she awoke, namely that Bernice lived with her now? "Oh yeah? How so?"

Helen explained. "I mean, I don't remember most of what I dreamed. I needed to be in control of my thoughts, and I don't know where my dreams led me or what's happened because of my dreams. You must be so confused. You see, Bernice, I didn't ask for it."

"Ask for what?" Bernice interrupted.

"I didn't ask to be the guardian of Uncegila's heart. But I have no choice. The elder Rose told me that the heart would give me strong powers until midnight last night, that the powers given to me by the heart would never be so strong for me again, and that I had some big decisions to make in a very short period of time. That's why I was so quiet on the way back to town last night."

"I know what the heart can do, Helen. I saw what you could do with it in my dreams. I remember everything from my dreams. You carried the leather book in each one. You told me your thoughts, and you told me that you could create major change with the power of the heart." Bernice went silent as she focused on speeding up her shoveling, hastily transferring the dirt into the hole, and only slowing when she could no longer see the box or the book. Helen watched Bernice in silence, afraid that Bernice was growing angry with some of the decisions Helen had made, whether they were conscious decisions or not. "Did you see the new house sitting where my house used to be?" Bernice asked.

"So you remember where you used to live? I wasn't sure if you would or if I decided or what was the best thing…damn it! I wanted to do the right thing by you, especially you, Bernice. I'm so sorry. I don't remember what I dreamed and what I asked for. I think I erased your home, and maybe I even erased your family," Helen confessed.

"Whoa, Helen, you didn't wish for that. I did."

Helen was stunned. "What? What do you mean you did? You don't have the powers of the heart. You couldn't have," Helen was baffled.

"I know. You explained the powers to me in your dreams. I joined your dreams. I'm surprised you don't remember any of it, really. It's like I knew I was in your dream but could keep sleeping. You explained everything to me."

Helen grabbed the spade from Bernice's hand and stuck it in the dirt. She took Bernice's hands in hers. Bernice could feel the urgency in Helen's words as she spoke. "Bernice, I don't know what I told you or explained in my dreams, but if you were there and you remember, you need to tell me. I need to know what I decided to do."

"I will. I will. Look, can we finish burying this thing first? I can't concentrate until it's done."

They both used their hands to push the rest of the dirt over the box. They stood up and stamped down on the soil. Helen slid her gardening toolbox over the spot. "We'll get some flowers to plant here. I don't plan on keeping it here, but it'll do for now." Helen and Bernice slapped the dirt from their knees and hands and walked over to Helen's front door. Helen walked in first. When she didn't hear Bernice follow her in, she turned around to find her standing outside at the door. "Coming in or what?" Helen asked her, puzzled.

"I'm sorry. It's just strange to see you walk right into your house. I mean, you didn't even hesitate! I think it's great. I just need to get used to it."

"You mean to tell me I didn't decide to have that memory erased?" Helen asked lightheartedly as Bernice came in.

"Actually, you specifically said not to take that memory away. You said you never wanted to forget how you used to live because you never wanted to repeat the things that made you so lonely. And you also told me you were proud of yourself and didn't want to hide from your, as you called it, crazy reputation."

Helen answered, "Huh, well, I suppose that's true. You know, I never really cared what everyone thought of me. Of course I knew everyone in town thought I was odd. I knew they talked. But I always figured that if they didn't take the time to get to know me, then I wouldn't waste time caring about them. It was awfully lonely living that way, though. It's funny. You were the first person to make an effort to get to know me. Even if it started with you spying on me, you tried. I'm glad you did." Once inside, Bernice sat on the sofa, a somber look spread across her face. Helen saw this and sat next to her. "You thinking about your family?" Bernice nodded yes, tears trickling down her cheeks. "Bernice, I need to know about one decision I made. I need you to be honest with me no matter what, all right?"

"No, you didn't," Bernice said.

"Didn't what?" Helen asked tentatively.

"You didn't wish them away. I did. You tried to talk me out of it. I thought you'd at least remember how upset you were over that part."

Helen apologized. "I'm so sorry, Bernice. I really don't. Please tell me."

"Well, in the dream, you told me that there was nothing you could do about the dead, that you could only help the living. Then you asked me if I had any grandparents or relatives around and if I wanted to live with them. When I said no, you reminded me that Marie and her mom said I could live with them. I said that that would be fine but that I'd rather live with you. You said you would love nothing more but that you weren't sure if that was the best thing for me, that it would be good for me to live with someone I already knew and was comfortable with. We agreed that I would go live with them unless something had happened to them at the hospital when it collapsed. When I woke up here this morning, I didn't know where I was. But I'd been to Marie's house before, and I knew it wasn't a room in her house. I figured out pretty quickly that, well, Marie and her mom must not have made it because I am here with you."

"You didn't wish them away! Please tell me that didn't happen!" Helen grew upset.

"No, no, not at all! That's not the 'them' I was talking about. I was talking about my family. I wished them away. You didn't want me to do it. That's what you were so upset about."

"I remember now," Helen said, remembering how upset she had been as she tried to explain to Bernice that it wouldn't be right to just forget her family. Helen told her that even if there were terrible memories of how they died and of bad times before that, there were still wonderful times to think of.

"And you said I was too young to make such a difficult decision, that you would regret erasing my memories of them. So we made a deal. You remember?"

Helen nodded and said, "That you would keep your memories of them and that I would erase everyone else's memories of them having ever existed, that as far as anyone knew, you'd always been my daughter. That's what I did, erased the entire town's memories of them, all except for Carson and Running Bear. I wanted them to have their memories of what happened yesterday and of who was involved. Maybe that was selfish on my part, but I knew Running Bear had to know because his family on the reservation would never forget. As for Carson, I just couldn't keep a secret like that from him."

Bernice said, "I understand that. And thank you for doing the other thing I asked you to do. When I went to Mandy and Lynne's this morning I wasn't sure if you'd done it."

"Everything was back to normal for them? No memories of Roy ever being institutionalized? James was back at work?"

"Yes, all that," Bernice said, adding, "but they also don't remember my mom and dad and brother or that I lived in the house across the alley from them. I never wanted to keep talking about it or explaining it to them or to anybody my entire life. It's enough to have the memories. And if I can talk to you about them, I'll be okay."

"Of course, Bernice. You can talk to me about absolutely anything, anytime."

"I know that. That's why I wanted to be here with you. And I remember the other part of the deal," Bernice said, a smirk forming on her lips.

"What's that?" Helen asked.

"That you refused to erase everyone's memories of your oddball reputation. That includes Mandy and Lynne. Now they think that my mom is crazy, and I'm going to have to live with that from them and everybody else in this town until the day I die!" Helen smiled and was about to explain herself again, but Bernice cut her off. "If I got through yesterday, I can get through a lifetime of defending you. I'll happily do that. Who knows? Maybe we can work on changing your reputation on our own without the help of the supernatural."

"Who says I want it changed?"

The End

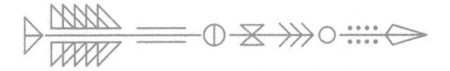

AUTHOR'S NOTE

Thank you to my husband, Darran, for being the first to read my finished product, for loving it before it was worthy of such praise, and for supporting me every step of the way. I am humbled and thankful for your unwavering belief in me. Thank you to my sons, Jack and Frank, two of the most kind, smart, funny, and brilliantly creative people I know. You inspire me every day, and I hope that my writing inspires both of you to always honor the gifts, talents, and creativity that is unique to each of you.

Thank you to my sister, Jessie, and to friends Mary H., Michelle M., and Ina M. who read early drafts of *Put It to Rest*. I appreciate your time, honesty, support, and constructive criticism.

Ina, with four sons, your youngest an infant at the time, you asked to read my book and I am still floored that you did it in less than a week! An extra special thanks goes out to you.

Thank you to everyone at Fulton Publishing, especially Trae Lynn and Megan. I appreciate your time, guidance, and attentiveness in getting my first book published.

Thank you to the talented students in the creative writing course at Rockland Center for the Arts. I appreciate your thoughtful and smart critiques of excerpts from my book as I worked on it.

A special thanks to instructor/poet/friend, Sally Lipton Derringer, whose keen eye and honest feedback of my first draft drove me forward to finish my novel. Sally, the content editing you provided was pivotal in preparing my manuscript for publishing. Your assessment gave me the confidence I needed to submit my draft for publishing.

Dr. Mellen Lovrin, your suggestion that I write is ultimately what got me to sit down and put pen to paper (or fingertips to keyboard, rather). Your guidance and advice have changed my life. I am forever grateful.

Thank you to my parents, Ronald and Michelle, and to my family and friends. Much love to you all.

Finally, it is important for me to honor the Lakota Sioux history and mythology of Uncegila that inspired the antagonist in my novel. I have tried to respect the legend and I acknowledge that wherever I have strayed from the myth, my sole purpose in doing so was to satisfy my storyline as a novelist. My intent was not to misinform, but to show humble deference to a rich cultural tradition by keeping the name of Uncegila alive.

ABOUT THE AUTHOR

Erin Mullahy was born and raised in North Dakota. As is apparent in *Put It to Rest*, her first published novel, Erin's writing bears the influence of her Midwestern upbringing. A lifelong avid reader of all genres, Erin loves a book she hates to put down, can't wait to get back to, and dreads finishing. It is the overarching theme in any novel she sets out to write regardless of genre. Erin currently resides in New York with her husband, their two sons, and their German shepherd, Stella.

CPSIA information can be obtained
at www.ICGtesting.com
Printed in the USA
BVHW080036060921
616101BV00001B/32